Butterflies
in the Storm

Also by this Author

That's Where You'll Find Her

THE WITCHES OF MARSTON DORNIE SERIES
A Far Cry from Summer
An Echo of Autumn
The Light from Winter Dark
The Spring Child's Whisper
Daughters of the Sunrise

Butterflies in the Storm

Gary Warner

Visit the Author's Website at
www.garywarner.co.uk

ISBN: 978-1-916981-56-0

PublishNation
www.publishnation.co.uk

Thank You

Elsbeth
For your invaluable help

Diane
For your infectious enthusiasm and
encouragement when I needed it most

and

Jenny
For being there

Chapter 1

"Thank you so much for coming. I know Julia would be very happy that you're here."

Melissa gave the woman, probably a family friend, a smile that she hoped showed nothing but heartfelt sympathy, and didn't betray even a hint of the bewilderment that she had felt ever since she'd received the invitation two weeks ago.

Was 'invitation' the correct word? It didn't seem right. After all, it wasn't a party was it? It was the funeral of a girl that she had apparently gone to school with some ten years previously. Melissa would never say as much to the grieving mother but, as hard as she tried to recall her, she had no memory of a Julia Storey who had, apparently, been in her year at secondary school.

The invitation, for want of a better word, had been lying in amongst a flurry of junk mail that she had found on her doormat when she'd arrived home from work on an overcast, depressing Thursday afternoon. Melissa had scooped it up, together with all the other unwelcome correspondence, and dropped it onto the kitchen table before going through to her bedroom to get changed. It hadn't been until the evening that the envelope, with its beautifully handwritten name and address, had been opened.

Melissa had torn at the pale lilac paper, recalling how she had thought it a pity to damage the delicate envelope, before carefully taking out the enclosed single page and unfolding it. Having read it several times, the rest of the evening had been spent searching her memory for any trace of the unfortunate, recently deceased Julia. However, she eventually decided, her remembering a long forgotten school friend wasn't what mattered, was it? Julia's parents had taken the trouble to track her down and it was obviously important to them that she attended their daughter's funeral. So here she was.

Melissa looked around the room, hoping to catch a glimpse of a face that might be vaguely familiar. She concentrated on the younger men and women, people of about her own age who might possibly have been at school with her. Strangely, there weren't that many. It hadn't occurred to her before but, for someone of Julia's age, there seemed to be a distinct lack of people who might have been in her peer group.

Maybe Julia hadn't made friends easily. Maybe her parents had struggled to find anyone who might possibly come. Suddenly Melissa felt both guilty and relieved. Her guilt driven by the thought that she had so nearly made her excuses and declined the invitation, and her relief that she had, ultimately, done the right thing.

She took another sip from her glass of orange juice, having politely refused the wine, before visiting the buffet to take a couple of sandwiches. Over in the far corner of the room Julia's mother was talking to an older couple. Ever since they had arrived back from the crematorium Melissa had been waiting for the chance to have a quick word, offer her condolences and, perhaps, learn a little more about her supposed connection with Julia. They had met very briefly before the cremation, but there had only been the opportunity to exchange a short greeting and no time for introductions. At last, the older couple moved away and Melissa took her cue, walking briskly across the room, wanting to reach Julia's mother before another guest could engage her in conversation.

"Mrs Storey. I'm Melissa Jones. I just wanted to say how deeply sorry I am for your loss and to thank you for inviting me here so that I might pay my respects."

The woman smiled sadly.

"Thank you. You're very kind."

Melissa considered leaving it there, not wanting to add to the woman's distress, but decided that perhaps there would be no harm in asking an innocent question.

"May I enquire how you found me? I haven't been in touch with Julia for years."

Melissa was sure that was kinder than saying 'I really have no recollection whatsoever of your late daughter.' Mrs Storey looked around the room before turning back to Melissa.

"You see all these people here? I recognise about a quarter of them. Julia seems to have so many friends that she never mentioned to me."

"So…?"

"So I'm admitting that I haven't been directly involved in contacting most of them. I smile and thank them for coming but really…."

She punctuated the unfinished sentence with a slight shrug.

"So would you have any idea who here might have asked me to Julia's funeral?"

Mrs Storey scanned the room once more.

"Perhaps one of her old university friends? She might have mentioned you to one of them."

"Mmm. Yes, you're probably right…."

Melissa wanted to push that further but felt she had already taken the gentle interrogation as far as she should.

"….well, anyway, I'm pleased to have been given the opportunity to come here today. Julia was a wonderful person."

Melissa hoped that sounded sufficiently convincing. Mrs Storey smiled her thanks before making her way over to a small group of people who had congregated near the buffet. As she was greeted with hugs and sympathy so Melissa returned her attention to the rest of the room, hoping that there might be a spark of recognition from someone. Anyone.

"Melissa? Melissa Jones?"

She turned to see an attractive woman, probably in her late twenties or early thirties, her brown hair swept back into a single ponytail, standing just a few feet from her. She was conservatively dressed in a dark trouser suit, as befitted the occasion, and had an unmistakeable air of self-confidence which Melissa immediately found herself envying.

"Yes."

"My name is Danika Pacek. If I had any friends they would call me Dani, but I don't, so no one does."

Melissa, slightly nonplussed, took the hand she was offering and gently shook it.

"Pleased to meet you, Danika."

"Likewise Melissa."

She just failed to disguise the merest hint of her Eastern European accent.

"I'm sorry, but you appear to have the advantage over me as I don't believe I know you."

Melissa had considered trying to continue to bluff her way through the whole experience in the hope she'd never see anyone she'd met today ever again. But, somehow, at this moment, telling the truth seemed more important.

"That's because we've never met."

Danika said this as though stating the blatantly obvious.

"Then…?"

But before Melissa could complete her question….

"And you don't recall Julia either, do you?"

Melissa shook her head.

"I didn't want to say anything, cause any embarrassment or further upset, but no, I don't remember her. How did you know?"

Danika moved closer, speaking in little more than a whisper.

"We'll discuss that later, but right now I have to tell you that you're right, you never knew her. She wasn't in your year. She didn't even attend your school. And we need to leave here right now…."

Danika glanced around her, wanting to ensure that there was no one within earshot.

"….because we don't have much time. Meet me in the toilet in five minutes. It's the second door on the left down the hallway."

"Excuse me?"

"I checked it out earlier. The window in there is just big enough for us to climb through and we can quickly make the trees to the rear of the house."

Melissa, at this point, was unsure whether to laugh or shout for help. She decided that humouring her might offer the best outcome. She smiled with as much fake warmth as she could muster.

"As chat up lines go I have to say that what it lacks in finesse it makes up for in originality."

But, far from having the desired disarming effect, this seemed to merely increase the urgency in Danika's voice.

"My car is parked in the road beyond the trees. I think we can reach it in under a minute if we run."

Melissa considered Danika's plan for a moment before deciding on a plan of her own.

4

"I have a better idea. You climb through the toilet window and make a dash for your car. I'm going to have another fruit juice, possibly apple this time, and maybe a daring third sandwich, then I shall offer further condolences and say my goodbyes before walking to my car which, strangely enough, is parked in one of the designated parking spaces to the side of this rather charming country house."

Danika shrugged.

"Ok. Try to leave. Go on. Give the extra drink and sandwich a miss and try to leave right now."

"But I don't want to leave 'right now', and besides, it would be rude to just walk out. And why am I even discussing this with you?"

Melissa inwardly winced because as soon as she'd said it she regretted how it had sounded. Although this woman, Danika, still standing a little too close for comfort, had approached her uninvited, displaying such overt irritation didn't sit well with Melissa. Throughout her life she had encountered many 'characters', but had always prided herself on never consciously displaying any sign of the annoyance that she might have felt.

"What I mean is…."

She added in a softer tone, hoping to blunt the edge to her previous question.

"….I appreciate your concern but I'm sure that everything's fine. However, I will bear in mind what you've said."

Danika moved closer still and gripped Melissa's arm, momentarily taking her by surprise.

"I accept your apology…."

Is that what it had been?

"….but I stand by what I said. If you doubt my sincerity, try to leave right now. They won't let you."

"They?"

Danika made no reply as, for the first time, Melissa looked, really looked, into her eyes and she saw something there that said maybe, just maybe, this woman was being serious.

"Ok. I'll leave. But I'm only doing this to prove you wrong."

Truth was, she wouldn't mind going anyway. There was no one here she knew and she still wasn't completely sure why she'd come in the first place. Melissa put her glass down and removed her car key from her jacket pocket. As she made her way over to where Julia's mother stood, still talking to the small group she had joined a few minutes ago, she looked around her, trying to spot anyone who might be watching her, but everyone seemed to be preoccupied with the food and quiet conversation.

"Thank you again, Mrs Storey. I'll never forget Julia."

That was, if she could ever remember her.

"Thank you for coming, Melissa. Pleased to have met you."

She offered no protestations, no demands that she should remain. So, if she was to be stopped, as Danika was so certain she would be, it wasn't going to be Julia's mother who would try to do the stopping.

Melissa smiled and turned, making her way down the hall, past the second door on the left which, she had been reliably informed, was the toilet, and on towards the front door. She reached out to turn the handle.

"Going so soon?"

She spun round to see an immaculately dressed young man walking down the corridor towards her.

"I….er….yes, unfortunately I have to be at a meeting this afternoon."

He was now standing beside her. Melissa tried to steady her breathing. He wasn't going to stop her was he? Why would he? She suddenly became aware that her heart was racing.

"That's a shame. We had hoped everyone would remain for a small presentation about Julia's tragically short life. You know, her academic achievements, her wonderful work for so many local charities. As one of her friends we thought perhaps you might like to say a few words?"

Melissa forced a smile while frantically trying to come up with some kind of believable response.

"I would have so loved to do that but, sadly, I really do have to attend this meeting. It is work related and therefore I must be there."

What would he say now? She had to be ready for another, perhaps more forceful, attempt to keep her there. She had to maintain her composure while sticking to her story, but what if he tried to physically stop her from leaving? She could call out, scream even….

"Well, that's a shame, but I understand. Mustn't upset the boss. I'll wish you 'good day' then, and thank you for coming."

He smiled as he turned away and, as she opened the door, walked through and out onto the wide driveway at the front of the house, she couldn't help feeling like a complete idiot. Of course they weren't going to keep her there. Why would they? It was a ridiculous idea. How could she have even begun to believe that woman? But, as she approached her car, Melissa thought that maybe, after all, she might have something to thank Danika for. By leaving now she had been spared the embarrassment of trying to 'say a few words' about a young woman of whom she had no recollection whatsoever.

Melissa unlocked the driver's door and climbed behind the wheel. As she fastened her seat belt she glanced back towards the house and wondered who Ms Danika Pacek would be talking to now. Perhaps she had already latched onto another unsuspecting guest. Melissa gave a wry smile as she pressed the car's ignition button. Nothing. She pressed it again. Still nothing. With a growing sense of panic, she jabbed at the button several more times although she now knew it was pointless. The car wasn't going to start.

She looked again to the house and thought she saw someone at one of the large windows, staring in her direction, but in a moment they were gone. She pushed open the door and got out. A part of her wanted to run, to not wait until she was dragged kicking and screaming back into the house. But, again, she had to remind herself that she had absolutely no reason to believe that there was any threat at all. Except why had her car failed to start? It was relatively new and had never let her down before today.

Melissa looked around her. She was alone on the driveway. What should she do? Maybe if she just walked away, down the drive and out onto the road. If they really didn't want her to leave, then surely someone would be bound to follow and try to stop her. But what if they didn't? She was miles from the nearest village and wasn't wearing shoes conducive to an unplanned route march. No. There really was no choice. She had to return to the house. She might even find someone in there who knew something about cars.

However, as she made her way back towards the large front door, she felt the first tingle of apprehension. What if…? As she turned the brass handle the 'what ifs' began to spin around in her mind, taking on a life of their own until the doubts drove all rational thinking away into the shadows. She re-entered the hallway. It was empty. She could hear voices coming from the room at the end of the corridor but no one had remained in the hall to see whether she had returned. Did that mean they didn't care, or that they knew she would?

Which door did Danika say was the toilet? Of course she had shown her from the opposite end of the hall hadn't she? Second on the left? Or was it third? And the left would now be her right, wouldn't it? It was the second, she was sure. Without hesitating, Melissa opened what she hoped was the correct door.

"Close it quickly and lock it."

Danika was sitting on the closed lid of the toilet. Melissa, now running on automatic, all reasoned thought gone, did as she was told. Behind Danika, the frosted window was swinging lazily on its hinges, its locking lever lying broken on the sill.

"I estimate we have a minute, maximum. Shall we?"

Danika stood and pulled herself up and through the open window. Melissa followed, not as gracefully it had to be said, but her endeavours achieved the desired result and they both now stood in the middle of a beautifully cultivated flower bed below the window.

"Follow me!"

Without turning to see if Melissa was obeying, Danika began to run across the well-manicured lawn towards a long line of oak trees that grew just inside the perimeter of the grounds. Melissa hesitated for a moment, glancing back at the window. At that moment she thought she heard someone knocking loudly on the toilet door. Did it sound as if they were about to break it in? Melissa spun away and sprinted after Danika, gradually closing the gap between them until, as they reached the trees, she was just a few strides behind her. Without waiting for her to catch up Danika continued on, pushing aside the smaller, lower branches and ducking under the larger, more unwieldy ones. She glanced back once to check that Melissa was still with her.

"I'm impressed!"

She called over her shoulder as she saw that Melissa was not only still with her but was now within touching distance.

"School two hundred metres champion three years in succession, and what the hell is going on!?"

Danika ignored her question.

"There's a high wall on the other side of these trees. I'll give you a leg up and then follow you. My car's parked just the other side of it."

As the wall came into view, Melissa kept hearing her own question replaying over and over in her mind. 'What the hell is going on?' But right now there was no time for questions or hesitation. Danika was already leaning with her back against the wall, her hands cupped together and ready to lift Melissa. In a moment she had placed her right foot into Danika's hands and was immediately raised so that the top of the wall was now within easy reach. Melissa pulled herself up and, with some effort, swung her legs over and dropped down onto the far side. She looked up and, after a couple of seconds, saw Danika's hands appear as they grasped the topmost line of bricks. In no time she too had hauled herself over and lowered herself down before dropping the remaining distance and landing quite elegantly beside Melissa.

"Been practising that. The secret's in the run up. There's my car."

She pointed to the blue Jaguar F Type parked on the country road's grass verge. Whatever Melissa had been expecting it somehow hadn't been that. As if she had read her mind, Danika said

"Oh, it's not mine. She lets me use it on jobs like this."

Melissa had wanted to immediately ask who 'she' was, and what she meant by 'jobs like this', but before she could say anything, Danika had raced around to the other side of the car, and moments later was behind the wheel with the engine running.

"Get in!"

Perhaps it was the urgency in Danika's voice, perhaps it was her own intuition, but Melissa did as Danika asked, or rather commanded, without hesitation. She accepted that this wasn't the moment for further indecision. As soon as Melissa had fastened her seat belt, Danika gunned the engine as she steered the Jaguar off the verge and onto the road, glancing into her rear view mirror. Seconds later, they were speeding along the country road and making good their escape, but from whom exactly, or what?

Chapter 2

Danika was still clearly concerned that they were being pursued, even though they had been travelling at high speed for some minutes, the countryside racing past in a blur of fields and trees. At first Melissa had been unsure whether she was merely reckless, as she took the shallow bends at high speed, often following what Melissa understood was called the 'racing line'. But it soon became clear to her that Danika was an expert driver and was using the Jaguar on the edge of its capabilities without pushing it beyond its limits.

At one point Melissa turned to look out of the back window. There was a car, some distance behind them. It was difficult to judge, but it seemed to be matching them for speed, just managing to keep them in sight.

Melissa sat in silence as they raced on, closing her eyes as the occasional vehicle came towards them, waiting for the crash that never came. She felt her seat belt tighten against her chest as Danika braked hard to take a particularly sharp corner, before she was pushed back into her seat when the accelerator was, once more, applied with controlled aggression. As the road straightened, Melissa turned again, scared that the following car might have gained on them. It was nowhere to be seen.

Some miles later Danika finally began to ease the speed down. Melissa took several deep, shuddering breaths, wanting to say something but, at that moment, knowing she wouldn't be able to form a coherent sentence. Danika glanced to her left, said nothing but pulled the car over into the entrance to a small woodland track, bringing it to a stop in front of a dilapidated wooden gate.

"They won't pursue us beyond a certain point, it won't be worth the risk. Do you want to get out for a moment?"

Danika reached across her and pushed the passenger door open. For some seconds Melissa remained in her seat, unable or unwilling to move. When, at last, she climbed from the car, she stood beside it for a moment before suddenly running over to an area of undergrowth, leaning over and retching onto the ground the other side of it. When she eventually stood up, Danika was standing beside her and offering her a large tissue. She took it and wiped her mouth before dropping it into a bin near the gate.

"You ok?"

Melissa nodded.

"My driving can have that effect."

"It's not that, it's…."

Melissa looked around her, struggling to find the words, looking bewildered and utterly lost. Danika put an arm around her shoulder and gently guided her back to the car. When she was sitting once more in the passenger seat, Danika opened the Jaguar's boot and removed a small bottle of water. She handed it to Melissa before climbing back behind the wheel.

"Take your time. We're safe now."

Danika rested a hand on Melissa's arm and, for the first time, there was a softness and compassion in her voice. Melissa took a sip of water and put her head back against her seat's headrest.

"Who are we safe from, Danika?"

She turned to face her, holding eye contact as she tried to put some weight behind her question. Except that she wasn't sure she wanted to hear the answer.

"You'll just have to believe me when I say that would be better coming from someone other than me."

"I don't *have* to believe you. If you can give me an answer, I think you should."

Melissa wasn't ready to let it go without being given something, but it was clear that Danika was not about to be any more forthcoming.

"I really don't mean this to sound brusque, but my remit begins and ends with your delivery to a place of safety. You've trusted me to get you this far. Please trust me for a little longer. I can't answer any of your questions."

"Can't or won't?"

Danika shrugged.

"The latter, I suppose."

11

Obviously any further pleas were going to be met with a similar polite refusal. Melissa turned away and stared out of the windscreen.

"Then I want you to take me home."

This prompted Danika to give a short, humourless laugh.

"I said my orders are to deliver you to a place of safety."

"So?"

Danika started the engine and steered the car back onto the country road.

"So, their failure to hold onto you today means they'll be watching for you anywhere you might be expected to show up. Your home will be quite near the top of their list I should think, wouldn't you?"

Melissa, in the light of what she'd just been told, or rather hadn't been told, began to consider her options. She knew full well she'd already made the decision to trust Danika, as far as her current situation was concerned. Thinking back, if she were really honest with herself, serious seeds of doubt had already been sown before her car's failure to start. For all her sarcasm and dismissive words to Danika, deep down, her intuition had already been telling her that the situation at the funeral was far from right, however much she had tried to ignore it. Therefore, she had no choice but to accept that she was being rescued. From who, and why, would be questions that she would have to put on the back burner until she met the 'someone' that Danika had referred to.

"You've done this sort of thing before, haven't you?"

Melissa considered that any conversation would be better than the silence that, she had the feeling, Danika might have preferred.

"A few times. Well, maybe more than a few."

Danika gave her a sideways glance. Did the hint of a smile find its way onto her lips? No, she must have imagined it. Melissa returned her gaze to the road ahead and saw that they were coming up to a T junction. The Jaguar slowed, Danika indicated left and they joined a much busier A road. Melissa hadn't come this way and didn't know the area well, having travelled for a little over an hour from the opposite direction to the funeral of her 'friend'.

"You look as if you could do with a little rest. Why don't you put your head back and close your eyes? We have some way to go yet."

It was broad daylight, and her body was only now beginning to recover from the adrenalin overload, so sleep, right then, seemed to Melissa to be neither desirable or possible.

"How far?"

She asked, more in hope than expectation.

"Far enough to ensure you'll be safe."

She could have predicted the response. Danika was well rehearsed in remaining polite and reassuring while giving away absolutely nothing. Any further attempts to elicit any kind of meaningful information would be futile, and would only serve to ensure they remained on this question and answer merry-go-round. But Melissa knew there was no way she would sleep, not a chance. She'd never felt more awake in her life.

Danika selected her playlist on the Jaguar's infotainment screen. Moments after Billie Eilish's 'No Time To Die' had begun to play, she glanced across to check that Melissa was still sleeping. It had taken only minutes from when she had first made the suggestion about 'putting her head back and closing her eyes' to Melissa falling into a deep, dreamless sleep, that had been aided by the mild sedative contained in the bottle of water she had given her.

Several tracks into her playlist, Danika lowered the volume and called up her phone's contact list, selecting the number that appeared at the top. There was no name to identify the owner of that number. She placed the call which was answered almost immediately.

"I have her and we're on our way home."

"Well done, Danika. Bring her to me as soon as you arrive."

"Of course."

Without further conversation Danika closed the call and brought the volume of the music back up. She pressed down on the accelerator and felt the surge of power as she reached the beginning of the dual carriageway. There were no other cars in the outside lane and so she let the Jaguar's speed build until she was flirting with breaking the limit. Now that she had Melissa safely in her care she wanted nothing more than to get her back to the house as quickly as she could. Traffic allowing, Danika estimated the journey would take a little under two hours and, hopefully, for most of that time Melissa would remain asleep.

She felt quietly satisfied because, on reflection, the potential for this one to go very wrong had been a real concern. Success, Danika had known from the outset, had depended completely upon her ability to persuade Melissa of the need to cooperate. Fortunately, she had predicted each step perfectly. The initial incredulity and absolute rejection, followed by the doubt which, of course, had already been there in the back of her mind. The biggest risk had been in allowing Melissa to attempt to leave the country house. There were, Danika had known at the time, a number of ways that could have gone badly. But experience had told her that, ultimately, it would be the quickest way to get her onside. Allow the panic to set in and then use it to achieve the desired outcome.

However, even given all of the obvious risks of her work, Danika knew that she wouldn't want to trade places with the one who had the task of sitting down with Melissa and explaining to her the likelihood was that, if she wanted to remain alive, she would never be able to return to her old life.

Chapter 3

"Melissa?"

The voice reached into the darkness and pulled her towards the light. Slowly, she opened her eyes. The Jaguar was nosing its way along a narrow road which wasn't much wider than the car. On either side were dense hedgerows that prevented her seeing what lay beyond. She turned to Danika.

"Are we here?"

Her voice was quiet and drowsy.

"Almost. You can wake up now."

Danika saw Melissa look down for the bottle of water. It wasn't there. Danika had removed it moments after she had fallen asleep.

"Only a few minutes and you can have a drink and something to eat, if you'd like."

Melissa sat upright, taking her head off the headrest as she tried to bring herself round. She stared out of the windows, looking for some clue as to her whereabouts, but all she could see was the road and the hedgerows. They were now travelling not much above twenty miles an hour as Danika steered the car into a shallow right bend. At the same moment she reached down to remove her mobile phone from its holder.

"My phone! I left it in my car!"

Seeing Danika's had suddenly reminded Melissa of her own mobile.

"Forget about it. You couldn't have brought it with you anyway."

"Why?"

Danika flicked her a glance that said 'are you really asking me that?'

"Because...."

She spoke as if to a young child.

15

"….it would have only served to provide another way of tracking you. You are now well and truly off grid, and we need to keep you that way."

"I need my phone."

But it was clear by the way Melissa uttered the words that she had abandoned any hope of seeing it again in the near future, if ever. She turned away from Danika to look out of the car's side window, and it was at that moment that the hedgerow ended, allowing her the first view of what, she assumed, was their destination.

Some hundred or so yards away, on the far side of a perfectly manicured lawn was what looked, at first sight, to be a large, sprawling, very modern building. One whole side seemed to comprise almost entirely of tinted glass interspersed at irregular intervals with bright red brickwork. The front door was also made of glass but with a much darker tint. However, as they drew nearer to the building, Melissa could see, through the glass, an open staircase in the middle of one of the rooms beyond and, moments later, noticed the large windows set in the slate covered roof.

The narrow country road, having now widened into a gravel covered drive, led to an open-fronted garage situated to the right of the main building. There were two other vehicles, a Range Rover and an Aston Martin, parked neatly under its shelter and, next to the furthest wall, a Kawasaki motorcycle. Danika steered the Jaguar into the space next to the Range Rover.

"Come with me Melissa. There's someone who's waiting to meet you."

She climbed from the car and walked around to where Melissa still sat, showing no inclination to get out. Danika leaned across her and pressed the seat belt release. She took her left hand and gently coaxed her out of the Jaguar. As they walked towards the house, Melissa felt Danika's grip on her hand tighten slightly. Was she expecting her to try to make a run for it? Unlikely. Where would she run?

"I know this is still difficult, but please believe me when I say this is the best place for you to be right now."

Melissa gave her a look that said 'I'll reserve judgement on that.'

In moments they were standing in front of the door with the dark tinted glass. Danika let go of Melissa's hand as she spoke into a small microphone near the door.

"Danika Pacek."

It took only a second for the door lock to be released with a soft click. Danika pushed it open and stepped into what seemed to Melissa like a luxury hotel reception. She looked around as Danika led her towards a door in the far corner. The tinted window that stretched from floor to ceiling gave a perfect view out across the lawn. She could see the entrance to the narrow road and the hedgerows that grew either side of it, concealing its existence. Beyond that was woodland that looked as if it surrounded the entire front of the building, but before Melissa could take in anything further they reached the door. The sensors above it had detected their approach and it was already fully open.

"Just down here."

Danika and Melissa made their way along the cool, dimly lit passageway as the door silently closed behind them. As they neared the further end of the corridor, Melissa noticed that there were no other doors in it except the one that they were heading towards. Danika stopped in front of it and gave the lightest of knocks.

"Enter."

The woman's voice came from beyond the door, which Danika then pushed open before stepping aside to allow Melissa to go in ahead of her.

"Hello Melissa. May I call you Melissa? I feel I already know you."

Before Melissa could answer she heard the door close behind her. She turned to see that Danika had not come in with her. The woman, who stood, silhouetted, in front of a large window, added

"Danika will join us again shortly. Please take a seat."

She pointed to a sofa that was placed against the opposite wall. Slowly, with her eyes all the time fixed upon the woman, Melissa made her way over to the sofa and sat down. The woman remained where she was for several seconds before walking over and lowering herself down beside Melissa. She hadn't expected that. She had expected her to sit in the impressive looking leather chair that was placed behind a large desk, close to where she had been standing.

As she sat, so the woman's features caught the light. Melissa's first impression was that of elegance and poise. Her posture was upright, her hands resting upon her lap, as if she were posing for a classy magazine photo shoot. She was in her late forties, Melissa guessed. Her hair was cut quite short in what could be described as an elfin style. Although its predominant colour was a mid-brown, there were flecks of grey at the sides which, Melissa was sure, were there by design, maybe to emphasise her seniority and, therefore, authority.

"Allow me to introduce myself…."

Her voice was quiet and soft, perfectly 'English', perfectly confident.

"….my name is Verity Trask, but please call me Verity. Everyone here does."

"And where exactly is 'here'?"

Melissa asked with much less confidence. Verity smiled. It was an attractive, natural smile.

"May I suggest, from your point of view, a more apposite question? I would ask not '*where* is here', but '*what* is here'. And if you were to ask that question, then I should reply that *what* this place is might best be described as a kind of sanctuary. A refuge for those who desperately need it, whether they are aware of that need or not."

For the first time since entering the room, Melissa noticed that placed around it were large vases of colourful cut flowers. She had no idea what they were but they had the most beautiful delicate scent.

"And you believe I'm in need of your sanctuary?"

Melissa felt as if she were in a dream, or a nightmare. Right at this moment she was far from sure which it might be.

Another smile.

"I don't *believe*, I *know*. I wouldn't have risked my lovely Danika or my equally lovely Jaguar had I not been sure that the threat to you was real and imminent."

There was a short silence before Melissa asked

"How long do you intend keeping me here?"

Of the many questions in her confused, weary mind that was the one that found its way onto her lips.

"I realise this is very difficult for you, that your life has taken a sudden, unexpected and unwelcome turn, but I'm afraid I can't answer that. I can't answer it because your question's basic premise is incorrect."

"I don't understand."

Verity took a moment before replying.

"I'm not keeping you here. You're free to go whenever you wish, however I would strongly advise against leaving, at least for the foreseeable future."

"Foreseeable future?!"

Melissa leapt to her feet and turned towards the door.

"I have a job! I have a life!"

Verity remained perfectly still, showing no outward reaction to Melissa's sudden panicked outburst.

"I do not exaggerate the threat you face, but I won't beg for your trust. However, if you decide to give it then you must give it freely and without reservation, otherwise I cannot help you."

Melissa was within a few paces of the door when she hesitated before stopping and turning back to face Verity.

"Do I have a choice?"

She spoke quietly as she slowly returned to the sofa, her words almost inaudible.

"You always have a choice, Melissa. All I ask is that you make the right one."

As she sat back down, Verity reached out and took her hand. It was a simple gesture but it had the effect of bringing a weak smile to Melissa's lips. She had no idea where the smile had come from. She felt wretched and still drowsy from the journey. Her mind was in turmoil as she tried, as best she could, to marshal some kind, any kind, of coherent thought. She knew she needed answers, knew that there were so many questions but....

"Listen to me. I'm going to call for Danika and she'll take you to your apartment. I suggest you rest until this evening. We'll be eating at seven and it would be lovely if you'd join us. There will be plenty of time for you to ask anything you wish, and nothing lost by delaying those questions until you feel a little better."

Verity punctuated the last sentence with a gentle squeeze of Melissa's hand before she stood, walked over to her desk and pressed a button on her telephone's base unit.

"Danika. Melissa's ready to be shown to her rooms now."

She returned to the sofa and sat back down.

"Thank you, I think."

Melissa managed to force what she hoped might pass for another smile. Before Verity could reply, the door opened and Danika entered. The first thing Melissa noticed was that her hair was no longer in a ponytail but had been allowed to fall freely onto her shoulders. Also gone was the trouser suit. It had been replaced by a loose fitting T shirt and a pair of pale blue denim jeans. In fact, she was almost unrecognisable from the woman she had met at the funeral.

"Come with me please, Melissa."

As Danika followed Melissa out of the office, she glanced over her shoulder and received the slightest of nods from Verity, who had already returned to the chair behind her desk.

Chapter 4

Together they walked along the corridor, Danika's hand resting lightly on Melissa's back, gently guiding her towards the reception room they had entered on their arrival.

"Through here."

Danika pointed to another door directly opposite. Melissa hadn't noticed it earlier, probably because it was recessed slightly, near an alcove. Beyond it was another room, and the staircase she had seen through the large window. Danika led her up the wide wooden steps onto the landing above. In front of them was another corridor, narrower than the one that led to Verity Trask's office. But this one was different in another respect. This one had doors all along its length. Melissa counted five as she followed Danika.

"Your apartment's just down here."

Sunlight was streaming in through several windows that were set into the sloping ceiling, and Melissa could see the bright blue sky beyond.

"Do others stay here?"

Danika smiled.

"Oh yes. Although not many. You're very lucky."

She stopped outside the fifth door.

"Here we are."

As Danika turned the brass handle and pushed the door open, so a movement at the furthest end of the corridor, near the landing, caught Melissa's eye. She turned in time to see a young girl looking out from one of the other doorways. But, in a moment, she had quickly retreated into her room and shut the door. It happened so quickly that Melissa wondered whether she had imagined her.

"Come in."

Danika had already entered but Melissa hesitated, remaining in the doorway.

"Don't you want to see your lovely rooms?"

She wasn't so sure that she did. Reluctantly, she joined Danika inside.

"I'm sure you'll be very comfortable. Let me show you. This is your living area…."

In one corner of the room was a small sofa and two armchairs. Set into the opposite wall was a large television.

"….you have access to Sky, Netflix, in fact all the major media providers. Follow me."

She led her through an archway in the centre of the room.

"Your bed, large single, and a wardrobe which we've taken the liberty of filling. We had to make an educated guess as to your size and I personally chose the clothes so any complaints should be directed to me."

She gave a quiet laugh as she opened the wardrobe's double doors.

"Underwear and night things are in the top drawer."

"Did you personally choose those too?"

Danika looked away momentarily as she closed the doors.

"En suite through there…."

She turned back to her.

"….I think that's all. And now I suggest you have some rest. I'll return later and take you down to the dining room."

"I….er….thank you."

Danika walked towards the door, but it was as she reached out to close it behind her that she saw Melissa's expression had changed. The look of resigned bewilderment had been replaced by something that stopped Danika dead in her tracks and, before she was able to return to her, the tears came as Melissa dropped to her knees, crying uncontrollably.

Danika knelt down and put both arms around her, holding her but saying nothing. She knew from experience that the best thing to do right at that moment was just to be there. No words of comfort or any attempts at explanation would cut through the maelstrom of emotions that had been waiting to overwhelm Melissa. Minutes passed until, eventually, her sobbing was replaced by deep, shuddering breaths. The tears may have stopped, but the fear and confusion that had been the trigger for them remained, as strong and as unbearable as in that first moment.

"I just want to go home" Melissa whispered as she fought hard to regain some kind of composure. Danika said nothing but slowly, gently, lifted her to her feet and guided her over to the bed. With her free hand she took hold of the duvet and threw it back.

"Lie down. Just for a while. Try to get some sleep. I'll come back later."

Melissa sat down on the edge of the bed and swung her legs up onto the mattress. Danika pulled the duvet back up over her and once more turned to leave the room.

"I don't want to be alone. Don't leave me alone."

Her words were spoken so softly that Danika almost didn't hear them. In response she picked up a nearby chair and placed it at the side of the bed. As Danika sat down so she reached out and let her hand brush Melissa's hair. That simple gesture seemed to calm her and, after some seconds, she allowed her eyes to close. It took a few minutes for her breathing to become steadier as she found some kind of peace in sleep. When she was sure that Melissa was indeed asleep, Danika settled back in her chair.

At that point it would have been easy for Danika to have quietly left the room, and she had considered doing just that. But if Melissa had woken up, found herself alone and panicked, then she would have felt that she'd betrayed her and any trust that now existed between them would have been damaged, possibly beyond repair.

Danika looked around the room, checking for anything that had been overlooked, any little touches that could have been added. Flowers! There were no flowers. She made a mental note to pick some from the garden that evening and bring them up before Melissa settled in for the night. Satisfied that nothing else was missing, Danika removed her phone from her pocket and found the book that she'd begun reading just the night before. It was a rather undemanding romance and perfect for her current mood. She needed something calming, something that would, temporarily, take her away from the here and now and thoughts of the earlier rescue.

It was always the same. However successful her assignment, Danika would always find herself going over the details in her mind. Could she have possibly done anything differently? Could she have made it less stressful for her assigned target? Were there lessons to be learned? She began reading her book, concentrating hard in an attempt to drive away any such thoughts. The job was done and she now needed to relax. Except it wasn't going to be that easy. It never had been. It never would be.

Every so often Danika would glance over to where Melissa lay, sleeping soundly. She would probably still be experiencing the effects of the sedative that Danika had given her. Although not a decision she had taken lightly, she had made a judgement call on giving her the water. And the end always justified the means. Didn't it?

It took just over two hours for Danika to finish her book. During that time Melissa had stirred on a few occasions but had quickly settled once more into a peaceful, silent sleep. Danika looked up at the clock on the opposite wall. Another half an hour and they'd be expected to make an appearance in the dining room. It was Verity's wish that Melissa be encouraged to eat with the others rather than have her meal in her room.

"Melissa?"

Danika spoke her name softly, not wanting to wake her suddenly.

"Melissa?" she repeated, this time a little louder. She stirred, rolling onto her side and slowly opening her eyes.

"We have a short while before we eat. I thought you'd appreciate the chance to maybe have a shower, perhaps change into something different?"

Danika wanted to avoid her suggestion sounding like an order. Melissa wearily sat up, swinging her legs off the bed.

"You....stayed."

Her voice faltered as she struggled to wake up.

"Of course I did. You wanted me to. Didn't you think I would?"

"No....I...."

Danika stood and held out a hand which Melissa, after a moment's hesitation, took as she helped her to her feet.

"Now I *will* leave you for a short time while you have that shower, and when I return we'll go and get something to eat."

Melissa wanted to say that she didn't feel particularly hungry but decided that would be neither wise nor polite. She needed to eat, whether she felt like it or not and she had no choice but to accept the hospitality that she was being offered. Whatever this place was and whatever she was doing here, she had been shown nothing but kindness and consideration up to this moment. There might come a time to question and oppose, but now was not that time.

Minutes later, as Melissa stood under the hot spray, her thoughts turned to what Danika had told her before she left. They would be dining with a few others as Verity felt it might provide a valuable opportunity to put her more at ease. Melissa was a long way from being convinced that it would do any such thing but she would admit that, beyond her own fears and concerns, there was a part of her that was intrigued to find out who else had been deemed to need this sanctuary.

After she had towelled herself dry, Melissa returned to the bedroom to take a closer look at the wardrobe full of clothes that Danika had shown her earlier. As she took out each outfit she was forced to admit that whoever had chosen them had impeccable taste. Each one was a designer label and probably cost way beyond anything she could have ever afforded on her modest income.

After some deliberation, Melissa settled on a silk blouse with a delicate pastel pattern and a pair of navy blue trousers that fitted perfectly. The underwear, that Danika had been reluctant to admit to choosing, was of equal quality and pedigree. *La Perla* and *Myla* were among the labels together with a few items by *Agent Provocateur*, which she wasn't going to even remove from the drawer.

Having dressed and reapplied some make up from the selection on the dressing table, Melissa dropped down into the chair that Danika had recently vacated. This morning, as she had dressed for the funeral, she had had her comfortable little life. Nothing spectacular, nothing that would change the world, but it had been secure, and it had been hers. Now who did it belong to?

But before her thoughts could take her any lower there was a quiet knock at the door.

"Come in."

Melissa stood as Danika pushed the door open and walked in, carrying a large vase of freshly cut flowers.

"They're from our garden. I picked them myself."

She placed the vase on the dressing table, moving a small hand mirror to make room.

"They're beautiful. Thank you."

Danika smiled. Melissa couldn't help thinking she should smile more often. It suited her.

"You're welcome and I approve, by the way."

"Mmm?"

"Your choice of clothes."

Melissa attempted to return the smile.

"Thank you again, but surely they're *your* choice?"

Danika ignored the remark as she proceeded to make small adjustments to the flowers.

"Ready for something to eat?"

"Oh yes, absolutely" she lied, trying her best to sound convincing.

"Excellent! Then follow me."

Chapter 5

Together they retraced their earlier walk, back along the corridor past the other doors that were still all closed.

"*Agent Provocateur*? Really?" Melissa asked.

"I'm sorry?" Danika's response was innocence personified.

"The underwear?" Melissa prompted, having no intention of letting her off that easily.

Danika shrugged.

"Oh that. Well, I didn't know, did I? Had to cover all possibilities."

"Some of those wouldn't cover anything" Melissa said, probably to herself.

Danika walked on, slightly ahead of Melissa, leading her back down the stairs and into the reception room. Whereas, previously, she had been taken along another, wider corridor to Verity's office, this time she was guided to an open doorway in the corner of the room. Beyond the doorway, Melissa could hear voices and Danika saw her hesitate.

"It's ok. None of them bite….much."

She smiled as she led her through the door. A large chandelier hung from the centre of the ceiling, bathing the room in a soft, subdued light. There were six small tables, each with two chairs, positioned at random around the dining area. Melissa's first impression was that of a high class restaurant, not that she had any first-hand experience of such places.

Seated at the table nearest the door, on her own, was a young girl, maybe thirteen or fourteen Melissa guessed. Could she have been the girl she caught a glimpse of earlier? It was certainly possible. The girl had her head down, her gaze fixed firmly on the plate of food in front of her and, although she must have been aware of them standing so near, she made no attempt to look up or offer any kind of greeting.

"Melissa! I'm so pleased you could join us!"

Verity, who had been sitting at one of the furthest tables, jumped up from her chair and walked over to greet them.

"Danika persuaded me."

Verity threw her an appreciative smile. She turned back to Melissa.

"Follow me. I know just the person to keep you company on your first evening."

"I thought I'd be eating with...."

She gave Danika a pleading look.

"Danika? Oh, you'll have plenty of time to spend with her."

Before there could be any further protest, Verity guided her over to a table where an elderly lady sat, eating a rather splendid-looking Caesar salad.

"Melissa? This is Harriet."

She put down her knife and fork and leant against the table, slowly pushing herself to her feet. Melissa was about to say something, to insist she remain seated, but Verity gave the slightest shake of her head. It was almost nothing but it was enough to prompt Melissa to stay silent.

"So pleased to meet you, my dear."

Harriet put out a slightly trembling hand which Melissa gently shook.

"I understand you're joining me for your meal this evening?"

If Melissa had any thoughts of arguing about that, or trying to politely decline, they were immediately dispelled by the elderly lady's warm smile. Verity pulled out the chair opposite and Melissa dutifully sat down.

"Harriet can tell you what's on the menu tonight. Danika and I will be at the corner table should you need us."

Before Melissa could reply, Verity turned away and left them alone.

"I'm not that hungry, actually."

Melissa received another smile, benevolent, understanding.

"However you may feel right now, you won't feel any better by not eating, will you?"

Melissa couldn't argue with that.

"Your salad looks good."

Harriet nodded.

"Excellent choice. Although there are alternatives. I believe there is a rather delicious vegetable curry on offer, or a lasagne, I think. Verity has more faith in my ability to recall these things than I do!"

She laughed.

"No, I think I'll go with the salad, thank you. Who do I….?"

Before Melissa could complete her question, Harriet had raised her hand and, as if by magic, they were joined by a young woman who had suddenly materialised beside them. She wore a black blouse and matching trousers and exuded efficiency.

"My friend Melissa will have the Caesar salad and…."

Harriet leaned over towards the waitress and added in a loud whisper

"….make it a bit bigger than mine."

The waitress smiled and nodded.

"And to drink?" she asked.

"I always have a nice glass of my favourite wine. Verity makes sure they always have some."

Harriet lifted her half empty glass.

"Not for me thank you. May I have an orange juice?"

"Of course."

The young woman was gone as quickly as she had appeared.

"I'll let you off with that as this is your first night, but I insist you do join me in a bottle of this lovely wine before the week is out."

Harriet gave her a conspiratorial wink as Melissa lowered her gaze. This prompted Harriet to place a reassuring hand on Melissa's arm.

"They *will* look after you here, you know. You'll be quite safe now."

"But safe from who? From what?"

Harriet nodded slowly.

"Ah, I see. Verity hasn't spoken with you yet?"

"Only briefly, just after I arrived."

Melissa threw a glance over to where Verity sat, deep in conversation with Danika. She turned back to Harriet.

"I need to know what's happening to me" she whispered.

Harriet took a mouthful of salad, maybe to avoid giving an immediate response, Melissa thought. While she waited she looked across the room and saw that the young girl had gone, leaving her chair pushed back against the wall. She noticed that she hadn't finished her meal. At the adjacent table, a woman, probably in her late twenties Melissa thought, sipped from her wine glass. Her black hair was in a perfectly cut bob. When she lowered her glass, Melissa saw the bright, raspberry red lips, but she hadn't made the mistake of going heavy on her eye makeup, which was minimal.

Harriet quietly put her knife and fork back onto her now empty plate and gently dabbed her lips with her white cotton napkin. She turned to Melissa and was about to speak when the waitress reappeared with a rather impressive looking Caesar salad. She carefully placed it in front of Melissa together with a tall glass of orange juice topped with crushed ice and a thin slice of blood orange. Melissa smiled her thanks. The waitress returned the smile before leaving as silently as she had appeared.

Although having initially denied having much appetite, Melissa had to admit that the salad that now sat in front of her was looking, she couldn't deny, annoyingly tempting. Begrudgingly she picked up her fork and speared a piece of romaine lettuce and an anchovy.

"The food here is rather good."

Harriet leant in towards her, as if imparting something of a highly confidential nature. Melissa continued eating the salad but gave the elderly lady a look that said 'I'd like to hear more than a culinary recommendation'. Harriet sat back in her chair, holding her now almost empty glass of wine. She stared at it for some moments.

"I'd love another one but I have to be good and resist such temptation. I hear you attended a funeral today."

It took a moment for Melissa to pick up on the last sentence. She stopped eating and looked at Harriet.

"Is that common knowledge?"

Harriet shook her head.

"Common knowledge? No. I very much doubt it. But there's little that goes on here without my knowing about it."

She said, with maybe just a hint of pride?

"So what do you know about the funeral?"

As she spoke so Melissa, for the second time, glanced over to Verity who was still talking to Danika. Harriet smiled.

"Are you concerned that you shouldn't be caught asking the question, or that I shouldn't be caught answering it?"

Melissa shook her head, possibly a little too vigorously.

"No. No, not at all. Well....maybe both, or neither."

Harriet laughed as Melissa failed in her attempt to give what she hoped was the right answer.

"I expect Verity told you *something* about this place, didn't she?"

Melissa thought for a moment.

"She said it's a kind of refuge, a sanctuary. But she didn't say why I should need such a thing."

"Did she say more than that?"

"She said I faced a threat."

Melissa tried to recall if Verity had actually said anything else, but was sure she hadn't and so she waited for Harriet to reply. There followed some moments of silence while the elderly woman seemed to be considering her choice of words. Eventually she spoke, her voice quiet and precise.

"I would not be exaggerating if I were to say that, were you not here with us this evening, it is highly likely that you would no longer be alive."

As she finished speaking so she took Melissa's hand in her own and held it in a gentle but firm grip. If there was a coherent response to what she had just been told, Melissa was struggling to find it. When Harriet spoke again Melissa saw in her eyes not only the truth of her words, but a wisdom and insight that she had seldom, if ever, sensed in another person.

"But you shouldn't dwell upon that thought, Melissa. I tell you so that, in moments when you find yourself questioning and, perhaps, lamenting your presence here, you will know that there is a reason. The greatest reason of all. Your very existence. Now...."

Harriet pushed herself unsteadily to her feet.

"....if you will excuse me I shall leave you for this evening, but I'm certain we shall talk again very soon. You may finish your meal in peace without an old woman continually wittering in your ear."

"Oh no, please...."

Melissa's protest was stopped before it had begun as Harriet held up her hand.

"You are a well-mannered, polite young lady and you will, of course, wish to argue the point but the time for my evening nap is fast approaching, and a little later there is a documentary about the artist Monet which promises to be rather good. So please continue with your salad. Thank you for your company Melissa, I very much look forward to our next meeting. It truly has been a pleasure to meet you. And don't forget what I told you."

She turned away and walked slowly over to the door. The waitress who had just served Melissa with her meal, appeared by Harriet's side and handed her a walking stick with an ornately carved handle. The elderly woman nodded her thanks as she took it.

"A pleasure to meet you too!" Melissa called after her as she suddenly remembered the manners she was supposed to have. Harriet, without turning around, lifted the stick in the air to acknowledge that she'd heard her. And then she was gone. Melissa returned her attention to her salad.

"May I sit here?"

She stopped her fork midway between her plate and mouth, turning to see who had spoken. Standing just behind her left shoulder was a young woman, her auburn hair styled in what Melissa recognised as 'curtain bangs'. She was wearing an elegant, midnight blue knee-length skirt and simple grey blouse. She wouldn't have looked out of place walking the corridors of some successful City finance company, on her way to oversee the takeover of a rival firm.

"Be my guest. Your turn to keep an eye on the new girl, is it?"

"I'm sorry?"

The young woman seemed genuinely puzzled by Melissa's words and she immediately regretted saying them.

"No. *I'm* sorry. Please...."

Melissa indicated to the chair that Harriet had just vacated. The woman lowered herself onto it and held out a hand.

"I'm Justine, by the way."

Melissa put down her cutlery and took her hand.

"Good to meet you. I'm Melissa."

Justine gave her a smile that seemed to brighten the room.

"I have to confess I already knew your name. Word gets round pretty quickly here."

"So I've noticed."

Justine looked down at Melissa's plate.

"That salad looks good, although I'm having the lasagne."

She spoke as though they were old friends.

"You're unique here, Melissa. Did you know that?"

Justine took a mouthful of the lasagne that had just been placed in front of her.

"How nice" she replied, having no idea what Justine meant.

"Of course! You don't know! Why would you?...."

Another room brightening smile.

"....Silly of me to think otherwise."

"You could enlighten me."

"Mmm, well...."

She swallowed and took a sip from her glass of mineral water.

"....as far as I'm aware, you're the only one who has no idea why she's here."

Melissa didn't immediately reply, perhaps hoping that Justine, having come out with such a statement, would see fit to elaborate upon it. Instead....

"But, then again, do any of us really know why we're here?"

Justine punctuated her pseudo philosophising with a wink as she resumed the attack on her lasagne, while Melissa considered whether she should ask the obvious question. Clearly Verity was happy for her to speak with the other 'guests', and so she surely must know that she was highly likely to be looking for answers from anyone and everyone.

"Are we all here for the same reason?"

Justine thought about this for a moment.

"Well, in the broadest sense, yes. We are all here because to be somewhere, anywhere, else would be....undesirable."

She had to search for the last word, and it hadn't been easy to find.

"Harriet said that if I wasn't here then I would probably be dead."

Justine shrugged.

"Well, that's pretty undesirable, isn't it?"

"Does that apply to all of you?"

She took another mouthful of lasagne and nearly a minute passed before she spoke again.

"Are you having a dessert? I shouldn't really but I will if you will."

Melissa had the feeling that the implication of that was 'yes', but also that the much clearer message was 'no more questions for now'.

"What would you recommend?"

Melissa wasn't completely sure that she wanted another course, but accepting Justine's suggestion would at least ensure that she had her company for a little while longer because, although she'd only known her for minutes, she had an overwhelming feeling that here was a person that, in the near future, she would wish to call a friend. Melissa couldn't explain that feeling. She just knew that it existed.

"The ice cream is so scrummy! It comes from a local farm. I nearly always have that."

"Sounds good."

Once more the waitress, with her quiet efficiency, appeared by Justine's side, ready to take her order.

"They will look after you here. I know how you feel, but all of this is for the best."

Justine had been right about the ice cream. It was the most delicious Melissa had ever tasted.

"How long have you been here?"

She decided to attempt another question, fully expecting it to be politely, but skilfully, brushed aside.

"Just over four months, and in answer to one of the questions you kindly haven't asked...."

Justine saw her eyes widen.

"....I can't give you any guesses about your own situation. Verity will discuss everything with you, but I can promise you one thing. She won't spare your feelings. She won't say stuff she thinks you *want* to hear. She'll lay it on the line and you'll have to accept it. Or not."

All thoughts of her ice cream, however delicious it was, had disappeared. All she could focus on were Justine's words and the expression on her face that spoke of her sincerity.

"Did you accept it?"

Justine smiled at Melissa's question.

"Accept it? I almost threw my arms around her. I was so bloody relieved. But then I knew things that, right now, you don't. And, as for the things you don't know, that, as I've just said, is Verity's province. Not anyone else's and certainly not mine. I'm sorry."

She added the apology as an afterthought, as if suddenly realising that what she'd said, and maybe how she'd said it, sounded much too abrupt and deliberately obstructive. She hadn't meant it to be. Another glance across the room confirmed that Verity and Danika were still sitting, talking and enjoying their meal. There was no sudden turning away, no indication at all that either woman had been surreptitiously observing her and Justine. Melissa momentarily wondered whether Justine was acting under instructions, and whether she had been too ready to accept her new 'friend' at face value.

"How about when we finish here we go and find somewhere a bit quieter? We can talk if you want, and you won't have to be continually thinking that we're being kept under surveillance."

"Is it that obvious?"

Justine smiled as she nodded.

"Afraid so."

"Ok. Yes, I'd like that. Where do you have in mind?"

There could be no harm in it, could there? And perhaps if she and Justine could be alone, just for a short while, there might be a chance she would be a little more forthcoming.

"Mine or yours? Or there's my favourite room in this whole place. Shall we go there?"

There was a genuine enthusiasm in her voice which intrigued Melissa.

"Ok by me. I've only seen Verity's office, my rooms and the corridors in between."

"I'm sure you'll get the full guided tour tomorrow. And you'll be impressed."

Justine saw the look on Melissa's face.

"Do you want to tell me?" she asked softly.

Melissa took a moment to bring her emotions under control.

"I can't do this. I can't pretend like this is some kind of holiday. I have a life. You have a life. We can't just disappear from….everything, no matter what the threat, real or imagined. Can we?"

Justine put her spoon down and stood up.

"Come on. Let's go."

As she spoke so Justine looked over to Verity who acknowledged her with a smile and a nod. Melissa noticed that short interaction but didn't say anything until they had left the dining room and were walking back through the reception.

"Did you have to get permission to leave?"

Justine stopped and turned to her.

"No. I thought, as a courtesy, that both Verity and Danika should be aware that you were coming with me and wouldn't need to be escorted back to your apartment."

Melissa looked suitably uncomfortable.

"It seems like I need to apologise again."

Justine shook her head.

"No. But what you do need to do is understand that this isn't some kind of five-star prison. Any of us can leave whenever we wish."

"That's what Verity told me. I'm not sure I believed her at the time."

"It's true. But we all know, and you'll get to know, that staying here is the better option by far."

Before Melissa could reply, Justine began climbing the stairway that led back to the corridor where Melissa's apartment, among others, was situated. They made their way past all of the doors to the end of the corridor that, when she had first seen it, Melissa thought was a dead end. However, she could now see, as they approached it, that it took a ninety degree turn to the right.

"Just down here."

They walked along another similar corridor, except that this one had large windows set, not in the sloping ceiling, but at regular intervals in the wall. Outside it was dusk, with the first stars appearing in a darkening sky.

"You don't have to eat down there all the time, by the way. You can have meals brought to your room. It's just that Verity likes anyone new to go to the dining room on their first night."

36

As Justine spoke, so the door that was now facing them at the end of the corridor began to swing inwards. For some seconds the room beyond remained in darkness but, as they approached, so the lights inside started to switch themselves on.

"Follow me."

Justine was the first through the doorway, glancing over her shoulder to ensure Melissa was close behind. The first thing that struck Melissa as she entered was not what she saw, but what she felt. The temperature was several degrees above that of the corridor they had just left. The air was warm but not uncomfortable. Everywhere there were plants and flowers, some in their own containers, others in raised beds that stretched along the length of each wall. In the centre of the room was a circle of larger plants and small trees that were just a few inches off touching the high ceiling.

Melissa's attention had been so taken by the amount and variety of plant life that it was some moments before she noticed the brightly coloured butterfly that had settled on one of the larger flowers. Its wings were gently fluttering as if being caught by a summer breeze. Then she saw that another, equally beautiful butterfly was resting on a leaf directly above the one she had first seen, and next to that another. In fact, Melissa quickly realised that each plant was home to several butterflies and, as she looked around her, she saw that there were so many that it would be impossible to count them all.

"Wow! This is amazing!"

Melissa slowly turned a full circle, taking in every corner of the room.

"It's all carefully controlled, right amount of daylight, heat, the appropriate flowers for them to feed. During the day the balcony doors are open...."

Justine pointed at two large patio doors that were now closed.

"....so they can fly away if they wish but, like all of us here, they choose not to."

As she spoke so she made her way over to a small bench that was placed under one of the trees. She sat down and beckoned Melissa to join her.

"You said Verity would talk to me about *my* situation, about why *I'm* here."

"Yes."

Justine said the word with more than a hint of suspicion, ready for an attempt to elicit information that she had already said she couldn't, and wouldn't, give. But she didn't blame her for trying. She'd do the same in her position.

"Then could we talk about *you*, and how *you* came to be here?"

Melissa asked more in hope than expectation, as one of the butterflies flew from a nearby flower and landed on her shoulder. In reply Justine laughed, as if Melissa had just told a mildly amusing joke.

"Are you just being polite, or are you really interested?"

"Oh, I'm interested. Believe me."

Justine smiled. Was that the truth? Did it matter?

"I'm happy to tell you, after all, we'll need to talk about something while we're in here, won't we?"

She held up a hand and, as if summoned, another butterfly fluttered from its resting place and settled in her palm, its colourfully patterned wings slowly opening and closing. Justine carefully lowered her hand onto her lap. The butterfly remained in her palm, showing no inclination to move from its new resting place. Justine turned to Melissa and, with another warm smile, began to tell her story, her voice quiet and clear. It was the only sound in the room.

Chapter 6

~Justine~

As she hung her coat on the stand, Justine glanced out of the window. There were storm clouds in the distance. Fortunately, she had managed the ten-minute walk from the tube station with only a hint of rain in the air, stopping at the coffee shop, a few doors away from the office, for her usual flat white. She placed the piping hot drink within easy reach of her desk, switched on her laptop and, while it booted up, took a sip of her coffee.

Justine was alone on the third floor, except for a few night cleaners who would soon be finishing their shift. But that was why she had left home an hour earlier. She wanted to arrive before anyone else in her department that morning. She had stuck to her usual routine, just in case she was seen by some early bird, maybe a conscientious employee from another section. She needed to buy her regular coffee. And her laptop needed to be on and logged into the system because, otherwise, what was she doing in the building so early? There were CCTV cameras everywhere, of course, but Justine had decided to gamble that they weren't being closely monitored at that time of the day. They wouldn't pay to have some security guy sit and watch the cleaners going about their work. All the secure stuff would be guarded by far more sophisticated and reliable means. No, the CCTV's recordings would only be checked if there was some reason to check them, and she had no intention of providing such a reason.

Had she been mistaken in what she saw, or thought she saw, yesterday? If she had misread the situation, and she didn't believe she had, she knew she certainly hadn't misread the look on the young woman's face, and the terror in her eyes. Yes, it had been only a glimpse, a fleeting moment, there and gone, but, having spent every waking second since going over and over that fleeting moment in her mind, she had convinced herself that she was right. That she couldn't just look away. But what if she was wrong? Then she would, in all likelihood, be risking losing a job that she not only enjoyed, but needed.

Her coffee had now cooled off enough for her to finish it. She took a deep breath as she walked from the room, dropping her empty cup into the recycling bin as she passed. There was still time to forget it, to go and sit back down and have another ordinary, safe day. But Justine knew that, if she did, those eyes, that had fixed upon hers for no more than a second, would haunt her forever. The two men either side of the young woman had tried to make it look as if they were merely walking together, perhaps heading to yet another meeting. And to the casual observer it might have appeared that way. If it hadn't been for that glance in her direction, that silent plea, then Justine too might have thought little more of it.

As she walked along the corridor, still illuminated its entire length by the dim night lighting, she knew she could turn back and no one would know. But she kept walking, no longer in any doubt that, ultimately, she had no choice. As she reached the stairwell where she had seen the young woman, Justine stopped, staring at the door that had been so hurriedly pulled shut the moment she had been marched through it. Justine tried to recall if she had been beyond that door before but quickly came to the conclusion she hadn't. It belonged, as far as she knew, to an entirely separate part of the company. Thinking back, she remembered being told that they dealt with highly sensitive data, and entry for unauthorised employees was strictly forbidden. Any further questions were actively discouraged.

She hesitated. What if the door was locked? But what was she expecting to find if it wasn't? Did she have any kind of plan? As she put out a hand to push it open, so more and more questions began to crowd in on her. It was as if, up until that moment, something had been pushing all the negatives into the background, hiding them from her view. She rested her hand against the door's frosted glass window for no more than a couple of seconds before leaning against it. It slowly swung inwards and she stepped through.

If Justine had expected to find some 'otherworld', a parallel universe, beyond that door, then she was to be sadly disappointed. In front of her there was a corridor very similar to the one she had just left. Nothing extraordinary, nothing sinister. It was then that she began to wonder if, somehow, her memory had been lying to her. Was she recalling the moment she saw the young woman accurately? Up until then she had never doubted herself but, suddenly, she was no longer sure. That new doubt, coupled with her earlier misgivings, almost stopped her dead in her tracks, and she had to make a conscious effort to continue on.

Another, longer corridor stretched out ahead of her. She was now, most definitely, in uncharted territory. Although similar to the part of the building she knew well, there was something different about where she now found herself. If asked to say what that difference was, she would have struggled to give it a name. Was it the building itself? Was it her imagination pulling her yet further into her own private fantasy? No. Focus on the girl. Just the girl. It was all about her, and nothing else.

There was another door in front of her. As she approached it she looked back over her shoulder. Was she expecting to be followed? If so, by whom? The men who had been with the girl? Justine stopped once more. Another chance to reconsider, another chance to walk away from this paranoia. Except she knew now, this wasn't some exaggerated, uncontrolled obsession. Whatever was driving her had direction and purpose.

This time, for no particular reason, she used her foot to push against the bottom of the door. It gave a little. Was it locked? No. It had opened far enough for her to see beyond it, except that she could see very little. There was no light at all, not even the low night lighting that was used in the rest of the building.

Justine removed her mobile phone from her jacket pocket and turned on its torch. As she shone its beam ahead of her and walked through the doorway she knew that she was now irrevocably committed. She cautiously moved forward, flicking the light from side to side, the shaking beam giving her an unwelcome reminder of just how much her hands were trembling. Behind her the door shut with a quiet 'click'.

She looked around her. As far as she could make out, she was in a large, square room. Was there a light switch? There had to be. But, as her mobile's beam scanned each wall in turn, she couldn't see one. It was as she was beginning another search of the room that something on the floor was momentarily illuminated, a sudden sparkle and then gone. It took her a few seconds to find it again. She held the phone as steadily as she was able as she walked over to where it lay. Justine knelt down and picked it up. It was a small diamond drop earring. She studied it closely, slowly turning it between her fingers. The diamond flashed and sparkled as it caught the light from her phone, its tiny heart burning with a blue and white flame.

Justine shone the beam across the floor, searching for the other earring. Perhaps if she'd been willing to venture a little further into the room she might have found it. But a little voice was telling her that she'd gone far enough, that she wasn't going to find the girl however hard she looked, and that she should get back to her office sooner rather than later. And she never ignored her little voice, except maybe....

She pushed the earring down into the depths of her jacket pocket as she stood up and took another few steps into the darkness. At that moment, from somewhere in front of her, she thought she heard a sound. Was it a door opening? And were those footsteps? She was sure she could hear footsteps.

Trying to keep the phone's light steady, Justine turned and began to walk quickly back the way she came. The beam reached into the darkness but failed to find the door she had used little more than a minute ago. In her near panic, had she not turned a full hundred and eighty degrees, or had she turned more than that? With her fear increasing with every breath and threatening to overwhelm any rational thought, she swung the mobile to the left and right, now desperate to find that door. She listened. The footsteps had stopped, if indeed they had ever existed other than in her own mind. But it was on the second sweep of the torch that she saw the metal handle as it momentarily reflected the light.

She moved forward, trying to keep the handle in the beam as she took the several paces needed to reach what she hoped was the door she had just used. She now realised that what scared her more than anything was the ease with which she had completely lost her bearings. It had taken just seconds for the darkness to frighten her to the point of panic, and she felt angry that she had allowed her curiosity and overactive imagination to put her in such a situation. The earring probably had nothing to do with the girl and, even if it did, it being on the floor didn't necessarily mean she had come to any harm.

Justine gripped the handle and pushed it down. It moved a fraction but then stopped dead. She pushed it again, harder this time. Same result. She placed her shoulder to the door, putting her full weight against it. It remained securely closed. It had let her into the room but would not let her out.

She rested, pressing her back against the door, taking deep breaths and fighting to remain calm. She brought her fist down hard against the door in frustration. What should she do? Losing what remained of her now fragile composure wasn't going to make her situation any better but, knowing that, wasn't helping. She listened again for any sound but all she could hear was her own breathing and the blood pounding in her ears. Did she have any choice now but to go on? She didn't want to, but neither did she want to remain in that room.

She turned and took a step away from the door, hoping that her phone's battery had enough charge in it to keep the torch going for as long as she might need it. Suddenly there was a sound behind her. It came from the door. As she aimed the beam once more towards it she stood frozen to the spot. Slowly the handle moved and a shaft of light from the corridor beyond shone into the room as the door was gradually pushed open.

"I heard you bang on the door. What're you doing in there?"

Without replying, Justine pushed past the cleaner, almost falling over her basket of detergents and sprays that she'd put down on the floor.

"I got lost!"

Justine didn't want to enter into a conversation with the woman but instead ran along the corridor, wanting to be back in her own office more than anything. She retraced her steps, slowing as she left the 'forbidden' area and returned to familiar surroundings. It wasn't until she sat at her desk, in a still empty office, that her panic began to slowly subside. She took several deep breaths, knowing that her work colleagues would soon begin to arrive, and she didn't want to appear anything other than calm and ready for the day ahead.

It was as she sat in front of her laptop that her thoughts turned to what exactly had just happened. And what *had* actually happened? Apart from spectres from her own imagination and a lost earring? No one had followed her, no one had been waiting for her. The only other person she had seen was one of the overnight cleaning staff. No young woman in distress, in fact no trace of her, except....she reached into her pocket and touched the earring. But, she told herself, there were countless female employees, many of whom must work in that part of the building. It could belong to any one of them. And the more she thought about it, the more she succeeded in convincing herself that the earring was probably of no significance whatsoever.

Minutes later the first of her work colleagues arrived, a serious, graceless young man who barely acknowledged her as he walked past and straight on to his own desk. When she had first met him, Justine recalled wondering if his brusque manner, which bordered on rudeness, was reserved exclusively for her, but quickly dismissed that idea when she saw that he was equally obnoxious to anyone below him on the pay scale.

She returned her attention to her laptop, quickly finding the spreadsheet she would need to continue with her work. Her heartbeat had now calmed and she was able to focus, sure now that she should try to rein in her overactive imagination in future. She even managed to smile as another two colleagues arrived, a pleasant couple who had met while working for the company. They were both excellent at their jobs and so, against company policy, they had been allowed to remain in the same department.

"Morning Ann. Hi Jez."

She received a cheery wave and broad smile in reply. And so another day at the office began. There were the usual unwelcome interruptions, with the sudden appearance of tasks that had to be done sooner rather than later. In fact, by mid-morning, Justine came to the conclusion that her spreadsheet work wasn't going to be receiving much attention for the best part of the day. It would mean another late finish, but it wasn't as if she had a hot date that night, or any other night for that matter.

One advantage of being busy was that the day seemed to fly by. Not that Justine ever wanted that. She loved the work, it was well paid and comfortably within her skill set. There were occasional opportunities for promotion and, apart from Mr Charmless, those she worked with were pleasant and easy going. And, as five thirty approached, she was asked several times if she needed any help with her remaining tasks. Each time she politely declined, knowing that those doing the asking would secretly be hoping she would turn down their offer. It didn't matter. She was relishing getting her head back into the spreadsheet and knew that without interruption she would make rapid progress.

Justine was now alone in the office. Every other laptop closed down, every other workstation empty. It would be at least a couple of hours before the night shift of cleaners and maintenance workers would begin to arrive, and she hoped to be finished well before then.

Her attention was so totally focussed on the laptop's screen that it was several seconds before she became aware of another presence in the room. She didn't look up immediately as she assumed it was one of the cleaners starting their shift early. Her concentration remained on the screen until she realised that the person, almost certainly not a cleaner, was standing right behind her, just a few feet away. She minimised the spreadsheet, ever mindful of protecting the company's data from prying eyes, before spinning her chair around to face whoever had decided to interrupt her work. But, before she could speak, a hand hit her hard across her face and, moments later, she tasted blood on her lips.

Chapter 7

~*Justine and Danika*~

"One chance. Give me the earring."

Justine had been so shocked by the sudden, unprovoked attack that for some seconds she remained silent, her hands clenched around the arms of her chair.

"The earring. Now!"

She looked into his eyes for the first time and saw no emotion. Nothing but a cold determination.

"I….I don't know….what you're talking about."

Was that the most stupid thing she could have said? Why lie? Why not just give it to him? She didn't have answers to those questions, and the only result of her denial was another, harder blow across her face. She thought she might pass out with the pain as she was roughly grasped by the arm. Her chair toppled over when he dragged her from it and pulled her towards the door where a second man was waiting. She quickly glanced from one to the other. Justine was sure they were the same men she had seen with the girl the day before. As she tried to regain her balance she was pushed hard into the arms of the other man who, in one swift movement, spun her round and slammed her against a glass partition. She felt the impact as the back of her head hit the toughened pane, her legs gave way under her and she fell to her knees.

"We know you have it."

The second man's voice was softer than that of his accomplice, more measured. He knelt down in front of her, his face level with hers. Should she continue to deny any knowledge of the earring? After all, it was only a nondescript little piece of jewellery. Was it something worth protecting? Why did she, subconsciously, believe it was?

"I….have no idea…."

He lifted her as if she were a rag doll. Justine, wanting to make herself believe she still had some degree of control over her situation, attempted to stand without support. The second man turned to the first.

"We can't do this here. We'll take her to The Room."

Without saying another word, he guided her into the corridor. She was hustled along it towards the door at the far end. Glancing around her, she desperately hoped to see someone who might come to her rescue. Suddenly, the door in front of them was pushed open and a very smart businesswoman appeared, with her sharp trouser suit and hair swept back into a single ponytail. She smiled as she walked briskly towards them, the two men doing their best to disguise the force they were using to move Justine along the corridor. Would the woman notice the smear of blood on her lips? It seemed not, as her gaze had now shifted from them to the lift at the other end of the corridor.

What happened next was still a blur to Justine. The woman brought her knee up with some force into the first man's groin and he dropped to the floor. Before the second man could react she had turned and landed her fist on the side of his head and, he too, fell. Without waiting to assess the extent of the damage she had inflicted, the woman grabbed Justine's arm and pulled her away.

"Come with me!"

Justine might have said something in response, or she might not. She couldn't remember. Not that it mattered because the woman wasn't waiting for a reply. She had now taken a firm grip of her arm and they were heading back along the corridor in the direction of the lift and stairs. The woman's preferred escape route had been the stairwell until, as they neared the lift, she saw that it was at their floor and its doors were open. She hadn't expected that. Without a word, she jerked Justine away from the stairs, into the lift and hit the basement button. It seemed an age before the doors began to close and, as they did, they saw the two men slowly and unsteadily getting to their feet. The woman turned to her.

"When we reach the basement you'll see a red car, an Audi, directly ahead of you. Run as fast as you can and get down behind it. Wait for me there."

"Is that your car?"

Justine was amazed that she had managed to ask a vaguely coherent question.

"No. We're not leaving by car. Just do as I say if you want to get out of here still breathing."

Before Justine could reply, the lift doors swished open.

"Go!"

The woman pushed her forward and Justine raced towards the red Audi, dropping down behind it. Seconds later she heard footsteps echoing around the basement car park as the two men entered from the stairwell. She glanced around her but could see no sign of the woman. The footsteps continued, and they were coming slowly, but inexorably, towards where she was hiding. There was nowhere to run. Either side of her was a wide open space, clear of cars and illuminated by bright neon lighting. Another few seconds and they couldn't fail to find her.

Justine began to fear that she had, for some reason, been abandoned by the woman but, just at that moment, a car over in the far corner of the basement suddenly came to life. It gave out several high pitched beeps, its lights came on and its engine started up. The men turned and ran towards the vehicle. A moment later the woman reappeared by Justine's side and pulled her to her feet.

"Over there. The pedestrian exit" she whispered urgently.

They ran together and made the swing doors before the men arrived at the car. By the time they realised there was no one inside it, the exit doors had closed behind the two women, and they were out onto the quiet side street. As they walked briskly away from the building, the woman reached into her pocket, removed a small card and pressed it into Justine's hand.

"Oyster card. We're taking the Tube."

Justine was about to say she had her own but suddenly realised that, in fact, she didn't. Her handbag was still under her desk, where it had been all day. With everything in it.

"My purse, my phone...."

"You won't need them."

As she replied she dropped a car keypad into a nearby bin.

"We won't need that either. It's served its purpose."

48

They were now out onto the main street and heading at a fast pace towards the London Underground sign. It was clear that the woman was not about to engage in any further conversation other than, as they entered the station....

"District Line Westbound."

There were the usual number of early evening passengers making their various ways home, but it took less than a minute for them to reach the platform. The overhead information display showed that the next train was the District Line service and was two minutes away. Justine looked up and down the platform, although unsure what she was actually looking for. The woman next to her was staring straight ahead, seemingly taking no interest at all in her surroundings.

It was while they were waiting for the train that Justine had the chance to reflect on what had happened since the men had appeared in her office. From that moment it was as if she had been watching a film, merely an observer. Because none of this could be happening to her, could it? She closed her eyes wondering if, when she opened them again, she'd be back in the office, safe and well.

The brush of warm air against her face announced the imminent arrival of their train. She opened her eyes. No office. No comforting normality. She felt the woman's hand close around her arm once more. Seconds later the train drew to a stop in front of them and its sliding doors opened. The woman stepped forward, pulling Justine with her into the carriage. Once inside, they found two seats next to each other and sat down. Another eight people joined them in the carriage, one man only just making it before the doors closed and the train moved off. Justine turned to the woman.

"Ok. I want answers. Who are you and where are we going?"

"We're getting off at Ravenscourt Park. That's all you need to know and all I'm prepared to tell you right now."

Her words were in perfectly formed English. Too perfect. And there was just a hint of something else. Eastern European? Yes, and if she were forced to take a guess, Justine would probably go with Polish. But that wasn't much help with her current situation, was it? At that moment there was no other option than to go along with whatever the woman said, Polish or not, because there was no denying that she had rescued her when there had been little hope of rescue.

The train pulled into Hammersmith. Ravenscourt Park would be the next stop. And then what? All Justine could do was wait, and put her trust in the stranger who sat next to her. She glanced over to the doors as they opened once more. Several people left the carriage and another three got on, each in their own little world. Two were wearing headphones and the third's attention was held by the screen of their phone, which turned Justine's thoughts again to her own mobile. It was all very well this woman telling her she wouldn't need it. But she ran her life from that phone. How could she not need it? The woman turned to her.

"Next station. You ok?"

The question was accompanied by a half smile. Justine nodded but said nothing.

"It's really important that you stay close to me when we get out."

Around her, the sights and sounds were so familiar, and yet she could take no comfort from that familiarity. And the woman's expression remained impassive. If she was feeling any anxiety or concern, then she hid it well. Maybe she was so confident in her planning and her abilities....except how could she have planned for such a seemingly random situation? Those men had wanted the earring that she had found, but that discovery had happened by pure chance. She might have decided to do nothing that morning, to forget about the girl she saw the day before. She could so easily have turned her back on whatever it was she had inadvertently become involved in. Thoughts of the earring prompted her to put a hand in her pocket and check it was still there, that she hadn't imagined it. It was still there, but how Justine wished it wasn't. Why couldn't she have kept her nose out of whatever this was? Why couldn't she still be quietly working on her beloved spreadsheet?

The train began to slow. The woman stood and took Justine's hand. They made their way over to the nearest doors. The only person in front of them was the man who, minutes earlier, had almost missed the train. Moments after it stopped the doors opened and they left the carriage, following the man. Just a few paces from the train the woman hesitated, seemingly waiting for something. Justine was about to ask her what the problem was when several things happened in a split second.

The train's doors started to close and, at that moment, the woman suddenly tightened her hold on Justine's hand and pulled her back into the carriage through the now nearly closed doors. They almost fell onto the floor of the train as the doors shut and it began to move out of Ravenscourt Park station. As Justine held onto one of the vertical bars near the door she saw the man who had got out of the carriage just ahead of them. He had turned back towards the train and moved forward, as if he too wanted to get back on. But he was too late and as the train left the station she saw him staring through the window, his gaze fixed upon her.

"Come and sit down. We're going to the end of the line."

"Richmond?"

The woman nodded.

"We always were. The Ravenscourt Park thing was just for our friend's benefit. We should be ok now."

Justine made her way over to the seat next to the woman.

"Perhaps I should now introduce myself properly...."

Yes, Polish. Justine was almost certain of it now.

"....my name is Danika Pacek. My friends would call me Dani, if I had any, which I don't, so no one does. And you are?"

She's done all this for me and she doesn't know who I am?

"I'm Justine. Justine Miller."

Her hand was offered and taken.

"Pleased to meet you Justine."

"Likewise....I think."

Danika gave her a sympathetic smile.

"And now, I need you to tell me exactly what happened today. Everything up to the moment I first saw you."

As she told her, as concisely as she could, so Justine realised just how much she needed to talk about it. Putting into words the events of that day was affording her a kind of release, taking the stopper out of a bottle that had been threatening to explode. When she had finished speaking, Justine reached into her pocket and removed the earring, offering it to Danika. She took it, holding it between her thumb and forefinger and, as she studied it, so her expression changed. Up until that moment, Danika had shown little in the way of emotion, just a confidence in her own ability to get them both out of a dangerous situation. But now a shadow had passed over her, taking away that confidence and replacing it with something that looked to Justine like a deep, heartfelt sadness.

"It was my fault. I was too late for her."

Justine remained silent, aware that Danika was, for some reason, struggling with her thoughts and needed to be given the chance to articulate them. Several people left the carriage at Stamford Brook and it was as the train pulled away from the station that she spoke again.

"Had I been there for her, got her away, then you wouldn't have become involved. For that, I deeply apologise to you....and to her. Events happened twenty-four hours earlier than anticipated. Once I was inside the building it didn't take long to establish that. My fault. My failure. But it was pure chance, and lucky for you, that I entered that corridor when I did. I was on my way out."

"But you haven't failed *me*. God knows what they'd have done to me if you hadn't shown up."

"I can tell you if you want to know."

"Tell me?"

Danika nodded.

"What they'd have done to you. Do you want to know?"

The question caught Justine off guard and she had to take a moment before replying.

"No, I don't believe I do, thank you."

She recalled the two men in the office and put a hand up to her mouth, feeling the place on her lips where she had been struck. No. She didn't want to know.

"May I keep this?"

Danika held up the earring. Justine nodded.

"Thank you, and thank you for caring about her. Now we must care for you."

"We?"

No answer was forthcoming. It was as if the question hadn't been asked. Danika's whole attention had, briefly, focussed upon the single earring that she had just been given. She looked at it for a few more seconds before carefully, almost reverentially, placing it into a breast pocket and pulling the zipper across, ensuring it was safe and secure.

The train was slowing and about to pull into Kew Gardens. One more stop. As it came to a halt so Justine looked across at the doors as they slid open. Should she get off here, make her own way home and call the police? Because the bottom line was, could she really trust Danika? And surely she was safe now. Then she remembered that she had no money, and no credit cards. Just the Oyster card that Danika had given her.

"There's nowhere you can go where they won't find you. Except one, and that's where I'm taking you. They fear you, Justine, and they fear what you might know."

It was if she had read her thoughts.

"But I don't know anything."

"You'll never convince them of that. They won't rest until they've found, and silenced, you. Your concern for the girl does you credit. You wanting to do something to help her, even more so. Unfortunately, in doing what you did, you have inadvertently focussed an extreme and unrelenting danger upon yourself. Only I, and those I'm taking you to, can keep you safe from that danger."

The train doors closed and the train left Kew Gardens. Justine looked around her. There was no one else at their end of the carriage. At the farther end there was a young woman. As Justine watched, she closed a folder she had been reading and placed it into a shoulder bag that lay on the seat next to her. She then picked up the bag and walked to the nearest door, holding onto the handrail. She continued to stare straight ahead, out of the door's window.

Justine turned her attention to the two other people in the carriage. After the incident at Ravenscourt Park she now saw every stranger as a potential threat and that made her feel angry. How long would she have to live with this paranoia, with no idea how all of this was to end? The teenage boy, his eyes fixed upon his phone's screen, totally disengaged from his immediate surroundings, stood and took his place behind the young woman. The last of the three, an older, well-dressed woman, looked more as if she belonged in a chauffeur driven Rolls than on the Tube. None of these people could possibly represent any threat to either

her or Danika, could they? As Danika wasn't showing the slightest interest in any of them then, in all probability, the answer was 'no'.

"We're heading for the NCP car park next to the station. This time we will be leaving by car and, again, stay close to me."

"Do you think we're still being followed?"

Danika didn't want to add to Justine's fears. But nor did she want her to believe that the danger was now over. She hoped it was, but past experience told her never to assume the game was won until it became impossible to lose, and Danika knew they were not there yet.

"It's unlikely, but possible."

The train was slowing once more, this time at the end of the line. Justine looked to Danika, not wanting to make a move without her say so. Danika remained in her seat, showing no desire to join the small queue by the doors. It wasn't until the train had stopped and every other person had left the carriage that she stood.

"Don't forget. Close."

Together they walked along the platform, on towards the adjacent car park and, as they walked, so Justine became aware that Danika was, all the time, glancing around her. Clearly she was still expecting some unwelcome attention, even though she was doing her best not to allow any serious concerns she might have to transmit to Justine, and there was no further conversation between them until they reached the car park.

"Over there."

Danika pointed towards a blue Jaguar parked halfway along the nearest row of cars. As they made their way over to it, Danika unzipped an inside pocket of her jacket and removed a keypad. Moments later Justine was sitting in the passenger seat while Danika remained standing by the closed driver's door. Justine leant forward to look through the window and saw that she was on her phone, although she couldn't hear what she was saying. The call had obviously been short and to the point because, seconds later, Danika climbed behind the wheel. If Justine had expected to be let in on the phone conversation that had just taken place, then she was to be disappointed. Danika remained silent as she started the engine.

The Jaguar nosed its way out of its parking space, following the 'Out' arrows. Justine glanced around her at the rows of cars. A little way off, the barrier at the entrance raised as a grey Land Rover Discovery drove into the car park. It continued on, past several empty parking spaces, until it drew to a stop about thirty yards in front of them.

"Stay down!"

Danika reached across and pulled Justine out of sight, low across the front seats.

"As soon as I'm gone, press that button. It'll lock all the doors. If things don't go well, hit the horn and stay on it. It'll hopefully attract some attention and keep you safe."

Before Justine could reply, Danika pushed her door open and was out of her seat. With the 'lock' button pressed, several seconds passed before Justine decided to disobey Danika's 'stay down' command. Slowly, very slowly, she lifted her head until she could just see out of the windscreen. Two men had got out of the Discovery and were standing and looking first towards the Jaguar and then to Danika, whose hands were now clenched into tight fists by her side. In the car, Justine lay across the front seats and closed her eyes.

Chapter 8

The butterfly that had been resting in Justine's palm while she had been speaking, suddenly took flight and fluttered to a nearby plant.

"I don't know how long it took for Danika to return to the car. I think my memory plays tricks on me regarding that. I felt it was an eternity but I'm sure that, in reality, it was maybe no more than a minute."

Melissa, who had listened in silence, watched as the butterfly settled, its wings open and showing off the delicate blue and white pattern that adorned them.

"And she was uninjured?"

"She had blood on her, but I'm pretty sure it wasn't hers. I think those men were treated with 'extreme prejudice'. I got the impression that they had to pay for the girl she believes she failed to save."

Justine smiled grimly before adding

"But you've seen her in action too."

Melissa nodded.

"True. But my rescue didn't involve any direct confrontation. We kind of just ran for it."

"She'd have got you out, no matter what. Or died trying."

"And she brought you here?"

"Yes. Just like you."

"Just like me" Melissa whispered under her breath. She looked around her. Everywhere in the room was green with life, the butterflies like tiny, sparkling jewels scattered among the small trees and plants.

"What did Danika tell you about the girl you saw, the one she was meant to save?"

"Nothing. She's hardly spoken of her since that day."

"Have you tried to find out? I don't think I could live with not knowing."

"I didn't say I didn't know anything about her, just that *Danika* wouldn't discuss her."

"So who....?"

Justine turned to Melissa, her expression prompting her to answer her own question.

"Verity?"

Justine nodded.

"Danika never spoke to me about her again. Verity told me that she still has the earring I found. She believes that Danika keeps it so that she never forgets what she sees as her personal failure. I've tried to talk to Danika about it but, on the few occasions I've had the opportunity, she either deftly changes the subject or refuses to speak at all."

"And what has Verity said about the girl?"

"Well, firstly, I'd wrongly assumed that she worked somewhere in the same building as me, but apparently she was taken there and, as Danika told me, they had expected her abduction to occur a day later than it did."

"Why did it occur at all? Has Verity told you that?"

Melissa couldn't prevent an edge of frustration showing in her voice and she immediately felt the need to apologise.

"You're seeing her tomorrow, aren't you?"

Melissa nodded.

"Then she'll give you some of the answers you're looking for."

"Only some? Look, I know you don't want to pre-empt what Verity might say but you have to give me something. Please."

Justine took a breath.

"I'm here because I was in the wrong place at the wrong time. But I quickly came to realise that there was no choice for me. However, I'm not what you are, Melissa. I'm not what the others here are. I'm here by an accident of circumstances. I just know that if I were anywhere other than here I would be dead by now. It really is that simple. Harriet was right in what she told you. If you hold onto nothing else, hold onto that. That is the 'something' that I can give you."

And so there it was again. She *had* to be here for nothing less than her own survival. But what had Justine meant by 'what you are'? There always seemed to be more questions than answers.

57

However, Melissa was now reluctantly resigned to the fact that those answers would have to wait until tomorrow's meeting with Verity.

"Who were the two others I saw in the dining room earlier?"

It was as good a question as any to change the course of the conversation and the answer, should Justine provide one, would be of some interest.

"The woman with the bobbed hair and the young girl" Melissa prompted as another butterfly flew over and came to rest on Justine's hand.

"The woman's name is Sophie. The teenager's called Layla. I believe her mother was a big fan of Eric Clapton."

Melissa was about to smile when she realised what Justine had just said.

"Was?"

"I understand that both her parents are dead."

"Poor girl. That's awful. Do you know what happened?"

Justine shook her head.

"Verity hasn't told us much, only that she's an orphan and, like the rest of us, is here for her own safety. Layla doesn't really interact with anyone. If you wish her a 'good morning' you might, if you're lucky, get a begrudging smile in return. She's a very frightened young girl who hides her fear and grief behind an overwhelming shyness and a barely controlled anger."

Melissa's expression couldn't hide her incredulity.

"That's a pretty impressive bit of amateur psychology if you haven't even spoken with her."

Justine smiled sadly.

"I'm not claiming any credit. I happened to overhear those exact words when Verity was discussing Layla's psychiatric report."

"Did you hear anything else?"

Melissa leant forward, suddenly feeling that she cared about this girl, but Justine was clearly unsure if she'd already said too much and whether she should say anymore.

"Nothing really. But I'm sure Verity wouldn't mind my saying that it's been decided to allow Layla the space it's felt she needs. I think they're hoping she'll open up if she's just given time."

Melissa decided not to ask anything else about her, sensing she had already pushed her luck.

"Does everyone here have a psychiatric report?" she enquired, perhaps hoping to surreptitiously get another piece of the jigsaw.

"You'd need to ask Verity a question like that. I wouldn't know."

And so it seemed Justine had stopped playing, at least for now.

"Thanks for your company this evening, and for sharing your story with me."

Justine smiled.

"I'd like to hear what happened to you today. Something about a funeral?"

Melissa frowned, and Justine felt obliged to add

"I might have overheard something. I'm quite good at that."

Justine's eyes glinted mischievously and, at that moment, Melissa was sure that, whatever her future might hold, she at least had one friend in this place. As they left the room Melissa took one last look around her.

"You can come back here anytime you want" Justine offered.

"I don't think I've ever been anywhere quite like it."

Once they were out into the corridor Justine asked again about 'the funeral' and so Melissa, looking on it as a sort of *quid pro quo*, proceeded to give her a short account of what had occurred earlier that day, right up to her arrival.

"Danika's quite something, isn't she?"

Justine had listened without interrupting as they walked, and only spoke when she was sure Melissa had finished her story.

"Do you think it's true what she says, about her not having any friends? I mean, at first I took it as a throwaway line, you know, just something to say to distract from the jeopardy of the situation, but now I'm not so sure."

Melissa realised that they were now standing outside her apartment door.

"As I told you, I've been here for a few months now, and I'm not sure about anything concerning Danika. Initially I thought I might be getting to know her but, as time went on, I slowly came to realise that she lets you in so far but no further. Maybe it's a subconscious thing, I don't know."

Justine punctuated the last sentence with a shrug of her shoulders.

"Would you like to come in for a while? I'm sure I recall seeing a coffee maker."

"Why not?"

Melissa had prepared herself for a polite refusal, so Justine's acceptance accompanied by a warm smile, came as a very pleasant surprise.

"Only thing is…."

Melissa walked over to the small table where the aforementioned coffee maker was standing, and knelt down in front of it, staring at the array of buttons and lights.

"….you might have to give me an hour or so to figure out how to get it to work."

Justine didn't seem to be listening but had picked up the handset of a wall mounted phone near the door.

"I'm feeling more adventurous than coffee" she said as she selected the '0' on the phone's touch pad. It was answered immediately.

"Hi. It's Justine. Could we have a nice chilled bottle of Rosé, please? That'd be lovely. Yes, Melissa's apartment, that's right. Thank you."

She replaced the handset in its cradle.

"So…."

Justine disappeared into the kitchen and re-emerged with two wine glasses. She placed them on a nearby table before sitting down on the sofa.

"….shall we watch something while we're waiting for our wine?"

She picked up the remote control and brought the television to life. Melissa watched as Justine worked the remote, various menus flicking up on the large screen.

"Something light and frothy…."

She lowered her voice into a mock sinister tone.

"….or something dark and disturbing?"

"You choose."

Justine thought for a moment before pressing the remote again, turning the screen off.

"Do you know what, let's just enjoy our wine and talk some more, if you'd like to?"

Melissa was quietly relieved. Although she hadn't wanted to say anything she really didn't feel like giving her attention to any kind of programme or film, frothy or disturbing. She nodded.

"Very much, yes…." She was about to add 'please' but realised, just in time, that might make her sound just a little too needy. And so they settled into some light, inconsequential chat, simply enjoying each other's company.

"Do you miss the life you had before you came here?"

But before Justine could reply, their conversation was interrupted by the arrival of the wine. And so they sat together on the sofa, both with full glasses of the chilled Rosé. Melissa's knowledge of wine was probably best described as limited but it was, unquestionably, delicious.

"It is good, isn't it? I knew you'd like it. And, in answer to your question, no. Not really. Things weren't great for me, if I'm honest. My work was the best thing in my life, and that's quite a sad thing to confess, isn't it?"

What could she say to that? Commiserate? Refuse to believe such a matter-of-fact dismissal of her old life? After some seconds all Melissa managed to come up with was

"Oh, I'm sorry."

"But I shouldn't be worrying you with my issues which, in any case, are in the past now. Suffice to say, I don't seem to be able to make anything good come from relationships. What about you, Melissa? Are you any good at relationships?"

She reached out to the wine bottle and topped up her glass before offering to do the same for Melissa.

"I'm fine thank you."

"Ok. So are you? Or you could tell me to mind my own business."

She laughed.

"No, I won't do that. But my answer's going to be pretty boring, I'm afraid."

"I'm listening."

Justine took a sip from her glass as she leant forward, giving Melissa her full attention.

"Well, apart from someone at uni that I suppose was semi-serious for a time, there hasn't been anyone for a while now. See, I told you it was boring."

But clearly Justine had no intention of leaving Melissa's love life, or lack of it, there.

"Is that through choice or....?"

In any other circumstances, with anyone else, she wouldn't have hesitated to politely close the conversation down but somehow she felt happy to talk about anything, however personal, with Justine.

"I suppose you could say that. I haven't been actively looking."

Melissa realised that she hadn't consciously thought about it before. Was that the case, or had it been something more than just 'not actively looking'? She knew, for some elusive reason, she wasn't prepared to face the answer to that right now, no matter how comfortable she was in Justine's company.

"That sounds like a bit of an excuse. I mean, do you want to be alone? Because a girl like you, I don't think you'd even need to try!"

Justine smiled as she spoke, knowing she'd made a blatant attempt to provoke a response from Melissa that might well be outside of her comfort zone. Her gaze flicked away, just for a moment. Had she touched a nerve?

"I believe that was a compliment, so thank you."

"So is it an excuse?"

"What if it is?"

Maybe, it occurred to Melissa, it might be a good option to admit the possibility rather than offer a flat denial.

"Well, if it is, then I'd be obliged to ask why you would choose to be alone, wouldn't I?"

Justine's eyes didn't leave her for a moment, looking for any tell-tale sign that she had pushed it too far, that she should back off.

"Can we talk about this another day?"

Melissa said after several seconds of silence, before adding

"It's not that I'm avoiding the question, really it's not, it's just that I'm not sure I know the answer. All I can tell you right now is that I'm not denying what you're suggesting. Will that do?"

Justine smiled apologetically.

"I'm sorry. I tend to do that. I pick up on things and I have to ask. Can't stop myself."

"No apology necessary. But I'd like to hear more about your relationships, if you want to tell me."

Justine contemplated her half empty wine glass.

"I could recite you a short, highly exclusive list of names. Some I knew would go nowhere but were fun at the time. If I'm honest, there really was only one. That 'someone' who seems right in every way, you know?"

Melissa nodded, not wanting to admit that, in all probability, she didn't know.

"What happened?"

Justine took another sip of wine, as if she needed its fortification before she could go on.

"I believed in them. I trusted them...."

She hesitated, her voice faltering with emotion and Melissa considered suggesting she stop. But maybe she needed this, to talk about something that obviously cut so deep.

"....usual story, I suppose. It turned out the commitment was all on my side. My fault. Shouldn't have been so naïve."

She gave a quiet, humourless laugh.

"No. You can't beat yourself up for offering unconditional trust and love. The fault was with them. No one else."

Melissa hoped that came out right. Justine emptied her glass, stood and reached out to take Melissa's hands, pulling her to her feet. She hugged her before gripping her shoulders and holding her at arms' length.

"Listen to us! We sound like people who've known each other for years! I think it's this place, it seems to bring people closer somehow....and now I'm going to wish you a goodnight, Melissa. Try to sleep well and I'll see you tomorrow."

Justine made her way over to the door and, without a backward glance, left the room, leaving Melissa alone with her thoughts....and fears.

Chapter 9

"Did you have a good night, in the circumstances?"

Verity rose from behind her desk as Melissa entered her office.

"In the circumstances, yes."

Actually Melissa had slept unexpectedly well, enjoying a deep and, as far as she could recall, dreamless sleep. Breakfast had been brought to her room by a pleasant young woman who, like the waitress of the previous evening, had little to say except to express the wish that she should enjoy her meal. And she had. It had been a continental breakfast, with coffee, fruit juice and various delicious pastries. The polite thing to do would be to thank Verity for it.

"I'm pleased you liked it. Danika chose it for you today but, of course, you're free to order whatever you wish from tomorrow onwards."

Tomorrow onwards. Those words served to remind Melissa that she was still unsure if she believed Verity when she told her that she was free to leave at any time.

"It's a lovely morning. Shall we go for a walk? I can show you everything we have to offer you here."

"That sounds....nice."

Melissa decided she wasn't going to immediately launch into a demand for answers. It looked as if Verity intended to spend some time with her, and hopefully those answers would come if she remained civil and patient.

"Good. Follow me."

Verity led her back to the reception, out of the building and onto the gravel drive. Melissa saw again the open fronted garage where the blue Jaguar was parked alongside the other vehicles. The sight of it brought back memories of the day before. She stopped for a moment to stare at it. Verity stood beside her but said nothing, not wanting to interrupt her thoughts. After some seconds her gaze moved from the car to look out across the vast lawn and to the woods beyond. Eventually Melissa turned back to her.

"Sorry. I didn't mean to drift off like that. I'm not normally given to daydreams."

Verity smiled.

"Not a problem."

She led her away from the main door, walking along the narrow path that ran parallel to the house.

"Let's try and give you something pleasant to think about, shall we?"

They turned the corner at the far end of the building. In the distance there were low hills that stretched away to the horizon, with wooded areas covering at least half of the visible landscape. But, in contrast to the wild, natural countryside of the distant woodland, where Melissa and Verity now stood were formal gardens set out in various geometric patterns. The flowerbeds were planted with careful attention to detail. No colour clashes, each plant and shrub having the space it needed to show itself off to maximum effect.

"These have all been chosen with insects and wildlife as the main consideration. I was most insistent upon that. You'll notice the small fountain and pond over there."

Melissa looked over in the direction that Verity was pointing as a colourful little bird flew down and perched on the pond's edge. It dipped its beak into the water several times before flying off, disappearing over the roof and out of sight.

"Did you design all of this?"

They continued to walk, on past the fountain and then along the path on the opposite side.

"I'd like to say yes but that would be stretching the truth. Let's just say that I had the vision and those with far more talent than I made it a reality."

"Verity's being too modest. This whole place's existence is down to her."

They turned to see Danika walking towards them. She was wearing jodhpurs and riding boots. In one hand she carried a riding hat, and in the other a pair of gloves. A white blouse and body protector completed a look that wouldn't have been out of place on the cover of *Horse and Hound* or *Tatler*.

"Good morning Danika. Which one are you on this morning?"

"Thought I'd give Firefly a bit more time in the outdoor school."

"Excellent. Do you mind if we watch?"

"No problem. See you there."

As Danika walked past them she gave Melissa a fleeting smile.

"She's very good with all of our horses, a real talent."

Verity sounded proud, as if she were talking about a well-loved daughter.

"All? How many do you have?"

"Twelve, with two in foal. Do you ride, Melissa?"

"Not since my school days. Been a while now, but I used to enjoy it."

The path ahead forked into two. Verity guided her to the right, leading them away from the gardens and towards the rear of the house.

"Then I shall ask Danika to take you out sometime."

The prospect of that caught Melissa off guard.

"Oh, I'm not sure…."

Verity interrupted before Melissa could build a credible argument against her suggestion.

"We have horses for all abilities and Danika would take good care of you."

Melissa gave her what she hoped was a polite but non-committal look as they reached a row of trees that obscured what lay beyond.

"Just through here."

Verity pushed aside a branch that was growing across the moss covered track. Seconds later they emerged into a wide open space that was surrounded on three sides by grassy banks.

"We can sit in the shade over there."

Verity pointed to a wooden bench that nestled against the large trunk of an oak tree and moments later they were sitting together, facing the arena.

"Well. Here we are."

"It seems so."

Melissa leant back, looking over towards the entrance to the school. Beyond the open gate she could just see another flat roofed building and a courtyard behind that. Verity followed her gaze.

"The stables. We'll show you around them later, if you're interested."

"I'd like that."

Melissa shifted uncomfortably on the bench, looking down at her hands and then back up to the arena. She heard Verity take a deep breath.

"However, although I'm sure you will enjoy the grand tour, my guess would be that it isn't at the top of your list of things you'd like to discuss right now?"

Melissa had wondered how long it might be before Verity would give her the opportunity to ask the questions she so desperately wanted answered. But now that the moment had come, Melissa found herself hesitating, suddenly unsure where or how to begin. She had gone over it again and again and thought she had it all clear in her mind. To her credit, Verity sensed that Melissa was struggling and picked up the conversation.

"So where shall I start? I believe I explained that you were here for your own safety?"

Melissa nodded.

"Therefore, I'm sure you'll agree, that then raises the question of who is threatening your safety, and why."

Melissa nodded again and Verity was about to continue when Danika entered the arena riding a magnificent looking bay gelding. Although Melissa was no expert she could see that Danika looked every inch the horsewoman.

"Firefly is quite young and still learning. She's schooling him in the basics at the moment, but she tells me he has great potential. Now, where was I?"

Melissa turned back to her.

"Who's threatening me, and why?"

She prompted, even though she knew Verity's question was probably rhetorical.

"They call themselves The Custodians."

Melissa's brow furrowed.

"The Custodians? Custodians of what?"

"Of their values, of their creed, believing that they need to avenge something they see as a centuries old crime in order to protect said values and creed. It's a present-day doctrine that has its origins rooted firmly in the past."

Melissa noticed that, even though they were sitting on a simple wooden bench that wasn't the last word in comfort, Verity still had the perfect poise and bearing that she had noticed on their first meeting.

"They don't sound very scary. More like they all work in a museum."

"Their beliefs certainly belong in one."

Verity allowed herself a half-smile, but her voice remained quiet and serious, and Melissa sensed there was worse to come. Much worse.

"But why would they be interested in me?"

Verity's attention was now on Danika and her horse. They had just begun to perform figures of eight in trot using the entire length of the arena. For a moment, Melissa wondered if Verity had completely lost interest in their conversation but, without diverting her gaze from Danika, she replied.

"For the same reason that they are 'interested' in every other woman who resides here. You, and they, represent a perceived threat. They believe that we must be destroyed before we destroy them."

"What makes them think that?"

Danika had now dropped Firefly back into a walk and was, at intervals, bringing him to a halt before walking him on while Melissa, in the seconds of silence before Verity continued, tried to make some kind of sense of what she had just heard.

"How's your English history, Melissa?"

"A comfortable pass at A Level. Didn't take it beyond that though. Why do you ask?"

"Seventeenth century, English Civil War."

Melissa attempted to dredge up anything she could recall of that time.

"Parliamentarians versus Royalists. Cromwell and Charles the First. Three main battles. Edgehill, Marston Moor and Naseby. Parliamentarians won and Charles was beheaded in

1649. The whole war took place between 1642 to 1651....I think I've got most of that right."

Verity seemed suitably impressed.

"Very good. Well, there you have the historical background. I mention it merely to give some context to what I need to tell you."

Melissa nodded as if she completely understood, but nothing could have been further from the truth. Just when she thought that her situation couldn't get any more surreal....

"As you seem to have a good grasp of the Civil War, perhaps your knowledge extends to other matters of the same period?"

Melissa began a deeper search of her memories from her sixth form days, trying to tease out any other relevant facts she might have momentarily forgotten. Verity remained silent, giving her the chance to complete that search. Eventually she began to recite some biographical facts about Charles the First and Oliver Cromwell, and how Charles marrying a French Catholic did not go down well with parliament....

"Forgive me...."

Verity allowed her to continue for a short while before gently interrupting.

"....I meant anything other than the politics of the time."

Several seconds passed before Verity decided to put Melissa out of her misery.

"Alongside the violence and tragedy of the war there was another smaller but no less tragic conflict playing out in towns and villages in the east of England and beyond. Although the persecution of witches had gone on before the Civil War and, of course, after it, the unrest, fear, and general collapse of society it generated gave rise to a fervour of witch hunting and led to many trials and executions."

She said it in a matter-of-fact way, a lecturer helping a student to revise a particularly problematic area of her subject. Melissa heard the words and understood them. She even realised she knew a little about it, recalling having seen that film with Vincent Price. What was it called? 'The Witchfinder General'? Yes, that was it. But why was Verity even mentioning this? What had witches got to do with anything? They didn't even exist! And even if they did, what could they possibly have to do with her?

But even as she asked herself the question, Melissa felt something deep down inside. Something that stopped her from voicing her incredulity and fear.

"But there was a specific incident in 1645, Melissa, at a place called Brathy Beck."

Danika had now coaxed Firefly into a gentle canter, describing a large circle in the centre of the school.

"Brathy Beck."

Melissa quietly repeated the words to herself. She knew she had never heard them before. So why did she sense faint echoes of something familiar in the back of her mind? Something that shouldn't be there. Something that had no way of being there. If Verity noticed the look in her eyes she made no mention of it.

"Repercussions from this incident were inevitable, and revenge, they say, is a dish best served cold. Nearly four hundred years is cold enough I would think. However, I'm acutely aware that all of this will be very difficult for you to take in at one go. Do you wish me to continue?"

It was at that moment, with those words spoken in such a compassionate way, that Melissa knew Verity genuinely cared. Whatever was going on, whatever the full picture was, she decided, there and then, to give her trust fully and without reservation to Verity. Only time would tell if she was making a mistake.

"I'd like to know more."

Melissa had been given just enough by Verity, sufficient to reel her in, like a trailer for a film that she then had to go and see.

"The Custodians are everywhere and nowhere. They are present in many areas of society. Small in number, but big in influence. Law makers, law enforcers, from the highest to the lowest. Organised and driven. I do, however, have hope that we may soon see light at the end of a long, dark tunnel. But that day is not yet with us. So we have to use our abilities to try to get lucky. Sometimes we do. Sometimes we don't. Take Justine, for example. You spent some time with her yesterday evening. Did she tell you her story?"

"Yes. She's not meant to be here, is she?"

Verity shook her head sadly.

"We failed to save that poor young girl, and Justine became involved by accident. That whole episode was a failure on our part."

"But you saved Justine."

Verity smiled, acknowledging Melissa's attempt to accentuate the positive.

"Yes. We did. And now we have you."

Her smile broadened and became warmer, and Melissa sensed that she was not only pleased but also relieved to be sitting next to her.

"I'm not here by accident though, am I? It was me they lured to that funeral, me they wanted, and me Danika was sent to rescue."

"Correct on all counts, Melissa. You were their intended target, as we knew you would be. It was only a matter of when, and fortunately on this occasion, our intelligence and timing was faultless. You will, therefore, have concluded that there is a provable and undeniable connection between you and the incident at Brathy Beck."

Another pause.

"What happened there? I feel I….I should know."

Melissa was now clearly struggling with the echoes that were getting louder, that were trying to force their way into her consciousness.

"Don't harbour any feelings of guilt for your ignorance, Melissa. Any memories of this have lay dormant and hidden from you for a reason. And the reason is that they may never have needed to surface. They didn't belong in the life you had. That not only applies to you, but to others you will meet here."

As a much needed distraction from the moment, Melissa looked out across the school to where Danika was still working Firefly, walking him on a few paces and then bringing him to a halt before repeating the sequence, again and again. Finally, she turned back to Verity.

"Do they all know? About Brathy Beck? About why?"

Verity nodded.

"They all know and they all understand."

"Then…."

Melissa looked up through the branches of the oak tree, to where the sunlight sparkled between the leaves.

"….it seems as though it's my turn."

71

Chapter 10

~*Brathy Beck*~

"It won't be long now. They'll be here soon, won't they?"

"Come away from the window, Isabel, and sit down. There is little point in fretting. They will be here in their own good time."

Isabel turned back into the room and walked reluctantly over to an empty armchair.

"You make them sound like welcome guests."

She threw Alice a disapproving glance.

"You know I didn't mean it like that."

Her words were followed by an awkward silence. The other young women in the room avoided each other's gaze until one of them walked forward, looking to each of her friends in turn.

"I don't understand you. Any of you. You all seem content to remain here and accept our fate."

"So what do you suggest, Helen? Look at us, look around you, and then tell me what do you suggest we do!?"

"They were in one of the nearby villages two days ago. Have we had news from there yet?" Helen asked.

"There is a rumour that they hanged four, but that may not be right. It was only a rumour."

Joan looked almost apologetic, as if she should have known for certain, but there was now a fire in Helen's eyes. With barely controlled anger, she spoke again.

"So it might have been three, or it might have been five. Does it matter? All that matters is that it will be us next unless we all agree to…."

She paused, wanting to be sure of her next words.

"….to confront and resist."

"Helen's right. We can't just wait here to die."

"But, Anne, don't you think all the others will have thought like that? All those that are now dead?"

It was Jane who had spoken as Anne turned back to Helen, silently imploring her to say something more. Helen's response was immediate as her anger threatened to overwhelm her.

"But we all know we're not like those others, don't we? Don't we?!"

Helen was daring them to disagree, but no argument was forthcoming. She turned to the woman standing in the furthest corner of the room, who, up until that moment, had said nothing.

"Cecily? Do you understand what I am saying?"

She nodded slowly and looked as if she was about to cry. Alice walked over to her and put a comforting arm around her shoulders as Helen began to pace the room, her thoughts now flying in ever darker directions.

"Anne? Shall we take a walk outside?"

Anne glanced around her before making her way to the door with Helen. All eyes followed them as they left the room, but not one of the young women uttered another word.

Once outside of the isolated farmhouse, Helen and Anne took the narrow path that led down to Brathy Beck, a small meandering stream that trickled its way gently over its stony bed. Together they headed for a moss speckled rock that rested on a grassy bank near the beck. They sat down close to each other.

"Beautiful place, isn't it? So peaceful."

Anne smiled in agreement, although she didn't feel in the least like smiling.

"Thank you for trying to support me."

Anne shrugged.

"I don't believe it made any difference. Do you?"

"Perhaps. Perhaps not. But whatever they think, I'm not about to meekly wait for their arrival and the end of a rope."

Anne looked up at the green sunlit hills. How could they be surrounded by such beauty and be awaiting such horror?

"I'm sure none of us would desire that. But what troubles them also troubles me, and I can see that you too, Helen, are tormented by your thoughts."

Above the two women a black crow swooped and circled, searching for its prey. Could it see the witch hunters approach from way up there?

"If there were any other way then we would take it, but I can't see one. Can you?"

She looked at Anne, almost begging her to come up with an answer she knew didn't exist.

"Have you truly considered the consequences of what you propose?"

Helen closed her eyes, at that moment wishing she and Anne were somewhere else. Anywhere. As long as they could live a peaceful, quiet life. But, of course, that wasn't the reality, was it? Their reality was that, in a short while, the witch hunters would be knocking on their door, and the inevitable outcome of that visit would be that not one of them would be left alive. Helen had heard the harrowing stories from other villages and knew she couldn't, she wouldn't, allow that to happen to those she cared about, and loved.

"But there is no choice, Anne. None. You have to help me make them understand. We must be as one if we are to succeed and save ourselves."

"You know I'll always be by your side. I'd walk with you through the gates of Hell if you were to ask me."

Helen stood, held her arms open wide and, as Anne fell into her embrace, she whispered

"It may come to that, my love. It may come to that."

"Helen, what you ask is….is unthinkable."

Alice's eyes never lifted from the floor in front of her as she spoke.

"But, nevertheless, I ask it. It is our only chance of salvation."

"Then, perhaps, it might be better if we do not survive."

Anne felt Helen's grip on her hand tighten at Alice's response.

"Do you all feel that way? Joan? Would you rather die than fight?"

She said nothing but shook her head.

"Jane? Cecily?"

They too, without speaking, shook their heads.

"You can't ask her, she's too young. She has no idea what you're asking, or what she's agreeing to."

Alice turned to Cecily with an accusatory look in her eyes. Anne looked as if she was about to say something but was prevented by a whispered 'no' from Helen. She released her hand and stepped forward into the centre of the room, slowly turning through a full circle.

"It has to be all of us, or none of us. We each understand that. And, as I see the present situation, we are all agreed except Alice. Cecily? You are now fourteen years of age. Your feelings on this matter will be considered with the same respect as those of any one of us. Do you wish to speak, or merely to give us a 'yes' or a 'no'?"

Cecily, still fighting back the tears, took several shuddering, shallow breaths before she felt composed enough to voice her thoughts.

"I'm frightened. I'm frightened if we do and I'm frightened if we don't."

Helen's smile showed her nothing but kindness and sympathy.

"I believe you are speaking for us all. However, none of us must allow that fear to cloud our vision. If we are to save ourselves, we must be resolute and free of any doubt or misgiving. So, I ask you again Cecily. Yes, or no?"

Helen's eyes fixed and held Cecily's. She wanted to keep her attention from wavering, wanted nothing to distract her from saying what she truly felt.

"I want to live, and I am prepared to do anything that will defeat those who wish us harm."

Helen nodded and turned to Alice.

"It is your turn to speak, and we will all listen to what you have to say."

She looked around the room, to each woman, ensuring that they would, indeed, all listen without attempting to interrupt or argue. But all eyes were now on Alice, and any doubt she had that she was in a minority of one would have evaporated in that moment.

"We are proposing murder, are we not?"

There was an uneasy silence, until Helen replied.

"The only way any of us will survive is to kill those who would kill us. And have you considered all the innocents who have met their death at the hands of these men? Don't they deserve some kind of retribution?"

Alice looked around her, searching for any glimmer of understanding for her position.

"So will this retribution undo their suffering and bring them back to life? And how many more will be made to pay for our actions? Surely we must consider more than just ourselves? Or is this all we have become, a channel for revenge?"

Another silence before Anne responded, speaking softly, wanting to prevent the disagreement escalating into something far more unpleasant.

"There is merit in what you say Alice and, clearly, none of us would normally have any desire to resort to such extremes...."

She consciously sought to avoid words such as 'kill' and 'murder', because they all knew the stark truth of the matter.

"....however, I believe there comes a time when it is no longer appropriate to turn the other cheek. This persecution cannot, and must not, be allowed to continue unchallenged, and it has fallen upon us to do this, whether we like it or not. The Coven of Brathy Beck will stand against these self-appointed witch hunters. We have to. We really do have no choice."

Anne threw a glance to Helen, who mouthed a quiet 'thank you'.

"So. Time is short. If no one else wishes to speak we must now come to a decision."

Helen paused, offering one last chance for any further opinions. There were none.

"Then we will now make that decision."

Helen looked first to Joan. She nodded. She turned to Isabel, who also nodded, as did Jane and Anne. Before she could catch Cecily's eye, the young girl had said 'yes', her voice now steady and certain. And this was the cue for them all to look once more to Alice. After taking a breath, she spoke.

"I am sure it is true to say that I will not succeed in changing the beliefs of any one of you and, likewise, my convictions on this matter are sincere and unshakeable. I abhor the thought of being involved in the infliction of pain upon others, be they good or evil, but there is one thing on this earth that would make me set aside such heartfelt convictions. What is that one thing? It is, quite simply, my love for you all. I have listened, I have watched. And I understand. We are one, or we are nothing. I will, therefore, stand with you and lend my voice to yours in order that we might bring about our salvation."

As one, they all surrounded Alice, each in turn embracing her and whispering their thanks. But it was Helen who was the next to speak, saying simply

"Then it is time. It is time to forsake the Light and to summon the Darkness that lies within us."

Helen led them all out of the old farmhouse and down to the Brathy Beck stone. The women formed a circle before kneeling down on the grassy bank. Then, at Helen's prompting, they held hands to close the circle, before bowing their heads while, above them, the crow continued to soar and swoop.

Chapter 11

Verity watched as Danika, today's lesson now over, dismounted from Firefly and led him out of the gate at the far end of the arena.

"It was nine men, in all, that died. Six locals and three who called themselves witchfinders."

"How did they die?" Melissa asked, unsure if she really wanted to know.

Verity smiled grimly. "Not well. The local men were each found hanged, except they were strung up in such a way that they could just touch the ground if they really tried. It is said they would have taken a long time to die."

"And the witchfinders?"

"Ah. The witchfinders. They were crucified inverted, and by the time they were found, the crows had been dining. Perhaps we should hope the birds found them post-mortem. Or perhaps not."

"And seven young women, one of them fourteen years old, were supposed to have done that?"

"There is no 'supposed', Melissa. It is a matter of record. We know it, and The Custodians know it. But, of course, your question naturally assumes it was seven women against nine men."

"Are you saying it wasn't?"

Verity shook her head. "Well, maybe in the physical sense, it was. But there was something else, something that those who came to that farmhouse on that day could not have foreseen."

"Which was?"

"Which was that this time they were not dealing with innocent village girls, but with those who had a power at their disposal. The real power of a real coven."

Verity knew Melissa would be trying to process what she'd just been told.

"I'm not a witch." Melissa whispered the words, to no one in particular.

"That may well be true, Melissa. It doesn't necessarily follow if you are a descendant of one, that you too have The Gift. However,

78

it is likely. And surely you would wish something positive to come out of this earthquake that has just hit your life?"

Melissa lifted her eyes and looked at Verity. "Have you got them all yet? The descendants of that coven? Are they all here now?"

Verity stood and beckoned Melissa to follow. "Let's continue our walk, shall we? There are more extensive grounds behind the stables."

She led her away from the bench and oak tree, and down to the side of the school. From where she now stood, Melissa could see a courtyard surrounded by stables, about half of which were occupied by some magnificent looking horses.

"I'll let Danika give you the equine tour later."

Verity walked on, glancing back to ensure Melissa was following.

"And you ask if we have scooped up all our little butterflies? The rather unsatisfactory answer is that we can't be certain. Good morning, Layla."

Walking towards them was the young girl who had been in the dining room the previous evening. Melissa thought she looked just as unhappy now as she did when she first saw her. As she drew level with them, Layla managed, with great effort, to force a smile onto her lips.

"She's a very troubled young lady," Verity confided as soon as Layla had disappeared from view, prompting Melissa's thoughts to turn to what Justine had told her. She recalled the words 'psychiatric report' and 'orphan' but wasn't going to repeat them out loud, especially in Verity's presence. She didn't want to get Justine into trouble for something she said she'd overheard.

"I'm sorry to hear that."

"We are attempting to help her, of course, but I will admit that making any progress is proving to be quite a challenge."

They walked on in silence. Melissa could see that despite Verity's measured, unemotional words, she held a deep concern for Layla and, undeniably, Melissa found herself sharing that concern.

"Do you like to play tennis?"

"I'm sorry?"

In answer to the question, Verity pointed over to their left where Melissa saw two grass courts. Four floodlights towered over them, and the whole set up looked very professional.

"You'll usually find someone willing to give you a game, just ask around. We can, of course, supply you with the appropriate clothing and equipment."

"Of course."

Melissa couldn't hide the edge in her voice and Verity couldn't fail to pick up on it.

"Do I detect....?"

Melissa turned to her.

"I don't want to seem ungrateful. Really I don't. But all of this...."

A sweep of her arm took in the buildings and entire grounds.

"....it's all just too good to be true, isn't it? I mean, everything, just for the likes of me, for women, who you may or may not find, connected to an incident that occurred centuries ago? Who would organise this, and pay for it?"

Verity seemed completely unfazed by Melissa's questions. Perhaps it was because she'd heard them before, from others who now lived in this place.

"Shall I take you to see the gymnasium, sauna, and indoor swimming pool...."

"How *do* you finance everything? I mean, a billionaire wouldn't be unhappy to live here."

Melissa repeated her question, determined to get at least one answer before the moment passed. For some seconds it seemed as if Verity was weighing up how much she was prepared to say.

"We have some very talented ladies who, um, remove money from those who don't deserve it and give it to us."

Was that an answer? Melissa didn't think so.

"Remove? How?"

Verity shrugged.

"How? They sit in front of a computer screen all day. I don't pretend to understand how it all works."

Melissa's eyes widened.

"Cyber crime?"

"Is that what they call it? I wouldn't know. Anyway, it's not really a crime is it, to take money away from bad people?"

Verity was innocence personified, but Melissa didn't, for one moment, believe that she wouldn't fully understand every single detail of what went on in the name of the sanctuary.

"And, to address the first part of your question, would you like to meet our 'visionary', the person responsible for the existence of this modest little home from home?"

Melissa hadn't expected such an offer or, at least, not so soon. She had assumed she would never see anyone higher in authority than Verity. Now she had learned that not only was there such a person, but that they were here, and it only took a moment for Melissa to accept Verity's offer.

"Good. Then we need to take the path down to the lake. I'm sure that's where we'll find her."

Verity pointed away from the main house, towards a tall hedgerow that ran from the back of the tennis courts to the furthest end of the adjacent gardens. A little way down it there was a narrow gap. Melissa tried to see what was on the other side of the opening but, from where she stood, the angle was too shallow for a clear view, however it seemed as if that was where they were heading. As they came nearer so Melissa saw the waist-high wooden gate that rested across the gap.

"Just through here."

Verity flipped up the latch and pushed the gate open before walking through and beckoning Melissa to follow. In front of her was a small wildflower meadow bordered by more oak trees and hedges, and beyond the meadow she saw the lake. On its surface, reflections of the surrounding trees and tall grasses shimmered in the morning sun. On the far side of the water, Melissa could see the silhouette of a person seated in front of what looked like an easel and canvas.

"I'll leave you now. Just continue to follow this path. I'm sure she'll be pleased to see you."

Before Melissa could reply, Verity had turned away and disappeared back through the gate. She remained rooted to the spot for some seconds, now unsure if indeed she did want to meet with this individual who, it seemed, wielded even more influence and power than Verity. What if they didn't want to see her? It looked as if they were enjoying a few hours of peaceful solitude and any interruption might be unwelcome. But, in that case, would Verity have suggested such a meeting? She had to believe not.

Melissa walked along the path that was bordered with a myriad of flowers on the meadow side and tall grasses and reeds nearest the lake. But although she was getting nearer, as she walked around the water's edge, so her view of the figure had become obscured by the easel and canvas. It wasn't until she was only yards away that she saw who the artist was.

"Ah. My dear. Good morning. How lovely to see you again. Did you sleep well?"

Melissa made her way to where Harriet was sitting, the easel and canvas in front of her and her tubes of paint and assorted brushes on a small table by her side. She sat on a wooden chair, her walking stick propped up against one of its arms.

"Yes....yes, thank you. I, er, that is, Verity suggested I come to see you. She said that you er...."

Melissa stumbled to an awkward halt, and Harriet decided to rescue her.

"And here you are."

From a bag near her feet she produced a blanket and handed it to Melissa.

"I always bring it in case the weather turns chilly. Put it down beside me and make yourself comfortable."

Melissa spread out the blanket and sat down.

"Thank you."

As she folded her legs under her, so she saw Harriet's painting. It was a faithful depiction of the lake and its surroundings, the colours vibrant and exaggerated, the brush strokes bold and confident. Melissa found it difficult to believe that it had been produced by the same hands that she had seen trembling and hesitant just the previous evening.

"I live for my painting. It makes me feel young again."

And as she spoke, Melissa could see a sparkle in her eyes that she hadn't seen when they had first met in the dining room.

"That is beautiful. You're very talented."

That heartfelt compliment brought a smile to Harriet's lips.

"You're being very kind to an old lady. But I have a feeling it wasn't my artistic talent, or lack of it, that brings you over to see me this morning. You've spent some time with Verity and, I'm guessing, you asked her a certain question to which I was the answer. Am I correct?"

Melissa nodded, unsure if she shouldn't have asked or if, having asked, she should have returned to the house and not interrupted

Harriet's peaceful morning. However, she was here now and, she assured herself, if her company was really not required then Harriet would tell her so.

"You're right. Verity told me about Brathy Beck, and that you're responsible for this place, for giving sanctuary to those being hunted because of what happened. Is that true?"

Harriet carefully replaced the small brush that she'd just picked up, and Melissa noticed that her hand was now once again betraying the slight tremor that hadn't been evident before.

"Well now, I expect that if Verity said such a thing, then it must be true."

Was that a mischievous glint in her eye?

"I'm sorry. Please forgive me. I don't mean to sound flippant, sometimes I can't resist. Yes. It is true. And that answer begs further questions, doesn't it, which is why you're here, sitting next to me now. Did you enjoy your salad last evening?"

This momentarily threw Melissa which might, she realised, have been the intention. Was she playing with her?

"Um, yes, it was delicious. Thank you."

"Good. I wonder what they'll have on the menu tonight? I do so look forward to finding out."

Melissa began to think that this might not have been such a good idea after all. Harriet's company was very pleasant, and she was undoubtedly a kind and considerate lady but, it seemed, she was not about to discuss....

"Still, that's for later, isn't it? Now what shall we talk about?"

Or perhaps she was.

"You?" Melissa offered, causing the glint to briefly return.

"Ah. Well, if you truly believe that such a subject could possibly hold any interest then I must do my best to ensure you are neither bored nor disappointed."

Melissa shifted her position slightly on the blanket, feeling its soft material as she rested her hands either side of her. She wanted to face Harriet and have no other distractions as she listened to what the elderly lady was about to tell her.

83

Chapter 12

~Harriet~

She looked again at the short message. It consisted of just a few sentences, but they were all that was needed to confirm her worst fears. She needed more wine but her glass was empty. She walked over to the cabinet and removed a bottle of red from one of the shelves, collecting another crystal goblet on her way back to the antique writing desk and its accompanying armchair. Once her glass was filled, she took several sips before sitting down, tipping her chair back and closing her eyes. But she had no intention of sleeping. Far from it. She had to think, to plan, and to run through each and every way that she might fail.

It was some thirty minutes later that Harriet opened her eyes, her mind now made up. For better or worse, she now knew what she was going to do. She pushed herself up from her chair and made her way to the large bookcase that stood against the furthest wall. Its four shelves were packed with volumes of all shapes and sizes but Harriet knew, more or less, where to find what she was looking for. She needed a particular book to remind herself of the facts. Running her finger along the next to top shelf, it took a few moments to locate the leather bound volume, its worn spine a testament to its age. Harriet removed it from its resting place and returned to her desk. With due reverence, she laid it onto the wooden surface, opened it, and picked up her reading glasses.

Carefully she leafed through the first twenty or so pages until she found the relevant piece of text. Its title was written in large, bold script at the head of the page. 'Brathy Beck'. As she read the writing beneath that title, so Harriet's sense of disbelief and dread grew. Although it had already been confirmed, she found herself struggling to accept that it could possibly be true.

When she had finished reading, she closed the book and replaced it on the shelf. There were other reference works and records she now needed to consult. She might have all the time in the world, or time may have already almost run out. She knew she had to work assuming the latter. Harriet reached out and lifted the handset from its cradle before dialling a number she knew off by heart.

"Thank you for your communication. It seems that rumour is about to become reality. I will, therefore, need certain information regarding descendants and their current whereabouts. Please prioritise those that your information suggests to be at the most immediate risk. I appreciate that some will inevitably slip through our net but we must do our very best and hope that, if they evade our efforts then, with some good fortune, they may also evade our enemy's. I do, however, wish to minimise our reliance upon luck."

It wasn't until she'd put the phone down that the potential magnitude of the task ahead hit her. It wouldn't be an overnight operation. It had the potential to last a very long time and would be fraught with difficulty and danger, but there really was no point in dwelling too much upon the many opportunities for failure. She quickly set about crystallising the basic outline of a plan, wanting to make sure, as best she could, that she'd missed nothing that might, at a later date, cost an innocent woman her life.

She worked deep into the night, trying to imagine the many ways in which this might play out, realising that protecting those in danger would require not only a single-minded determination, but much, much more. The hours passed and, as the first light of a new day began to shine through the window of her study, Harriet had, at last, given in to her fatigue and fallen asleep, her head resting on the desk, her notepad and pen beside her. If she had hoped that her dreams would give her some respite from the looming terrors of the real world, then that hope was destined not to be fulfilled. Those dreams were a landscape of shadows that hid unfathomable horrors waiting for her to venture too close, or to fail to hear the tell-tale whisper, taken away on the wind, before it could warn her of the approaching evil. She looked around her, searching for some glimmer of light, but there was nothing. It was as the darkness began to close in on her, that she was snatched away from that otherworld by the telephone ringing. Still half asleep, Harriet lifted the receiver and placed it unsteadily against her ear.

"Harriet" she said, trying to sound as awake as she could. However, she didn't have to say much more than the odd 'mmm', 'yes', or 'ok' for the next few minutes. She listened with increasing concern, quickly scribbling down a word or phrase every so often until, on the last line of her notebook's page, she wrote down the name she had just been given and circled it several times.

"Right. Fax me anything you've got as soon as you can. A photo would be helpful, if you can find one."

When the call ended, she left the study and walked through to the bathroom. She turned on the shower and, for the next five minutes, stood under the hot spray, facing the powerful jets of water. As she sat on the side of the bath, wrapped in the largest towel she could find, her thoughts returned to the telephone conversation, and what she now knew she had to do. Harriet had hoped that this moment wouldn't have come so soon or, if she were honest, would never have come at all.

She dressed, choosing practical outdoor clothing, and trying all the time to focus on the task ahead. She couldn't deny she had her doubts, and one in particular. It wasn't her resolve that troubled her, but something far more practical. Physically, was she capable of doing this? She quickly admonished herself. She was forty-seven, not eighty-seven! However, she was well aware that she couldn't be certain exactly what she would face. She would *have* to be up to it, physically and mentally, and that was the beginning and end of it.

Perhaps it wouldn't play out as badly as she was imagining. People told her she was inclined to be pessimistic and possibly they were right. Maybe this first one would be a simple case of location and observation, with a removal option if necessary. Maybe.

But it was the last of those that was now giving Harriet real cause for concern. Removal to where? There was clearly a moral duty upon their Order to do something. These women had a right to expect their help in protecting them from this threat. Or, at least, they would expect help if any of them were aware of the threat's existence. And there lay another big problem. Convincing them that they needed such an intervention.

Harriet also recalled several inconclusive discussions regarding the 'where'. But all those past meetings had been in the abstract, about a danger yet to materialise. Not only would they now need to find that 'where', but they had to have the means to keep it safe from prying eyes. Harriet had her own ideas about that but, right now, she doubted very much if anyone within their Order would countenance what she was considering proposing.

She made her way out of her apartment, pausing only to grab a fax message that was lying in the tray beneath the printer, and across the road to where her VW Golf was parked. As she climbed in she placed her open notepad onto the passenger seat next to her road atlas and fax, before putting the key into the ignition. She picked up the atlas and used her index finger to trace her route, occasionally glancing at the address she had written on the notepad. When she was completely happy she took a moment to glance at the photo on the fax before starting the Golf and guiding it out into the early morning traffic.

And so it had begun. The price for Brathy Beck was about to be paid, but Harriet couldn't help thinking that everything needed to deal with this should have already been in place, they shouldn't only now be attempting to make this right for these women. But if there were to be an inquest into duty of care failures, then now wasn't the time. Any distraction could only serve to assist their enemy.

As the traffic came to a halt at a T-junction, Harriet took the opportunity to look again at the road atlas. If her chosen route was reasonably clear, she estimated that her journey would take a little over three hours. Plenty of time to think again about her plan of action, such as it was. She had always believed in allowing room to react to events in real time, rather than slavishly adhering to a predetermined course. 'Winging it' was a phrase she'd often heard thrown in her direction, usually as criticism rather than praise. But experience had told her not to become too obsessed with fine detail. She had a basic knowledge of the locale, her target and her target's circumstances. She knew the endgame might well involve removal to a safe house, such as it was. Other than that, yes, guilty as charged. She'd be winging it.

Chapter 13

~Harriet and The Young Girl~

The small town of Markham on the south coast is one of those picture postcard places beloved of the wealthy retired, or merely wealthy. Property prices had risen way beyond the means of most locals, given the town's idyllic coastal setting and a direct rail link to Central London.

Harriet dropped her Golf's speed as she drove past the Markham Old Town Orphanage, allowing herself a glance through the large wrought iron gates. The cold, forbidding building beyond looked like something out of a Dickens novel. She hadn't been prepared for the effect its initial sighting would have on her, feeling an overwhelming sense of pity for those who, through no fault of their own, were forced to live in a place like that.

She drove on, towards a nearby car park that she had marked on her map. Having parked and bought her ticket, Harriet took one last look at the blurry, black and white photo on the fax message before making her way out onto the quiet side street. The orphanage was a few minutes' walk away, and she had decided she wanted to take a closer look straightaway. All previous thoughts of remaining in the shadows were gone. Something was telling her that every second mattered, that merely observing was no longer an option. Perhaps the sense of urgency was coming from nothing more than instinct, but Harriet had learned never to ignore her instinct.

Harriet walked on, past several antique shops and a very inviting tearoom, with an impressive assortment of cakes on display in its front window. Some moments later, the iron gates of the orphanage came into view once more. She approached them slowly, intending to give the impression that she was just a passer-by, casually taking in her surroundings. She was hoping that she had jumped to the wrong conclusion with her first impression but, as she paused by the entrance and looked at the building beyond, she saw nothing to change her original feeling of deep concern for those within.

Harriet continued on past the house with the intention of gathering as much knowledge as she could about routes in and out, especially anything that might lend itself to a covert approach. There had been little time to obtain any useful information before her journey and, anyway, she would always want to rely on her own first hand observations.

Following the perimeter fence into a narrower road to the side of the orphanage, Harriet's attention was suddenly taken by a car parked at the further end. She could just make out, behind the reflections in the windscreen, a man who, at first glance, appeared to be reading a book. But, as she neared the vehicle, Harriet became less and less sure that the scene was as innocent as it first seemed. She walked slowly past the car, turning back as she neared the corner. In that brief moment she was sure that he had put the book down, his attention now directed towards the orphanage.

She took a left turn at the end of the narrow road, still following the fence. The car was now out of sight, but definitely not out of mind. However, she knew she needed to return her concentration back to the building. Before the distraction, she had noticed that a path led to the rear, ending up at an ordinary, drab-looking door, some distance from the imposing main entrance. It was surrounded by climbing roses which had the effect of partially hiding it from view, and she decided that it would be worth a second look, having not seen anything else that might offer a less public route in or out.

Harriet stopped and waited, not wanting to retrace her steps straightaway. From where she stood she was as certain as she could be that it wasn't possible to observe her from the house, but she needed a moment to remind herself not to do anything impulsive. Take a step back and assess the situation. That would be the sensible, safe course of action. But the car was still bothering her.

She turned and walked back the way she had come just minutes earlier. Might the man in the car wonder what she was doing? What if he did? It was none of his business where she took her morning stroll.

The car was still there. She hadn't noticed before but it was parked illegally, the road markings clearly prohibiting waiting at any time. And the alarm bells she had heard when she first saw it began to ring again, this time a little louder. She increased her pace slightly, wanting to satisfy herself that the man was still inside the vehicle, either reading or otherwise. He wasn't. She bent down to look in through the driver's side window, all pretence at discretion now gone. The book lay on the passenger seat. For a moment Harriet considered breaking into the car in the hope of finding something that might give her a clue as to his identity. Her eyes fixed on the closed glove compartment, and she was tempted. However, she reminded herself, right now he wasn't the priority.

She looked around her, hoping to catch sight of the man, but he was nowhere to be seen. Without hesitation, Harriet jogged back to where she had seen the partly hidden door. Maybe he had seen it too. She reached up and grabbed the iron rail that ran along the top of the perimeter fence, placing her hands carefully between the equidistant spikes that were at the end of each vertical metal post. With one deft movement, she pulled herself up and over, clearing the spikes with millimetres to spare before dropping into the undergrowth on the far side. As security fences went it wasn't the most difficult she'd encountered, built more to deter, than prevent, unlawful entry.

Harriet looked around her, needing to be sure she hadn't attracted any unwanted attention. Whether or not the man represented any threat was now irrelevant. She was committed to her chosen course of action and the outcome, good or bad, would be down to her and her alone.

She calculated it would take her about five seconds to cover the distance to the door. It appeared to be slightly recessed into the wall, which might give her some cover, maybe buying her precious moments to attempt to gain access to the building. After another glance at her surroundings, she took a deep breath and then ran across the gap between her and the door as quickly as she could, doing her best to avoid the dips and bumps in the uneven ground.

90

She tried to stop before she reached the door but still hit it with some force. If someone was anywhere near the other side of it, they couldn't fail to hear the impact. Harriet waited, wanting to be sure no one was going to suddenly open it and challenge her or raise the alarm. All remained quiet, which was a relief because, in order to gain entry, she now knew she was going to have to break in.

She knelt down so that she might get a better view of the lock, frequently glancing behind her and back towards the road, in case the missing man were to suddenly reappear. The lock was a simple mortice. Nothing special. Harriet considered trying to pick it, but success wasn't guaranteed and the attempt would eat up precious seconds. She stood up and faced the door. With one swift, hard, well-aimed kick, the wood near the lock cracked and splintered. She then hit the door with the heel of her hand, causing the lock to break away from its fastenings. Harriet pushed the door open and walked through into the building.

The neon lit passageway in which she now stood had another door at the far end. It was the only way in or out. She moved towards it, all the time listening for any sound that might indicate another person's presence. Pressing an ear against the still closed door, she could hear only silence. She gripped the handle, hoping that this one wouldn't require any degree of force to open it, as she had no wish to test her luck again so soon.

The handle was stiff to move and, for a moment, Harriet thought that it too might be locked. But, as she gradually increased the amount of force she was applying, so it moved downwards, releasing the catch that had held the door closed. She opened it an inch or so and peered through the crack. From what she could see, there was a staircase that led both up to the next floor and down to what, Harriet assumed, must be the basement. When she was as sure as she could be that there was no one around, she slowly pushed the door fully open and walked through onto the landing. She turned and gently closed the door, taking great care not to make any sound.

There were several portraits on the wall. The subject of each painting looked as if they were eminently suited to this place that, at first glance, seemed to be as austere on the inside as it was on the outside. So, up or down? Harriet leant over the age-worn bannister. The descending stairs disappeared into darkness, and she couldn't believe anyone would be down there, at least not through choice.

From what she knew of the orphanage, there were ten young boys and girls in its care including her target, with three staff and an unknown number of visiting tutors and domestic workers. She hoped that luck would continue to be on her side and the number of staff on duty that morning would be minimal.

With one more glance down into the gloom, she decided to try upstairs. If, subsequently, she was forced to explore the lower floor, she could use the torch that nestled in an outside pocket of her jacket. She pressed her hand against the pocket to reassure herself that it was still there.

Carefully, she put her weight on each step, pausing before moving up to the next one, wanting to be sure that there wasn't going to be a tell-tale creak from either the staircase or bannister. She continued her ascent until, several steps from the next landing, she heard the faint sound of a voice coming from one of the rooms on the first floor.

Once she reached the landing she was able to see that there were three doors. She stopped to listen again. She had to give herself the best possible chance of discovering exactly who was on this floor, and precisely where they were. Of course she was aware that just listening was nowhere near a guarantee of being sure, but it was all she had.

Harriet found a recess near the stairs and remained there, hidden in the shadows. It took some minutes before she was convinced that any voices she had heard were coming from only one of the rooms. There had been nothing but silence behind the two nearest doors. She knew she shouldn't discount the possibility that those rooms were not empty, but felt she now needed to concentrate on what she could hear and not what she couldn't.

In fact, there was only one voice that was predominant. If it was a conversation, then the other party was contributing very little to it. The person doing most of the talking was a woman, well-spoken, confident. She spoke in a level tone, but emphasising certain words as if to add an extra authority to what she was saying. That was it. Authority. She had authority over whoever was in that room with her. And then, for the first time, she heard the other voice clearly. It was that of a young girl. Could she possibly be her target? Maybe, if the conversation continued, there might be some clue, a word, phrase, or better still a name that would confirm her identity. If only Harriet could get closer to the door....

She was on the verge of risking a few steps out of the shadows when she heard, almost too late, someone else on the stairs. She pressed herself hard against the wall, trying to keep her breathing shallow and silent. The person, another woman, had now reached the landing and was making for the door closest to Harriet. At any moment she expected them to look towards the recess and raise the alarm. But a second later, the door was opened and then quickly closed.

Harriet waited, hoping that whoever had just entered the nearest room would soon leave it. Until they did there was no way she could move from her hiding place. She returned her attention to the voices coming from the third room, trying again to catch anything she could of the conversation. The woman was still the one doing most of the talking.

"....remain here until I return. You will be silent while you wait, and any disobedience will be punished, just as before. Do you understand?"

There was a pause, followed by a very subdued

"I understand."

The young girl sounded scared and Harriet so wanted to burst into that room and put a stop to whatever was going on. But she knew to do that would not only be the height of stupidity, but also counter-productive. If that girl was the reason she was here, then she needed to learn as much as she could before revealing her presence to either her, or anyone else.

But there was nothing more to hear because, just a moment later, the door opened and the woman, a tall, stern looking individual with no trace of humanity in her expression, left the room. Harriet had expected her to head down the staircase, but instead she walked quickly over to the third door and knocked twice. She heard footsteps from within the room as the person made their way to the door.

"She's in there."

The stern woman nodded in the direction of the room she had just left.

"Good. Have you locked her in?"

"No. She won't go anywhere. She's probably even too scared to get up from her chair."

Did one of them laugh? Harriet felt the anger rising inside her but fought the desire to take that anger out on them, at least not yet.

"He'll be here soon and we need to hand her over as quickly as possible."

"Right. Is he bringing the payment?"

"Cash on delivery."

Another laugh.

"We should be downstairs."

"Are you sure she'll stay put?"

"Oh yes."

"Ok. Let's go."

Without further conversation, they both headed for the stairs. Harriet attempted to get a good look at the second woman but she was gone before a clear view was possible. She waited until the sound of their footsteps had receded and all was quiet before moving out of the shadows. She stood outside the furthest door, pausing just for a moment before entering. Instantly Harriet knew that the young girl now staring at her, eyes wide with fear, was the same girl whose photo she'd been faxed hours earlier.

"Please don't be frightened. I'm here to help you."

As she took a step towards her, so the girl cowered in her chair, as if expecting to be struck at any moment.

"I can get you out of this place. You do want that, don't you?"

Harriet saw her eyes flick towards the doorway.

"They've gone for now, but I don't think we have long. Will you trust me? Please?"

She could see in the girl's expression the difficulty she was having deciding what she should do. To her eternal credit, facing a situation that no ten-year-old should have to confront, she made her choice. She stood and held out a hand to the stranger. Harriet smiled as she took the small hand, wondering just how scared she must be to be willing to put herself in the care of someone she had known for seconds.

94

Harriet led the girl over to the door and opened it a crack. There was no one on the landing. Together they left the room and made their way to the top of the staircase, as Harriet became aware just how tightly the girl was gripping her hand. They waited, listening for any approaching footsteps, but there was only silence, and so they began to descend to the ground floor. Harriet had in mind that they would exit the way she had entered however, once outside, she would have to find another way to leave the grounds. There would be no way of getting the girl over the fence. The phrase 'winging it' again came to mind.

It wasn't until they had almost reached the ground floor, and the passageway to the damaged outer door, that the voices could be heard once more. Harriet knew they had just moments to get to that door but, before she could guide the girl in its direction, she had let go of Harriet's hand. The child hesitated for a moment, summoning every ounce of courage she possessed, before she began taking the stairs down into the darkness of the basement.

Harriet wanted to call out to her, to get her to turn back, but she knew any sound they made now might prove fatal. She had no choice but to follow her into the gloom. Suddenly remembering her torch, she reached into her pocket, removed it and pointed its narrow beam down the stairway.

The light picked the girl out against the bare brick wall. She had already reached the bottom of the stairs and was waiting by another door, shielding her eyes against the intense beam. Harriet hurried down to her side.

"Can we get out through there?" she whispered knowing that, if the answer was 'no', then they were trapped and their attempted escape would be over before it had begun. There were now two people, possibly more, on the landing above and on their way up to the room where they had left the girl.

In answer to Harriet's question, she nodded and pushed at the door, which didn't budge. Harriet took a step back before giving it a hard kick and, for the second time that day, forced her way past a locked door. She grabbed the girl's hand and pulled her through the doorway, flicking the torch's beam around them to get an idea of their surroundings.

They were standing in a large cellar. Against one wall were old cobweb covered packing crates. Leant against the furthest wall was what had once been a beautiful dressing table. Its large mirror was now cracked and had a substantial piece of glass missing from a top corner, and the whole thing looked as if it hadn't been treated kindly on its journey to its present resting place. Harriet wouldn't have given it a second thought except that the girl had run over to it and pulled out one of the drawers, throwing it behind her on the dust-covered stone floor. The noise it made prompted Harriet to glance behind her at the open door, expecting someone to burst through it at any moment.

The girl had put her hand into the space left by the discarded drawer, using it as a place where she could get a good grip on the dresser. She was attempting to pull it away from the wall. Harriet ran over to add her strength to the effort. There was no time to ask any questions. She estimated they had, at most, about a minute before the women would think to search the cellar.

Slowly, too slowly, they succeeded in moving the dressing table away from the wall, just far enough for Harriet to be able to shine her torch behind it. There was a square hole in the brickwork. It looked just large enough for a child and slender adult to crawl through. The girl turned to her.

"I think it's an old way out, like a secret passageway."

Harriet was sceptical, but now was not the time to argue the point or ask how she knew of its existence. It was either a long-forgotten escape route, or it wasn't.

"Ok. Go."

She gestured to the girl and, in an instant, she had disappeared from sight. Harriet attempted to be as fast as her through the hole but she was quickly reminded that she was somewhat larger and it wouldn't be nearly as easy. However, with some effort and determination, she managed to pull herself through.

Once on the other side of the wall, Harriet used her torch again to get some idea of what they now faced. It was a good thing that she didn't suffer from claustrophobia. If she'd hoped that the passageway might have opened out into something more easily negotiable, then she would have been bitterly disappointed. It remained very narrow, with a low ceiling that was less than four feet from the uneven floor. But there was no going back. The girl's disappearance would have been discovered by now and it would only be a short time before their escape route, if that's what it was, would be found.

They moved forward, the torch's beam picking out the way ahead of them. At one point the girl stopped as what looked like a rat darted from its hiding place and scuttled off into the darkness. But, to her eternal credit, she remained completely silent, and Harriet said a quiet 'thank you' that the creature had not run in her direction.

"Do you have any idea where this might come out?" Harriet asked, more in hope than expectation, as she got closer to the girl who, she was sure, had deliberately slowed down so that she might catch up.

The girl turned and shook her head.

"No. But it'll come out somewhere, won't it?" she added helpfully.

They continued on. Fortunately, it seemed that the rat didn't have any friends or relatives, at least not in that part of the tunnel. After what seemed an age, but in reality was probably no more than a few minutes, they came across a thin shaft of light cutting through the darkness ahead. The sight of it prompted the girl to increase her pace and Harriet had to call after her.

"Wait for me when you get there."

Harriet tried to keep up with her but only succeeded in hitting her head on the ceiling, which seemed to be getting lower. In front of her, the girl had done as she was asked, and had stopped just short of the light. As Harriet drew closer to her she tried to see where the light was coming from and, on reaching her, she was able to make out a narrow crack in the wall. She gestured that the girl should move aside. There was no way Harriet was going to allow her to go through first, and still wasn't convinced that going through at all was a good idea. But they couldn't go back.

Harriet pushed against both sides of the narrow opening, gently at first and then with more force. For a moment she thought that it wasn't going to move. She knew she had to remain calm for the sake of the girl, but something close to panic began to rise inside her. She pushed harder, aware that the girl was watching closely.

She felt it give slightly. Creaking and cracking, it sounded as if it was a small wooden door on hinges that had seen better days. This had to be the way out, didn't it? Harriet was now sure she could get it open and was about to give it one final, hard push when a large spider dropped from the ceiling above the door and landed on her hand. She managed to stop herself from crying out and quickly brushed it away, refocussing her efforts on getting them out. Dispensing with any pretence of stealth, Harriet hit the door with both hands, managing to keep hold of the torch as she struck the wood. It splintered and flew outwards. She turned to the girl and took her hand.

"Whatever happens, stay close to me."

Without hesitation, Harriet forced her way out, pulling the girl after her. The sudden change from the torch lit darkness into bright daylight momentarily blinded them. But Harriet knew they couldn't waste a single second. Assessing their situation and considering what might be the best plan was a luxury they couldn't afford.

Harriet glanced behind her and saw that they had emerged from what looked like the side of a small shed, partially hidden by thick undergrowth. The shed was, in fact, in a state of disrepair and was probably only there to disguise the existence of the passageway. But what was ahead? As they moved forward, Harriet's heart sank to see the high fence looming in front of them. Had she hoped that they would somehow, magically, come out on the other side of it? She felt the girl now pulling *her* onwards towards it, seemingly undeterred.

There would be no way of walking out through the main gate unobserved, so Harriet had to try to think of a way of getting the girl over the fence. But who was she trying to fool? She had already considered the possibility and quickly dismissed it. So there had to be another way, didn't there? But in the moments it took Harriet to run through alternatives, if there were any, the girl had let go of her hand and had run over to the foot of the fence, where she knelt, in front of a low clump of bushes, pulling at the leaves and small branches. Without considering the logic of this, Harriet joined her and together they cleared some of the undergrowth. The girl's single-minded fixation on this task was enough to convince her that this was more than just pure desperation. She was focussed and had purpose and, once there was a gap in the vegetation, Harriet was able to see the reason for the girl's actions.

The hole that had been cut in the fence had been there for some time. On the other side, it was concealed from the road by a privet hedge which grew a few feet from the line of the fence. The girl, once again, wasn't going to wait for any prompt from Harriet. Before she could make any attempt to stop her, or to advise caution, the girl was through, beckoning frantically for Harriet to follow.

'Who's rescuing whom?' was a question that occurred to Harriet as she scrambled on all fours to join the young girl. But, regardless of any misgivings Harriet still had, she couldn't deny that they were now out of the orphanage grounds and not far from where her Volkswagen was parked. She took the girl's hand once more as they made their way along the length of the hedge, moving as fast as they could to avoid being seen from the building.

It was as they reached the far end that, without warning, the girl was grabbed by her free arm and snatched away from Harriet's grasp. She tried to hold onto her but failed, and she was unable to see at that moment who it was who had taken the girl so quickly and so violently.

"As you can see, child, you aren't the only one who knows of that tunnel's existence…."

It was the stern-looking woman Harriet had seen in the orphanage but, worse still, standing a few paces behind her was the man she had seen earlier, sitting in the car.

"….and I have been hoping so much that, one day, you'd use it. All those times I locked you in that cellar weren't wasted after all, and I do so enjoy the thrill of the chase. Don't you?"

The woman smiled at the girl, but it was a cruel smile, devoid of any humanity and even Harriet, who had seen evil in many forms throughout the years, felt a chill run down her spine. The woman turned to the man, who was now beside her.

"Take her and go. Our business here is concluded."

She pushed the girl into his arms as Harriet walked slowly towards them.

"I don't know whether to be angry, or just hurt."

99

Harriet moved closer still as she spoke, holding eye contact with the woman.

"What do you mean?"

The woman was clearly irritated and made no effort to disguise the fact. Harriet merely shrugged.

"That you dismiss my presence here so readily because, I have to tell you, I'm not going to let either of you take this girl anywhere, especially as you seem to see her as nothing more than an object for your twisted idea of amusement."

The man remained silent but tightened his hold on the young girl, while the woman seemed to be relishing the situation.

"Not just amusement. Don't forget the rather substantial sum of money I've just received for her. But I do admire your optimism. By the way, I assume I'm talking to someone of her kind?"

She looked at the girl and then back at Harriet, who said nothing, knowing that her only chance was to remain calm and focussed.

"I'll take your silence as a 'yes'. You see...."

She turned to the man.

"....they don't want you to have her."

The fear in the young girl's eyes was heart-breaking, more so because Harriet now knew that being threatened and afraid was probably something she had encountered all too often in her short life.

It was the man's turn to smile.

"She's bought and paid for. She belongs to The Custodians now."

"Because you believe this young lady should pay the price for something that happened centuries ago? Really?"

Harriet wasn't so naïve as to believe that she could talk either of them into handing the girl back to her, but she was attempting to buy herself precious seconds, well aware that it was two against one and there would only be one chance to achieve the desired outcome.

"I won't be lectured by your kind! The descendants of the Brathy Beck Coven will be punished for their inherited sins!"

She had clearly succeeded in touching a nerve, which had been the intention. If he was angry then he would be distracted, and his reactions should be fractionally slowed. At least, that was the theory.

"Well, witch hunters would know all about sins, wouldn't they?"

Must keep going, wait for the chance. It will come. And it was at that moment that Harriet's chance did come, but not in the way she had expected. Without any warning, the girl managed to free one of her arms and lashed out at the man, her hand landing a hard punch on his chest. As he cried out, his hold on her weakened and she broke free but, instead of running as Harriet hoped she would, the girl turned and kicked the man hard on one of his knees.

"The town car park! Go!"

Harriet called out, but the girl hesitated for just a split-second, giving the man the opportunity to make a grab for her, however, she just managed to evade his outstretched hand and, with one last glance back to Harriet, she ran. Harriet had to hope that the girl not only knew the way to the car park but, more importantly, that she would be able to join her which, at that moment, was far from certain.

The man was still holding his knee and struggling to walk. The woman, however, had turned her attention to the girl, who was fast disappearing from sight but, before she could think about giving chase, Harriet launched herself at her. She collided with her in a rugby tackle and together they hit the ground hard. Without waiting to check whether she was injured, Harriet pushed herself up. A sharp pain in her left shoulder made her wince, but she couldn't afford to let up on her attack. The woman had rolled away and was now on her knees. Harriet aimed a kick at her body and she fell back, clutching her side. But before Harriet could land any further blows, the man had seized her arm and whipped her around, wrenching her already damaged shoulder.

Still limping from the girl's kick, he pulled Harriet close, his arms exerting a fierce pressure on her chest. She struggled to try and break his hold but felt herself growing weaker as breathing became more and more difficult. If she was unable to free herself in the next few seconds, then she would lose consciousness and it would be over for her and for the young girl. The best she could hope for was that there might be someone else in the car park, a random member of the public, who could take pity on her and get her away to some sort of safety. Harriet desperately tried to convince herself that might happen but she knew that her first instinct was right. If she failed, here and now, then it was the end for them both.

Her vision began to blur and she felt her strength fading. As her hand dropped to her side, she remembered the torch that she'd used in the tunnel. Could she find it? She pushed her hand into her pocket and touched the small metal cylinder. Channelling every last ounce of strength, she removed the torch, gripping it tightly, before lifting it up and ramming its handle as hard as she could into the man's right eye. He dropped to his knees and fell forward, silent and still.

Harriet gasped for air. Seconds passed, she managed to calm her breathing and, moments later, climbed unsteadily to her feet. The woman was nowhere to be seen. She had to get to the car park and hope to find the young girl there. Because that was all she had now. Hope.

Harriet ran. The effort was almost too much for her. Each time her feet hit the ground, the jolt caused the pain in her shoulder to give her a sharp reminder that she was not in good shape.

The car park was now in sight. Harriet looked around her for any sign of the girl. Was there another car park in Markham? Had she, through lack of local knowledge, inadvertently misdirected her? There were several other parked cars near her Golf, but there were no other people to be seen. She considered calling out but stayed silent for fear of attracting the wrong kind of attention.

Harriet unlocked her Volkswagen and leant down to put the key in the ignition. Suddenly there was a sharp tug on her jacket. She spun round and saw the young girl standing behind her.

"I hid until you got here."

'Your faith in me is touching' Harriet wanted to say but, instead, wasted no time in getting her into the car. As she climbed behind the wheel and started the engine, she managed to give her a reassuring smile.

The loud bang on the side window caused Harriet to flinch away as the woman smashed her fist again and again onto the glass. The girl gave a short, terrified scream and covered her face with her hands. Harriet's first instinct was to floor the accelerator and drive out forwards, making a sharp left turn before she hit the perimeter wall of the car park. But, at the moment she was about to press the pedal down, she realised that she wouldn't make the turn. There was another hard blow and the window shattered, showering them both with small fragments of glass.

The woman tried to reach in and get her hands around Harriet's neck but, before she could close her grip, Harriet found reverse gear and came down hard on the accelerator. It took a second for the tyres to bite before the car shot backwards. The woman, her hands dripping with blood, began to run after them, this time making for the passenger side.

Harriet leant over and pulled the young girl as far as she could away from the window, but her seat belt locked and held her. She brought her foot down on the brake, bringing the Volkswagen to a sudden stop. As the woman reached the passenger door, Harriet found first gear, and then very quickly, second, as the car picked up forward momentum. She wrenched the steering wheel around, pointing the car at the exit.

The girl screamed again as her door flew open and the woman threw herself at her, her arms flailing as she tried to find the seat belt release. Harriet knew that if she attempted to fight the woman off she couldn't hope to control the car. Shutting out the girl's cries and the woman's angry shouts, Harriet put all her concentration into steering the VW as accurately, and as fast as possible, out of the car park. The woman was still pulling at the seat belt and running to keep pace with the car's acceleration. There was a loud noise as the open passenger door hit one of the concrete bollards that stood on either side of the exit. The impact sent it slamming shut onto the woman's outstretched arm, cutting through flesh and shattering bone. She gave an agonised scream and fell back onto the ground, her head hitting the concrete. She lay still, her eyes wide open, staring up at the blue sky but seeing nothing.

They were now out onto the main road. Harriet glanced into her rear view mirror. She saw the woman lying motionless in a growing pool of blood. Steering right to take the shortest route out of Markham, Harriet turned to the young girl who, now she was sure that she was free and safe, managed a weak smile.

103

"You ok?"

The girl nodded.

"Yes. Thank you."

Harriet returned the smile.

"I don't think I've properly introduced myself. I'm Harriet."

The young girl nodded before replying.

"Thank you for saving me, Harriet. I expect you know that my name is Verity. Verity Trask."

Chapter 14

"I'm pretty sure the woman died...."

Harriet glanced at Melissa before turning back to her canvas and picking up one of the smaller paint brushes.

"....and the man. I killed them, and I'm not sorry."

Melissa saw a shadow pass over her, and she remained silent, instead looking out over the lake. It was so calm and beautiful.

"They both deserved it, especially the woman. Locking a young girl in a dark cellar, hoping that she'd find an escape route you already knew was there, and hoping that, one day, she'd use it so you could punish her even more severely. Can you imagine that?"

Melissa shook her head, still sitting beside Harriet, not having moved since she had started speaking.

"It all fell perfectly for her. She was in charge of the orphanage and used her position to torment those unfortunate enough to end up in her care. So, when she was approached by the witch hunters, not only did she have the opportunity to inflict even more misery upon Verity, but the poor girl had also suddenly become a valuable asset."

"Do you think it was just luck that you went up those stairs instead of down?"

It was a question that had occurred to Melissa as she had listened to Harriet's account.

"Your choice of words suggests that you don't?"

She shrugged.

"I'm not sure."

Harriet dipped her brush into some particularly vibrant azure blue.

"I have thought about it over the years. I did once ask Verity, although I rarely talk to her about her time at the orphanage. No point in revisiting memories that only hold pain and fear for her."

It was becoming clear to Melissa just how much Harriet cared for Verity and how, even now, all these years later, she still wanted to protect her from the horrors of her childhood.

"What did she say?"

"She said she recalled, in her darkest moments, wishing for some kind of deliverance. She said she didn't care in what form it came."

"What do you think she meant by that?"

The sorrow in Harriet's eyes told Melissa the answer and, moments later, she confirmed it.

"I think Verity wanted to die rather than continue to live the life she had. For a ten-year-old that's quite something, isn't it?"

Melissa reached out and rested her hand on Harriet's arm.

"But she didn't die, did she? You saved her. Her wish was for deliverance. You were that deliverance, and you must be so proud of her."

She wanted her words to deflect from the sorrow, to get Harriet to see nothing but the overwhelming positive in an incident that obviously still held such a deep sadness for her.

"Yes, I am proud of her, and I'm proud of what we've achieved here together. You see, it quickly became clear that Verity was only the first. There were going to be others who would need our help and protection, and The Custodians would only become more accomplished in their methods to find and take these women, or girls. Not only did we have to 'up our game', as I believe the phrase goes, but we knew that we needed somewhere to bring them, somewhere that safety was guaranteed. Would you like a drink?"

From the bag next to her, Harriet produced two tumblers followed by a bottle of white wine and a corkscrew. From the condensation forming on the glass it looked as if the wine was suitably chilled.

"That would be lovely. Thank you."

Melissa could have taken or left the alcohol but, more than anything, she wanted to hear as much as Harriet was willing to tell her, and sharing the bottle could only serve to encourage further conversation.

"My dear Melissa, would you be willing to do the honours? My hands are not as steady as they once were. If I'm on my own I don't care about the odd spillage, but…."

"Of course."

Melissa removed the cork and poured two glasses of wine before handing one to Harriet. They sat in silence for some minutes, enjoying the Chablis and their peaceful surroundings.

"Do you always ensure you can cater for two?"

Melissa lifted her glass as Harriet gave a quiet laugh.

"It would be embarrassing if one could not, wouldn't it?"

"Yes, I suppose it would."

Melissa took another sip.

"Now, where was I?"

"You were just going to tell me about your 'somewhere'."

Harriet thought for a moment.

"Ah yes. Well, there's not much more to tell. It was decided that we had to find a special place, an invisible place, where no one could find us."

"Forgive me, but someone, someday, will be bound to find…."

Harriet held up a hand to stop her mid-sentence.

"I understand why you would think so however, please be assured, this place and everyone here, will never be found by those who intend us harm. That I can guarantee."

Melissa couldn't see how she could make such a promise and, briefly, considered gently arguing the point but something stopped her, something in the way Harriet spoke, and the look in her eyes. There was a certainty, an unshakeable confidence in her words. Was she fooling herself? Melissa quickly discounted that idea.

"I can see from your expression that you are unconvinced. Therefore, when you have finished your wine we shall take a short walk."

And she said nothing more until Melissa's glass was empty, instead returning her attention to the canvas and adding a few more brush strokes to one of the trees that bordered her painting. As soon as Melissa had placed her almost finished glass onto the grass by the blanket, Harriet replaced her brush and, with some effort, stood up. Melissa was about to reach out to help her, but

107

recalled the previous evening when Verity had discouraged her from assisting. Although now struggling with what Melissa guessed to be age-related arthritis, there was a definite 'I will not give in to this' attitude, and good for her, Melissa thought.

Together they made their way across the lawn, walking away from the lake and towards a wooden bridge over a gently flowing stream which, Melissa could now see, fed into the lake a little way downstream. They paused in the middle of the bridge as Harriet pointed out a female duck with several ducklings in tow. They didn't seem to notice the two women watching them as they swam on in the direction of the lake. On the other side of the bridge there was a path, lined with rose bushes laden with deep red blooms, their powerful scent drifting on the summer breeze.

"We've cultivated our own variety. Quite wonderful, aren't they?"

There was pride in Harriet's voice, not only for the roses but for it all, this whole new, beautiful, enigma of a world. Rightly so. And now it was Melissa's world, if she chose to accept it.

"Magnificent" was all she could think to say as they continued along the scented path, the sound of the stream receding with every step. In front of them there was another thicket of shrubs. The path disappeared into the undergrowth that was itself in deep shadow, most of the sunlight being blocked out by several tall trees, each one heavy with deep green leaves. Whereas, up until this moment, all had been beauty and light, the place where they were now heading felt somehow more forbidding to Melissa, somewhere apart. Harriet must have sensed her growing anxiety.

"There's no need to be frightened. There is love here, I promise you, and you are part of that love. You always have been and you always will be."

Harriet stood beside her, waiting, giving Melissa the time she needed to calm herself and to be sure that she was ready to walk on into the shadows. Because now it was a matter of trust, wasn't it? Melissa had to trust all that she'd been told, to accept that she was part of something, and to try to gain an understanding of that something. Give nothing, or give it all.

"I'd like you to show me. I want to know."

Harriet took her hand.

"You already know, Melissa."

If she expected Harriet to elaborate on that statement, then she was to be disappointed. Instead, she was led on along the path, slowly but with purpose. They entered the half-light beneath the trees, where the path took them around some dense shrubbery until, glancing back, Melissa could no longer see the sunshine and the birds and the lake. The temperature had dropped now that they were in unbroken shade, to the point where Melissa gave a slight shiver. She turned to Harriet, who didn't seem to be affected by the colder atmosphere at all.

"You will, of course, now understand why this place must never be found and, I'm sure, you are beginning to see that here the ordinary does not apply. You know of Brathy Beck. That was the catalyst. And, you seem to have accepted all that you have seen and heard, and your own situation. Is that so? I ask because I need to be sure before we continue."

Had she accepted it? Melissa recalled the funeral and her first meeting with Danika. Her mocking incredulity, quickly followed by fear and trepidation as she saw her old life, and the prospect of returning to it, moving ever further out of her reach. And, if she did believe without question everything she had been told then she had to acknowledge that she was not the person she had thought herself to be. She was descended from an infamous coven of witches, and this 'fact' had now put her life in danger. But was she truly among friends, her own kind, who would offer her comfort and protection? Verity had told her she was free to leave but, truthfully, she had absolutely no desire to do that. And the sudden realisation of being sure she wanted to remain told her everything she needed to know about her true feelings.

"I want to continue."

Melissa looked her in the eyes as she spoke, so that Harriet might see beyond her words. If there had been any doubt in her mind then, she hoped, that doubt might be completely removed.

"Then we shall."

There was no hesitation before Harriet's reply. She had seen into Melissa's heart, and was content.

The grey, angular rock, a weather-worn, moss covered piece of limestone, rested against a high wall that rose up out of the long grass and wild tangle of undergrowth. Melissa stood in front of it, unsure whether to remain where she was or move closer, perhaps to within touching distance.

"You don't need to ask me what it is, do you?"

In response to Harriet's question, Melissa slowly shook her head as her eyes remained fixed upon the rock. Instinctively, she reached out to it, feeling its pull. It wanted her. It wanted her touch. She rested both palms on its rough, cold surface and closed her eyes. In that moment Melissa felt the shock run through her and she almost broke her contact with the stone. But she knew that she had to hold the connection. She had no choice.

Emotions flooded her thoughts, driving out the present and replacing it with echoes of the past, a past that was now no stranger to her. And through it all, like a golden thread woven intricately into each recovered memory, the sense of belonging. Should she be afraid? She no longer felt any fear. Perhaps because she knew that the souls that now embraced her offered nothing but love and protection. And she also knew that the 'belonging' that she now felt so strongly was what had been hidden away in her subconscious, telling her that this place was where she needed to be, where she *had* to be. It was what had quietly helped to suppress her initial panic, and to fight her natural desire to push back against the shock of her arrival at the sanctuary, silently encouraging her to accept and to learn. She understood that now.

"I can hear the beck."

Melissa whispered, her eyes still tightly shut.

"This stone was near it, close to Brathy Beck, wasn't it?"

She didn't need Harriet to reply. She knew.

"There is a force that is channelled through the stone, a desire that reaches across the centuries."

Harriet spoke softly, not wanting to distract Melissa from the moment.

"They are watching over us, aren't they?"

"Yes. They know there is a debt to be repaid, and they are doing that in the only way they are able. By keeping our sanctuary safe from the outside world."

A short time ago Melissa would have had questions, but not now. Now she understood. Harriet took a step back, resting a hand on the branch of a tree to steady herself. Close to her hand, a butterfly had settled. Melissa saw the flash of colour out of the corner of her eye, and her thoughts returned to the room where she had sat with Justine. She had experienced something then, but she hadn't recognised that 'something' for what it was. Even now, she would struggle to describe it. All she could say was that it was beautiful. Truly beautiful. And she no longer felt the cold.

Chapter 15

"Great shot!"

Justine patted her racket while her opponent, the young woman that Melissa now knew was called Sophie, acknowledged the compliment. Melissa sat on the grass near the tennis court, enjoying the afternoon sun and the well-contested match. If she'd been expecting a gentle, good-humoured game played purely for fun, then she would have been mistaken. This was a real, meaningful encounter between two women who both believed they could win.

"They're very good, aren't they?"

Verity elegantly lowered herself down beside Melissa, tucking her legs underneath her. It was doubtful that she could do anything other than gracefully.

"You should charge to watch it!"

Verity laughed.

"I believe they both played for their colleges."

She returned her attention to the court, leaving Melissa to decide whether to continue with the conversation or to be quiet and concentrate on the match. As excellent as the tennis was however....

"Harriet's quite a lady, isn't she?"

Melissa's choice of words had been deliberately vague, allowing Verity the choice to either engage, or give a one syllable answer and close the subject down.

"I'm pleased you found her agreeable company. Did she have an interesting story to tell?"

Melissa was unsure how she should answer, not wanting to get Harriet into trouble for saying too much. But Verity, reading the look on Melissa's face, quickly put an end to her uncertainty in a way that she couldn't have expected.

"I still hate the dark. I don't give in to my fear, but it's there. Always. All those times I was shut in that wretched cellar...."

Verity returned her attention to the two women playing tennis and, for a moment, it was as if she hadn't said anything.

"I'm sorry for what you went through."

Melissa felt her words were inadequate. Since she had left Harriet she had gone over and over in her mind what she might say when she met Verity again. Fortunately, Verity herself had swept away any concerns Melissa was harbouring regarding what she could and, more importantly, couldn't mention. By acknowledging the psychological damage she had suffered Verity was, in her own way, dealing with her nightmares.

"Thank you. But it was a long time ago and we must try to move on, mustn't we?"

Melissa could see that she was trying to put on a braver face, but were her eyes just a little moister, and was there a slight tremor in her voice when she spoke? Melissa's thoughts returned to the moment when she had walked into Verity's office and met her for the first time. Confident, perfect poise, comfortable with the authority she had. She had presented a formidable emotional barrier and, therefore, Melissa had to decide whether to give her the chance to allow the barrier to slip again, or to pretend the barrier hadn't slipped at all and walk away.

"Nevertheless…."

Offer her the chance. If she wants to take it, she'll take it. The last thing Melissa wanted was to push Verity into a subject she would very much prefer to avoid. Maybe those words about hating the dark were just a slip, a private thought mistakenly spoken out loud. Melissa made a conscious effort to avoid eye contact and instead turned her attention back to the tennis. Justine and Sophie were still battling, neither wanting to concede an advantage and both hitting the ball harder than ever.

"Everyone has their demons, Melissa. I'm no different. But I've never asked for sympathy, and I never will."

Verity's defiance was spoken softly, her voice even and controlled.

"I'm sorry…."

She continued after a short pause.

"….that sounded rude. It wasn't meant to."

"It didn't. It sounded honest."

"Thank you. Honesty is something that Harriet told me to value."

"Did she bring you up?"

Melissa expected her question to be politely rebuffed, but she felt she had to ask. The implication of what Harriet had told her suggested such a relationship and, if *she* were honest, she really wanted to know.

"In a manner of speaking...."

No rebuff then, at least not yet.

"....she was always around, either with me, or in the background, overseeing my education."

"She found you a school?"

Verity smiled.

"When I say 'education' I'm not just referring to the academic although, of course, that was addressed. Perhaps, after this morning, you understand what I mean?"

Melissa nodded.

"To appreciate who you are, and what you are, is one of the most important lessons of all, don't you think?"

Verity shifted her position slightly, making herself more comfortable. In front of them, Justine and Sophie were still locked in battle.

"Yes. But I had no idea of my....ancestry."

Melissa wondered if that was the right word.

"Neither did I, as a young girl in that orphanage all I knew was I hated my life and wanted a way out, one way or another. Some days, the worst days, I would try to wish myself dead."

So there was the confirmation from Verity herself. Harriet had been right.

"But in a twisted sort of way...."

Verity continued

"....I suppose I have The Custodians to thank for my eventual salvation. If they hadn't tracked me down to the orphanage thereby prompting Harriet's intervention, I dare not think what might have become of me. Except, of course, I do. Every day."

Melissa saw her eyes fix upon an imaginary point in the distance, as her thoughts took her to a place hidden away in the darkest corners of her mind. She might have been physically liberated from that desperate childhood but, Melissa could now

114

see, Verity had no escape from the memories of it and the darkness they held.

"Did Harriet bring you here, after she'd rescued you?"

Melissa hoped the question would take her away from thoughts of the orphanage and maybe onto happier times.

"Goodness me, no. This place is a result of Harriet's vision and determination over many years. No, I was initially taken to a small town house. I lived in an attic room for some time, I can't be sure for how long. It wasn't a mansion, but I was protected, and I was loved, and that was all that mattered to me. The ground and first floor were used by a secretarial business, as I recall."

"A cover?"

Verity shook her head.

"No. It was a genuine business, with genuine clients. But the situation was far from ideal. Harriet knew there was always the possibility of being discovered. As further targets were identified by The Custodians, so there was an increased need for more safe houses with, obviously, a similarly increased risk of those houses becoming compromised. Hence the vision and determination to find a place more suitable to our unique needs."

Melissa could well believe that if Harriet wanted something to happen, it would happen. But her vision, her sanctuary, was so much more than buildings and beautiful grounds. Melissa understood that now.

"I've seen the stone."

"And you felt the affinity?"

"Yes. I sensed their presence."

"Good. Then you'll know that we're protected here. Those who wish us harm will never find us because our sanctuary is in the care of the Brathy Beck Coven."

Melissa's thoughts momentarily turned to her old life, and everything she had believed herself to be. That all belonged to another world now, a world that seemed to be dissolving into nothing and would soon be gone forever.

There was a cry of frustration from the tennis court as Justine was passed down the line by a perfectly hit half-volley.

"Looks like it's going to a third set."

115

Melissa wasn't unhappy about that as she was enjoying the whole scene, the tennis, the warm afternoon sun, and Verity's company.

"How many more times do you think you'll have to send Danika out to save others like me?"

"I can't answer that, not because I don't want to but because I don't have an answer. Experience has taught me to assume nothing."

"She's good at what she does, isn't she?"

"Danika? Oh yes, as several, including you, can testify."

"Don't you worry for her safety when she's out doing what she does?"

A cloud momentarily passed over Verity's expression.

"I don't put her at risk on a whim. She's a competent young woman. Supremely capable of looking after herself, and others, and yes, of course I worry. I try not to let her see it but, if you care about someone, you can't help it, can you? She's like a daughter to me."

Verity's honesty was raw and heartfelt.

"So she does have at least one friend, even if you don't call her Dani."

Verity smiled, suggesting she knew the reference Melissa was making.

"Yes, she has a friend…."

Verity said softly

"….and I still think about the day we first met, and how it all so nearly ended in tragedy…."

Chapter 16

~*Verity and Danika*~

The rain was falling harder, prompting Verity to fasten another two buttons on her coat. The courtyard was almost empty except for the occasional office worker hurrying to the train station or car park. It was now dark and the lights from the surrounding buildings were shining brightly out onto the large expanse of pavement, adding to the neon glow from the street lamps.

It had been some time since Danika had called her on the burner phone she had sent her, and Verity was now beginning to worry. Danika should be with her by now, but she was nowhere to be seen. One part of the plan seemed to be playing out as expected, but had she been too optimistic in believing that it could all go well? Might it be that Danika's choice of lover would prove to be fatal for her? If that turned out to be the case, then Verity knew that she would be responsible. She had taken the decision and would have to live with the consequences.

But how much longer should she, or could she, wait? Verity checked her phone. Nothing since Danika's call. If she remained in the courtyard for much longer, Verity was sure that her own safety might become compromised. And so, it was almost time to make up her mind. Should she continue to hope that Danika would show up, or should she face reality and save herself?

Danika knew she was going to be late but, as she waited at the kerbside, she had the feeling that she was being followed. Had they pursued her from the castle? She hadn't seen anyone, she hadn't heard anyone, but she sensed an approaching threat.

It was a split second decision to suddenly dash out into the traffic. Amid the sound of car horns and screeching brakes, she reached the other side of the road. Behind her the cars had begun to move again, with several drivers making various gestures in her direction. Without hesitating, she ran on, taking the first turning off the main street, desperate to lose herself in one of the many side roads.

Danika had briefly thought that she should stay on the high street, but it would have been a much easier proposition to follow her under the bright lights. And she had to make it to where, she hoped, someone called Verity Trask would still be waiting. She began to jog. Maybe, if she tried, she could make it to the courtyard only a few minutes late. But what if those few minutes meant that Verity was no longer there? She hadn't considered the possibility before, perhaps because the thought was too frightening to contemplate.

The jog turned into a run. Maybe if it hadn't, the blow that landed moments later wouldn't have had quite such a devastating effect. Danika was thrown sideways against a garden wall, the impact knocking the breath out of her. Before she could react several more blows sent her sprawling across the pavement.

"Pick her up. I'll get the car."

Danika heard the voice come from somewhere within her world of pain. She wanted, more than anything, to lose consciousness and to cheat the hurt by giving herself to an oblivion that was ready to take her. The sound of a car pulling up nearby cut through the welcoming darkness and, as she was roughly lifted to her feet, she knew that in seconds it would all be over.

Verity was now alone in the courtyard. The sporadic flow of office workers had all but dried up as they were now either on their trains and buses, in their cars, or enjoying the hospitality of one of the local pubs. Standing near one of the street lamps, she had a clear view of the path that led into, and out of, the courtyard.

She would wait another ten minutes. She owed Danika that. But what if she didn't show up, and she had to leave without her? As the minutes ticked by, Verity began to fear the worst. Had she failed her? Should she have done this differently? She tried to shut out the negative feelings, but couldn't help thinking of the frightened young women she'd been unable to save.

The rain had now eased off to a steady drizzle, and it was through the drizzle that Verity first saw the young woman's silhouette against the street lighting. She watched as she walked slowly towards her. Too slowly. Verity was about to call out to her when the woman, after trying to take another step, fell forward onto her hands and knees. Verity ran over and, as she knelt beside her on the wet pavement, she saw that her face was covered with cuts and bruises.

"Danika?"

With some effort, Danika forced a smile onto her blood-spattered lips.

"Verity, I hope."

Verity nodded.

"Let's get you out of here. Can you stand?"

She didn't wait for a reply, putting an arm around her waist and lifting her to her feet. She knew the by-the-book way would have been to assess her, check for broken bones, concussion, and any one of countless injuries Danika might have sustained. But Verity also knew there was no time for that. It was quite possible that whoever did this to her was only seconds away and wouldn't hesitate to finish the job.

"My car's very near. Lean on me. Carefully. That's right."

It was clear that the act of walking was both difficult and painful for Danika, but Verity could sense her determination and the effort she was making to move as quickly as she possibly could. As they left the courtyard they were overtaken by a middle aged man who threw them a cursory glance, but walked quickly on, deciding not to get involved with the woman and her intoxicated friend.

"Nearly there. You're doing really well."

Verity received another laboured smile in response as they reached the car without incident. She had spent the duration of their short walk looking both in front and behind them for any possible threat but, for whatever reason, none materialised.

Danika leant against the side of the car while Verity opened the passenger door. Moments later she was in her seat with her safety belt fastened.

"They....they won't have followed us."

"I'm sorry?"

"You keep looking in your rear view mirror. There's no need. They won't have followed us."

Verity gave her a fleeting glance.

"How can you be so sure?"

Danika gave a short laugh which caused her to cough painfully.

"Because I left them both in a worse state than I am."

"You…?"

"I know it doesn't look like it right now, but I can take care of myself."

"Do you want to tell me?"

Verity again glanced to her left. Danika shook her head as she took a short, painful breath.

"About what happened? No. I just knew I had to get away from them. I was scared you wouldn't wait for me."

"But I did, and now you're safe."

Verity wanted not only to reassure her, but to keep her talking, concerned that she might drift into unconsciousness.

"Yes. I'm safe. Thank you."

Danika was trying hard to remain calm, to keep it together, but the relief she felt was threatening to overwhelm her. Minutes passed and they were leaving the city behind them. The traffic had thinned considerably in the suburbs and, by the time they were deep into the countryside, it seemed as if they were the only people for miles around.

"You haven't asked where I'm taking you."

"I don't care. It won't be where I've come from. That's all that matters."

Verity already knew something of Danika's background, various random facts that had come to light as she had carried out her research. Danika had left Poland, alone, in her teens. Having an English mother meant she was permitted residence in the UK. She had achieved high grades at college and, after leaving further education, had trained to work in Personal Security. So, yes, it was quite possible that Danika was able to 'take care of herself'.

"Fine, but would you like an answer to the question you haven't asked?"

Verity waited for a response but none was forthcoming.

"Danika?"

Her eyes had closed. Verity slowed the car, steering it onto a grass verge and bringing it to a stop.

"Danika?"

Verity rested a hand on her shoulder and gently rocked her to and fro several times. She stirred and her eyes opened briefly.

"I....I'm sorry. I suddenly felt really tired. I'll try and stay awake....but...."

Danika slipped into unconsciousness again. Verity quickly removed her phone from its resting place in the car door. In a few seconds she had placed the call, a call she had been considering making for the best part of the journey.

"Pamela? Yes, good to hear you too. Listen, I need an urgent favour. Are you alone?"

Verity parked directly outside the cottage's front door. Before she could attempt to wake Danika, the porch light came on and the front door was thrown open. The woman, wearing jogging trousers, a loose-fitting sweatshirt, and a pair of well-worn white trainers, ran over to the car, making straight for the passenger side. She didn't immediately acknowledge Verity, but opened the door and leant in to release Danika's seat belt.

"Doctor Pamela Flynn, I presume?"

Verity enquired from the driver's seat. She received a warm smile in return.

"Danika? Wake up, love. Danika. Wake up."

Pamela quietly repeated the words until Danika slowly opened her eyes.

"Hi. My name is Pamela. I'm a doctor and I'm going to help you. I'm just going to do a few little checks before we get you out of the car."

Verity remained in her seat while Pamela gave Danika a short, preliminary examination. When she was content that it was safe to move her, she nodded to Verity and together they assisted her into the cottage.

"We'll go into the living room. Just through here."

Pamela, with the utmost care, guided Danika to a large sofa.

"We'll need to keep our voices down. My daughter's asleep...."

She pointed to one of the upstairs bedrooms.

"I'm fine. Really."

"Doctor Flynn will be the judge of that, Danika. Do you still keep the coffee in the same cupboard?"

Pamela nodded before retrieving a small brown leather bag from the side of the sofa as Verity left the room and headed to the kitchen. She paused in the doorway. It was just as she remembered it. The sight of the kitchen table, with the rather uncomfortable wooden chairs placed around it, made her smile. She walked over to the row of wall-cupboards and opened the middle one, took down the jar of coffee and three mugs.

Verity had decided not to hurry making the coffee, wanting to give Pamela plenty of time to give Danika a thorough examination. As she busied herself with the drinks and began a search for Pamela's secret hoard of shortbread biscuits, Verity's thoughts returned to the first time she had met Doctor Pamela Flynn. It had been at a dinner party hosted by a mutual friend that they had initially enjoyed each other's company and conversation. Several meetings later and it had been as if they had known each other all of their lives, although neither of them had planned, or expected, the path that their consequent relationship had taken.

At the time it had seemed like a natural evolution from a close, trusting friendship to something intensely intimate and physical. Looking back on it now, Verity still wondered why she hadn't asked, or had her suspicions, about Pamela's home life. And so when she eventually told her about her husband and young daughter, Verity knew it had to end. Not for the husband's sake, not even for the daughter's, but for her own, and there had been no drama, no arguments. It had all been very civilised. Maybe too civilised. Sometime later, Pamela called Verity to tell her that her husband had left her, and they had considered trying again. But, deep down, both had known it wouldn't be the same, that those earlier days, and nights, could never return in the way they both wanted. It would have been easy to pretend, to want it so much that they ignored what they knew to be true. Or, at least, that's what they told themselves because, to accept that it was the end, meant they could avoid any further heartache. It was the easier option, wasn't it? But did the feelings that had originally brought them together still exist in both Verity and Pamela? Sadly, it was unlikely they would ever find out.

They had remained friends, very good friends, but Verity's work with the sanctuary and Pamela's NHS commitments meant that time spent together had diminished to the occasional phone call. Verity had never told her of the true nature of her work but had scattered small truths in amongst the bigger lie. As far as Pamela understood, Verity worked at a secret hideaway for women in physical danger. Actually, not far from the truth at all. The lie, as is often the case, existed in omission rather than any blatant fabrication.

The idea of calling Pamela had come to Verity early in their journey from the city, and the longer she spent talking to Danika and observing her, the more she had become increasingly convinced that she needed to see a doctor sooner rather than later. The diversion to Pamela's cottage had added at least an hour to their journey and it hadn't been a decision taken lightly, because all the time they were not at that ultimate safe house, they both remained in danger. But Verity had made the call and, for better or worse, here they were.

She placed the three mugs of hot coffee and a plate of delicious-looking shortbread onto a tray and carried it back through to the living room, carefully balancing it as she gave a light knock on the closed door. Moments later it was opened by Pamela.

"You found my best biscuits, I see."

"Should've changed the hiding place."

They laughed and, for just a second, the years fell away.

"I've examined Danika, treated her wounds, and I'm happy there's nothing too serious. She's taken quite a beating though, but rest and time should see her ok. Sanctuary girl?"

Verity nodded, and no more needed to be said. Total trust. Total discretion. Always. Pamela took the tray from Verity and followed her into the room, where Danika was sitting up at one end of the sofa. She put the tray onto a low table and passed a coffee to Danika. As she took it, Verity saw the various dressings on her face, hands, and arms.

"Can I make a suggestion?"

Pamela asked as she sat down in the chair opposite. Verity picked up her mug and settled herself onto the sofa next to Danika.

"Go ahead."

Verity took a sip and silently congratulated herself for making something so enjoyable. Maybe Pamela's choice of coffee might have played a small part, but still....

"My spare room's free. Why don't you both stay here tonight and finish your journey tomorrow? I think a night's sleep would be beneficial, especially for you Danika."

Verity was about to politely decline, before she turned to Danika and saw her face. She had a look of total fatigue. It was as if, not only the events of that evening, but all that had gone before, had suddenly swept over her like a wave that she had been trying to outrun but that had now overwhelmed her.

"That's so kind, thank you."

"Yes. Thank you."

Danika added, and there was a definite feeling of relief in her voice.

"Excellent. There's a single bed and a futon, up to you who has which."

Verity knew she had no intention of denying Danika the bed and anyway, the futon was bound to be more than comfortable enough.

"Verity knows where everything is...."

A brief exchange of smiles between Pamela and Verity.

"....and, please be assured, you are quite safe here."

Those words were directed at Danika, who said nothing but nodded her thanks as she pulled a hand roughly across her eyes. Verity picked up the plate of shortbread and offered it to her, wanting to give her something else to think about.

"I can find you some cereal, maybe egg on toast, if you'd prefer?"

"Or maybe just a warm bed?"

Verity asked while looking at Danika, fairly sure what she would prefer. And so, some ten minutes later and after a combined effort converting the futon into a very passable bed, Verity and Danika were settled in their room. Verity lay on the futon, having just removed her jacket and shoes. Maybe she would undress later and submit to the warm, inviting duvet, but she doubted it. She didn't expect to sleep very much, if at all. Deep, restful sleep was something that had eluded her since childhood. Another legacy from those days was a fear of the dark. Every night at the sanctuary she would leave her bedroom light on, and she hoped that Danika would be ok with that for the few hours they would be spending together. But, on looking over to the bed, she saw that she needn't have worried. Danika had her eyes closed and was fast asleep. Verity smiled to herself, pleased that she'd made the right decision in accepting Pamela's offer. So, maybe if she tried closing her eyes just for a little while....

"It's alright, Danika. It's alright."

Verity, jolted from her sleep by Danika's sobs, sat beside her on the bed and gently rocked her into consciousness. As soon as she was awake, her crying subsided until she was calm and quiet once more.

"Nightmare?"

It took some seconds before Danika was able to reply.

"I'm sorry."

"Please don't be. It's ok. You were calling for Elise. Do you want to talk about her?"

Danika shook her head, and Verity had no intention of causing her more distress by asking her again about the friend she had lost just hours ago. She pushed herself up from the bed, intending to return to the futon to see if she could find sleep again.

"Stay with me. Just for a little while. Please."

Saying nothing, Verity lay down beside her, on top of the duvet. It was a large single bed and so there was just enough room for two to lie comfortably side by side. As Verity rested next to Danika, she couldn't help but reflect that they were both damaged goods, and that they both needed the sanctuary to save them from their own personal hell.

Chapter 17

"I don't think either of us slept much more that night. We were both too preoccupied with our own demons. As I recall, it took Danika a month or more to fully recover. Not from the nightmares, of course, I honestly don't believe either of us will ever escape those."

Melissa had listened intently while Verity had been quietly talking but now, after all that she'd heard, she had to say something.

"But Danika is so confident, so assured. I owe her my life, so does Justine…."

"And others, but we can never truly know someone, can we? I believe she *has* to do what she does. The rescues seem to be a kind of catharsis for her."

Melissa turned her attention back to the tennis court where it looked as if Sophie was serving for the match.

"What about you, Verity? Are you like her? Do you need your work?"

With someone else, under other circumstances, Melissa wouldn't have dreamt of asking. But, somehow, with all that Verity had given her, with her honesty and her willingness to hold nothing back, it seemed to Melissa that it would be wrong not to want to know more about a woman who was now the driving force behind the sanctuary.

"Yes…."

Verity took a moment before adding

"….this is my universe, my *raison d'etre* and….I think Sophie's won!"

They looked across to the court where Sophie and Justine were hugging and laughing. All the competitive aggression that had been on show had evaporated as soon as the match was over, and it was clear to see that, away from the court, the two women were the best of friends. They left the court and walked over to where Verity and Melissa were sitting, and Melissa knew that, for now, their conversation was over.

"Well played both of you!"

Verity and Melissa gave them a very polite round of applause as Sophie dropped her racket onto the grass before sitting down next to Melissa. Justine, holding her racket in one hand and her towel in the other, nodded in acknowledgement of their appreciation.

"I need a shower and a lie down! She's too good!"

"Won't you join us?" Melissa asked, recalling how much she had enjoyed Justine's company the previous evening.

"If I sit down I may never get up again!"

"And I need to get back to my office. Thank you for your company, Melissa, and for listening. See you later, Sophie."

Verity got to her feet and followed Justine back along the path to the house. Melissa wondered if Sophie would join them, but she showed no inclination to leave her just yet.

"I saw you in the dining room last night, didn't I?"

Melissa asked, recalling the black hair that was cut into a bob, the raspberry red lipstick, minimal eye makeup, and the air of understated chic. It had to be said that some of that chic was looking a little the worse for wear after the intense three sets she'd just played but, nevertheless, it was still there.

"Yes. I don't go every evening, but it's a pleasant enough place to be. Your first night, wasn't it?"

"I still can't believe how much, and how suddenly, everything can change."

Sophie lay back on the grass, looking up at the deep blue, cloudless sky. For a while she seemed to be in a world of her own, until she turned her head towards Melissa.

"It's changed for the better though, don't you think? I mean, it's preferable to being dead, isn't it?"

She gave Melissa a broad smile, lending her words a lighter touch than they might have otherwise had. She then closed her eyes, and Melissa wondered if that meant she had said all that she wanted to say.

"What about you?"

No harm in trying to keep the conversation going.

"What about me?"

Her eyes remained closed.

"How did you cope with losing everything you had and coming here?"

"Well now, I wonder, does that question mean you'd like to get to know me better?"

Did it?

"No, I mean, yes, I suppose so."

The eyes were now open and regarding her with an unmistakeably mischievous twinkle.

"Well, that's clear enough then."

Without warning, Sophie leapt to her feet and picked up her racket.

"You're going? We don't have to talk if you'd rather not."

Sophie stood in front of the still sitting Melissa, throwing a shadow across her.

"I'm sweaty, I'm tired, I'm hungry and thirsty. When I've dealt with each one of those, I'd be delighted to spend some quality time with you, lovely Melissa. I'll find you later."

As she turned away she blew her a kiss and, without looking back, waved her hand above her head in farewell, leaving a somewhat bemused, and intrigued, Melissa. She watched Sophie disappear from view. But now she was alone, she knew that all she wanted was to return to the place where Harriet had taken her some hours earlier, to the Brathy Beck stone.

Melissa walked away from the tennis courts, retracing her steps. She stopped several times to look over to the lake and the woodland beyond. As the afternoon shadows lengthened and the sunlight was slowly becoming less harsh, she found herself drawn into the peaceful beauty of her surroundings. A peaceful beauty that hid well its sad purpose.

Approaching the shadowy clearing where the stone rested, Melissa could hear the sound of a young girl's voice. She was talking softly, as if to a close friend. But, as Melissa drew closer, she could see that the girl, who had her back to her, appeared to be alone.

"Layla?"

She spun round, a look of panic on her face. Clearly, she hadn't expected to be disturbed. She had been kneeling in front of the stone, but was now on her feet and looking ready to run away.

"Please stay. I can come back later."

Layla's eyes flicked from Melissa to the pathway out of the clearing as she weighed up her options. After some moments she seemed to relax a little and even managed to force a smile. But, if the smile said a begrudging 'hello', the body language was saying a definite 'go away', or words to that effect. Melissa was about to do just that, but something made her hesitate. Justine's and Verity's words flashed into her mind, of the description of a deeply troubled young girl who had lost both of her parents. She wondered if that was the usual reaction when confronted with Layla, to bail out before things got too complicated. Melissa took a deep breath.

"I'm Melissa, by the way. Pleased to meet you."

She held out a hand, and Layla looked at her as if she were holding a gun. Melissa quickly dropped her arm to her side, not wanting the prospect of having to shake hands be Layla's reason to leave. Her demeanour remained one of deep suspicion bordering on outright dislike but, undeterred, Melissa stood her ground, waiting to see what kind of reaction her presence would eventually provoke.

"You already know my name. What have they said? Watch out for the weird kid who hates everyone?"

Well, that was more than Melissa had expected, and she still hadn't run away.

"No one has said anything like that. But the people here are concerned for you. They care, Layla."

The look on the thirteen-year-old's face suggested that she didn't believe a word of that.

"I think I'll go now."

Her gaze lowered and she took several paces towards the path that led back to the lake.

"Who were you talking to?"

Melissa hadn't intended to mention that she'd heard her, but she felt that now there was nothing to lose. She would either continue on her way or....

"What did you hear me say?"

She seemed to be asking more in fear than anger.

"Oh, I just heard your voice, I couldn't actually make out any words."

Melissa hoped that would be enough to allay any worries Layla might have had about being overheard. Another suspicious look as she weighed up this woman called Melissa who had so rudely interrupted her. Finally, she gave a reluctant 'Ok' and, much to Melissa's relief, looked as if she had decided to stay. For now.

"Is this one of your favourite places?"

Melissa asked, more to see how Layla would react to another question rather than having any expectation of starting a meaningful conversation.

"I don't have any favourite places."

It seemed to Melissa that although her words and attitude were outwardly negative, the fact that she hadn't run off was a small victory. She didn't want to engage with Melissa, and yet....

"But there must be a place you'd like to be, more than anywhere else? I know when I was your age...."

"There's nowhere. Not anymore. There's nowhere."

Should she pursue it? The 'not anymore'? Melissa knew that the expert advice would probably be to say a few kind words and back off, move onto safer ground as soon as possible therefore avoiding further distress for Layla. But it seemed that's what had been tried, and it didn't seem to have worked, did it?

Melissa walked over to a bed of grass and wild flowers that grew near the stone. She sat down and wanted to beckon Layla to come and sit beside her, but felt that might be asking too much too soon. Instead, she simply looked up at her, inviting her to make up her own mind.

"But you had a special place once, didn't you? Somewhere with happy memories?"

Was that a good guess? She'd soon find out. Layla, again, gave her 'that' look, but this time there was something else, something that hadn't been there before. Just for a moment Melissa thought she saw a softening in her eyes. Maybe the hint of a desire to talk to her, or was that just wishful thinking? She wasn't going to push the question any harder but, instead, waited for Layla to make her decision. When it came, her response was hurried, spoken quickly, as if she needed to get her words out before she changed her mind.

"I come here to talk to my Mum. That's who I was talking to."

Melissa was momentarily thrown by what she'd said and, before she could think of a fitting response, Layla had turned away and was gone. Melissa waited, but it soon became apparent that she wasn't coming back. With some reluctance, she stood, no longer wanting to stay in the limestone clearing. Somehow, given what Layla had just told her, it didn't seem right to be there on her own, in a place that obviously meant so much to the young girl. Melissa took one last look over her shoulder at the stone as she followed the path into the woods and, eventually, back to the house.

Chapter 18

"I said I'd find you!"

Sophie sat down next to Melissa. The hair was, once more, salon perfect and the minimum make-up reapplied to maximum effect. Chic had been fully restored.

"Actually…."

She leant towards her with an air of exaggerated confidentiality.

"….I have a confession to make. I cheated. I asked Justine and she told me where you'd be."

Melissa looked down at the butterfly that was sitting on her hand. The patterns on its wings were a bright, iridescent blue.

"She brought me here last night. Wonderful, isn't it?"

Another butterfly had the temerity to try to settle on Sophie's perfect bob of hair, but soon realised the error of its ways and fluttered down to her shoulder.

"Quite therapeutic, which is the point, I suppose."

Sophie gently put a hand up to her shoulder and coaxed the butterfly onto it before carefully bringing it down onto her lap.

"I don't think this room is here just for our benefit. I get the feeling that there's something far more to it than that."

"Says the lady who's been here five minutes."

Sophie accompanied her words with a wink, ensuring that Melissa knew they were being said with more than a degree of humour.

"No, you're right. What do I know?"

"Actually, lovely Melissa, I believe you know more than you think you do, and that probably applies to most of us here."

Melissa waited to see if some kind of explanation would follow, but Sophie's attention now seemed completely focussed on her butterfly.

"I'm not sure I understand."

She looked up, as if woken from a daydream.

"Mmm?"

"What do most of us know?"

Melissa prompted.

"Oh...."

Sophie turned to her.

"....sorry, I just meant that we, most of us, ultimately know what we are. It might be buried in our subconscious, but it is there."

Melissa thought for a moment.

"After your match with Justine this afternoon, when I was alone, I felt I wanted to go back to the stone. I'm still not sure why, if I'm honest."

Sophie smiled.

"Because you belong and, as I said, something inside you knows it. How long did you stay?"

"Not long, as it turned out. There was someone already there."

Melissa hadn't intended to say who that 'someone' was but Sophie was in no doubt.

"Layla?"

"That wasn't a guess, was it?"

Sophie shook her head.

"I thought it was quite likely to be her. She goes there a lot. It's common knowledge."

"Does anyone know why?"

Sophie shrugged.

"Maybe somebody does. I don't. Did she tell you?"

Melissa thought it best not to say too much.

"No. No, she didn't say anything. Well, not anything specific."

The remark about talking to her mother might have been made in confidence, or it might not, but it wasn't worth taking the chance, Melissa decided.

"That sounds like Layla. Did she talk about anything at all?"

"We chatted for a short while but she left quite soon after I arrived."

"What did you think of her? First impression?"

Melissa could say that she hadn't been with her long enough to form an opinion, to deflect the question, but instead she chose to give Sophie an honest answer.

"I liked her."

"I'm not surprised. We all do. We all want to help her, but she won't let anyone in."

Melissa lifted her hand and let the butterfly flutter to a nearby plant where it settled.

"That's so sad. I was told she's lost both parents. That's enough to make anyone bring down the shutters isn't it?"

"Verity's doing all she can, but her worry is that the longer those shutters remain closed, the more our chances of ever reaching her diminish."

Melissa's thoughts flashed back to her earlier brief meeting with Layla. She recalled that look in her eyes, the look that she thought she might have imagined.

"I want to talk to her again. Or do you think I shouldn't?"

Sophie made no effort to hide her scepticism.

"I wouldn't say that exactly, after all, I don't believe she could be in a much worse place. No, I'm more thinking, how would failure sit with you?"

Melissa wasn't sure how she should answer that.

"I only ask...."

Sophie continued.

"....because I've experienced it. Failure. And I've tried my best to find a way in, believe me."

Somehow Melissa couldn't imagine Sophie failing at anything.

"Did Verity ask you to talk to her?"

Sophie nodded.

"And you said you believe you failed? Can you tell me what happened, where you think things went wrong?"

Sophie watched as her butterfly joined Melissa's on the plant.

"No. I'm afraid I can't, for two reasons."

"Which are?"

"One, I think it would be better the less you know, thus avoiding any preconceptions that might affect your judgement."

"And the second?"

Sophie smiled.

"Oh, the second is far more straightforward. Patient confidentiality. Layla's psychiatric report? I wrote it."

While Melissa struggled to come up with an appropriate response, Sophie looked over to one of the small trees. She hadn't noticed before how beautiful the leaves were, so intricate, so delicate.

"What about you, Sophie? What would a report about you say?"

Melissa, having now adjusted her thinking, decided that changing the subject was probably the best way forward.

"The lake's rather lovely in the evening, and the pathways are beautifully lit. Shall we?"

And Melissa couldn't think of a single reason why they shouldn't.

The water shimmered and sparkled, reflecting the lights that illuminated the lake and surrounding grounds. Melissa and Sophie followed the path, stopping occasionally to take in the scene, which looked so different at night.

"I can think of worse places to be."

Melissa looked beyond the lake to the trees, stark silhouettes against the night sky.

"Good. Hold onto that thought and you'll be fine."

Sophie gave her a wry smile.

"Is that what keeps you happy here?"

Melissa turned to her, wanting to look into her eyes when she answered, hoping to see the truth. Not that she expected her to consciously lie, but she would want to put her at ease by saying what she thought she needed to hear, and Melissa very much wanted to see past anything like that. She wanted to know the real Sophie.

"In the end, there's always a price to pay. We can't be protected out there, in that big bad world. The clock would be ticking for all of us, and we would be blissfully unaware until, one day, it stops. You, Melissa, would have disappeared by now. 'She went to a funeral' they'd say, 'no, I don't know exactly where' they'd say. Those with an interest would ensure that any enquiry into your disappearance hit a dead end. You have, of course, worked all of that out for yourself by now. So, as I'm sure others have said although perhaps not in quite the same way, it's not a case of being happy here, or unhappy. There is, quite simply, no choice for any of us. The price we pay for our survival is our freedom. Is it fair that something that happened centuries ago has denied us that freedom? No, probably not. But neither is there any point in bemoaning our fate. We are what we are."

Melissa listened to her soft, calm voice, drawn in by its gentle, even tone. She could hear the lake quietly lapping against the water's edge, and a warm evening breeze had picked up, lightly ruffling their hair. As they walked on, Sophie continued to talk, her words drifting into the night air.

Chapter 19

~Sophie~

"Dance?!"

Although the girl with the caramel blonde hair was shouting, she could barely make herself heard above the music. She tapped Sophie on the shoulder and repeated her question.

"Why not?!"

Sophie yelled back as she followed her into the crowd. She momentarily lost sight of the girl, but as she approached the centre of the dancefloor she saw her again, already dancing wildly, seemingly oblivious to anyone around her. However, as Sophie reached her side she received a broad smile as the girl grabbed her arm and pulled her closer. Any conversation was impossible and so there was nothing else to do but dance, which they both did as if their lives depended on it.

They stayed out on the floor for another half an hour until the girl gestured that she wanted to get a drink, and so they made their way out of the dance room and over to the bar. Although the music there was still loud it was now possible to hear above it. The girl caught the barman's attention.

"Two French 75s please!"

"Oh really, no…."

Sophie's protests were silenced by a finger pressed onto her lips.

"Oh really, yes!"

"You're buying me cocktails and I don't even know your name!"

The girl laughed.

"Well, I don't know yours either, so that's ok!"

"Sophie."

The girl nodded.

"Nice name. I like it. I'm Caz. Now we know each other are you happy to accept the drink?"

Sophie smiled.

"I suppose I am. You're a great dancer, Caz."

She accepted the compliment as nothing more or less than her due.

"Yeah, I am. You're not bad. Probably benefit from a bit of time in the gym though."

Caz followed up her advice with a broad grin, thereby avoiding an equally acerbic response. Sophie, meanwhile, had already decided that this bright young thing called Caz was someone worth spending more time with. She liked women with an edge, who might not always play by the rules. Whether she could make an equally good impression on Caz remained to be seen, although she had picked her out from the crowd, hadn't she?

The cocktails duly arrived and Caz beckoned Sophie to follow her. She led the way through to an annexe that was even further away from the dancefloor. In the far corner there was an empty table which they quickly claimed before anyone else could take it. Sophie sat down opposite Caz and took a sip from her glass.

"Delicious. Thank you."

Although it wouldn't have been top of Sophie's list of favourite drinks, the blend of gin, champagne, lemon juice and sugar proved to be a very agreeable combination, and she made a mental note to definitely add it to that list.

"You're welcome. Of course, I shall want something in return."

She looked her directly in the eyes, challenging her to ask the question.

"Go on."

Sophie said with some degree of apprehension. Caz took a long, slow drink from her glass, showing no sign of being in a hurry to answer. Eventually, she placed the champagne flute back on the table.

"Another half an hour on the dancefloor."

Sophie wasn't sure whether she was relieved, or not.

"Of course, if you think I'm up to it."

"I'll get you another French 75, then you will be."

Sophie looked at her two-thirds full glass.

"If you do that I'm not sure I'll be up to anything."

138

"Oh, I definitely won't then."

This time Sophie thought it best to avoid her gaze, unsure what her own eyes might betray.

"So tell me, Caz, tell me all about you."

She had the feeling that this very confident, full-on young woman might welcome the chance to talk about herself.

"Not a great deal to tell...."

Ok, so she might be wrong.

"....I'm from London, come here nearly every week...."

And so, for the next minute or so, Caz continued to talk. Sophie, although giving her the impression that she had her full attention, found herself looking at, rather than listening to, this captivating, vivacious individual who had so suddenly appeared from the crowd.

"....and now, what about you, Sophie?"

Caz sat back, looking ready to hear a comprehensive life history. What she got, however, were very brief details from Sophie's last cv, as best as she could recall it. To her credit, she did attempt to make it sound interesting but, as Caz was now finding out, Sophie was not Sophie's favourite subject.

"You don't look like a psychiatrist."

Sophie's expression suggested it wasn't the first time she'd heard a comment like that, but she decided to play anyway.

"And what might a psychiatrist look like?" was the standard response.

"Older."

Sophie was suitably impressed with such quick thinking diplomacy, but should she go on to explain that she'd completed her six years of training, three core and a further three in higher specialty? Maybe not. Instead she thanked her and suggested that she might nearly be ready to revisit the dancefloor. Whether that was true or not, she was about to find out.

At ten minutes past one in the morning Sophie and Caz, who had gradually become a little the worse for wear as the evening had progressed, left the nightclub. With others looking for a taxi directly outside the club, Caz suggested they walked for a few blocks in the hope of picking one up in a quieter part of the city.

Sophie had her doubts that they would be successful but didn't feel like arguing with her new friend and, after a few minutes, was glad she'd kept quiet. Just as they turned a corner and the club disappeared from view, Caz leapt out into the road in time to hail a taxi, its 'For Hire' sign brightly lit against its dark interior.

"Your place?"

Caz asked as they climbed into the back of the cab. Without hesitation, Sophie nodded, prompting Caz to give the address to the driver. It seemed to her like a natural way to end the evening, so why not? They said very little on the journey to Sophie's apartment. There probably wasn't very much left to say, although there was something nagging in the back of Sophie's mind. It was that thing where you know there's something but, however hard you try, you can't quite grasp it, and the recent alcohol intake wasn't helping.

The taxi pulled into the kerb outside of the small apartment block and it was while Caz was paying the driver that the 'something' suddenly occurred to Sophie. As the cab drew away, leaving them on the tree-lined pavement, she asked

"How did you know my address, to tell the driver?"

There was a moment's silence before Caz answered.

"You told me."

Had she? Sophie attempted to recall but, however much she tried, she was unable to remember their conversation in sufficient detail, again, probably something to do with the French 75s. Well, she must have told her. Simple as that.

"Fine" seemed to be the best response Sophie could come up with as she led her into the building, the question of her address now fast disappearing and being replaced by far more agreeable thoughts. They walked together across the small foyer and into the lift. As the doors swished closed, Sophie turned to Caz.

"Are you still ok with this?"

Had she expected her to suddenly decide it was all a big mistake, that she had never really wanted things to happen so quickly between them…?

"I wouldn't be here with you if I wasn't. I don't think it would be right to finish our evening off any other way."

As they stepped from the lift Caz stumbled, almost colliding with the opposite wall. She giggled.

"I think I'm just a little bit drunk."

Sophie laughed, for no other reason than she felt ecstatically happy.

"Just along here."

Sophie led her towards the door of the apartment. She reached into her pocket for the key but, in the moment it took her to find it, Caz had put her hand out and pushed at the door. It slowly swung inwards.

"But I know I locked…."

Caz held a finger up to her lips which stopped Sophie from completing her sentence. Then, without waiting for Sophie, Caz entered through the now open door. Sophie followed, flicking the light on as she passed the switch. It took a moment to take in the scene that faced them as they entered the lounge.

Standing over by the closed curtains was a man, tall, well-built. His arms were by his side and in one hand he was holding a knife. A second man was sitting in one of the two armchairs. He had unbuttoned his jacket and seemed to be enjoying the comfort of the chair. A third stood just to the right of the door, ready to cut off any attempt to run back towards the stairwell or lift.

As Sophie remained rooted to the spot, scared to move or say anything, Caz made to step forward but stumbled again. She fell on top of the man in the chair, laughing uncontrollably as she landed on him. The other two men seemed briefly transfixed, amused by this little unexpected sideshow, while the man under Caz barely moved as the short needle slipped silently into his heart. His eyes, already open, remained staring ahead.

Caz rolled away from him and grabbed a bottle that stood on a nearby drinks cabinet. She smashed it hard against the chair as she stood, sending red wine spraying across the room. The moment the man holding the knife saw the blood slowly spreading over his dead colleague's shirt, he raised the blade and moved towards Caz, while the third man threw his arms around Sophie and pulled her nearer the door. But there was no chance to deal with the immediate threat to Sophie as the knife was now just inches from Caz's face. She backed away, desperately trying

141

not to break eye contact with her attacker. On the periphery of her vision she saw Sophie being dragged through the open door and into the hallway.

Caz tightened her grip on the broken bottle, holding it down by her side, the jagged glass glinting as it caught the light. She continued to move away, until she felt the wall behind her pressing against her back. He had moved with her, keeping the steel blade up at eye level. Caz couldn't be sure if he was about to attack, or if his intention was to keep her in that room until Sophie had been taken from the building.

Caz, knowing time was fast running out, dropped to her knees and in the same movement brought the broken bottle up into the man's groin, hoping that her aim would be somewhere near the femoral artery. She drove the jagged glass in as hard as she could before rolling away, across the floor. When she looked back she saw that his trousers were soaked with blood, and although obviously in great pain, through absolute, fanatical determination, he remained on his feet and was still holding the knife.

Could she run? Leave him to eventually bleed out? If she waited for even a short time, she knew that Sophie might then be beyond her help. But he was now between her and the door and clearly had only one goal, to prevent her leaving the apartment. Caz stood and moved towards him. It was a response based purely on instinct. She had to get past him, and quickly.

He took a clumsy step forward, wanting to bring her within range of the knife. He thrust the blade towards her face, missing by fractions of an inch. Caz pushed his hand away and glanced down to see where she'd dropped the broken bottle. Was it just out of reach or could she…?

He saw what Caz was about to do and attempted to kick her hand away, but he failed to connect and instead fell to his knees, where he remained for a moment before the knife dropped from his hand and he collapsed to the floor where he stayed, lying perfectly still. Caz jumped over his body and in a moment was back out into the hallway. There was no sign of Sophie or her abductor. Caz ran to the lift in time to see the light above the doors counting down to the ground floor.

At the far end of the hallway was the stairwell. It was her only chance of catching up with them but, as she flung the fire doors open and began to descend as fast as she could, she knew that it was highly likely there would be a car waiting outside the building. If that was the case, then her only opportunity to stop them would be to prevent them getting to the street. She took the last flight two steps at a time but, as she ran into the foyer, she saw that the main door was already closing. Caz pushed it open and ran out onto the pavement. She looked left and right along the empty street. In the distance she could hear a car and her heart sank. Could he have got her away so quickly? Sophie would have put up some kind of struggle, wouldn't she?

Caz reached for her mobile, ready to make the call and report her failure. It was as she lifted it to her ear that she heard a sound. It had come from the other side of the road. Quickly replacing her phone, she ran across the street before stopping to listen again. There was only silence. Had she imagined it? She walked on a few paces, into the shadows cast by one of the roadside trees. It was then that she noticed the entrance to a narrow alley. She couldn't have possibly seen it from her viewpoint directly outside the apartment block as it was almost completely obscured from view by, not only the tree itself, but also by the shadow it threw across the alley's entrance.

As she took a few paces towards the darkness, Caz realised that she was now unarmed. The poisoned needle had done its job but remained embedded in the first man's heart, while the broken bottle lay on the carpet in Sophie's apartment. Removing her phone once more, she switched on its torch and shone its beam down the alleyway.

"Move back or I'll kill her here!"

He had one arm wrapped tightly around Sophie's neck, while his free hand was holding a small flick knife against her side.

"Ok. Ok."

Caz held up a hand and took a step back but kept the torch trained on them, not wanting to allow him to retreat into the darkness. She took some solace from the fact that he clearly wanted Sophie alive, but Caz wondered if it might be better if she attempted to stop him and they both died in that alleyway, rather than allow Sophie to be taken away to face whatever horrors The Custodians had waiting for her.

"What do you want me to do?"

It occurred to Caz that if she could start some kind of dialogue, any kind of dialogue, then she might possibly manage to buy a few precious seconds. What exactly she would do with those seconds she, at that moment, had no idea.

"You? Absolutely nothing. I think you've done enough, don't you?"

Good. He was talking, and while he was doing that he wasn't harming Sophie.

"Well, not really. One can rarely do enough, don't you find?"

She decided to turn the Englishness up a notch, hoping that the faux politeness might possibly help to dial down the current hair-trigger tension.

"I meant what I said. I *will* kill her right now if you don't move away."

Or maybe politeness was grossly overrated. Maybe another approach was required. Caz still held her mobile, its light catching the look of terror in Sophie's eyes, silently imploring her to do something. Anything. The sound of a vehicle from the street at the far end of the alleyway momentarily took the man's attention, his head turning to try to catch a glimpse of the car, and in that second Caz made her decision. She threw the phone as hard as she could. Her aim wasn't perfect, but it was good enough. Its edge caught him a glancing blow on the side of his head. The shock of the impact was sufficient to cause his hold on Sophie to loosen at the same moment that Caz collided with him using her full bodyweight.

As Caz and the man fell to the ground, Sophie managed to break free and scramble away. Once clear, she turned back in time to see that Caz had a hold of his arm and was trying to get to the knife that he was still holding. Instinctively, Sophie ran back to where they were struggling and brought her foot hard down onto the man's wrist, breaking his grip on the knife. Caz was lightning fast in seizing the weapon.

"Don't kill him! Please!"

Caz had the blade poised above his throat when Sophie cried out. She hesitated for a moment, before bringing the knife down hard into his shoulder, leaving it deeply embedded.

"Come with me, now!"

Before Sophie could respond, Caz had grabbed her hand and was dragging her to the far end of the alleyway, pausing only to scoop up her phone from where it had fallen. The man was now frantically clawing at the knife's handle, trying to remove it. Sophie looked over her shoulder at him as they ran, but Caz wasn't going to allow her to slow down and in seconds they reached the street at the furthest end of the alley. Caz looked up and down the road.

"This way!"

"Where are we going?"

Sophie managed to ask as they dashed along the pavement.

"See that Range Rover? That's where!"

Caz pointed to the car that was parked some way down on the opposite side of the road. Sophie felt the jolt on her arm as Caz almost wrenched her off her feet in her eagerness to increase their pace. Thankfully, Sophie was able to keep up and they quickly closed the gap between them and the Range Rover.

As they drew level with the car, Caz pulled one of the rear doors open and virtually threw Sophie in before slamming the door shut. She then ran around to the other side and climbed in to the seat next to Sophie.

"Ok! Go!"

The woman sitting in the driver's seat revved the engine. At exactly the same moment as the car began to move, a blood-covered hand hit the window next to Sophie. She screamed in shock and flinched away as the man, blood flowing from his shoulder wound, tried to pull the car door open but the driver was quicker and had already hit the 'door lock' button. As he continued his attack on Sophie's side of the Range Rover, so the woman released the brake and they shot forward, leaving the man on his knees, wounded and bleeding, in the road.

"You ok?"

Caz asked Sophie as soon as they were clear of the immediate threat.

"I….I think so. But, if you don't mind my asking, what the fuck is happening?"

"Mmm, well, first of all I think I should make a couple of introductions…."

As she was speaking, Caz set about undoing her jacket before removing the caramel blonde wig she was wearing, revealing her own brown, swept back hair.

"….our driver for this evening is called Verity…."

The woman glanced over her shoulder and smiled.

"….and…."

The perfect, pure English accent had gone. There was now just a hint of Eastern European.

"….I'm afraid I lied to you. My name isn't Caz, it's Danika, Danika Pacek. As to what's happening, well, that might take a little longer to explain."

Chapter 20

Melissa opened her eyes and lifted her head from the soft down pillow. Lying next to her, still asleep, was Sophie. She lay back down, but her eyes remained open and her thoughts turned to the night before. She recalled their walk by the lake, the warm night air, and Sophie's voice.

Was this supposed to have happened? As the memories gradually returned, Melissa smiled and she became aware, once more, of the warmth of Sophie's body as she lay beside her. Without the question being asked by either of them, they had made their way back to Sophie's room sometime after midnight. A bottle of chilled White Zinfandel had been enjoyed, while Erik Satie's 'Piano Dreams' played softly in the background as the night had taken them, body and soul.

And now the night was giving way to a cloudless dawn while, on the lake, the swans were gliding across the still, clear water. Once more, the early morning sun shone between the trees and touched the ancient Brathy stone, bringing the promise of a new day.

Melissa rolled onto her side to face Sophie, who was now awake, her eyes still holding the sparkle she recalled from the night before.

"Good morning."

Sophie smiled as she reached out to touch Melissa's hair, letting it fall through her fingers.

"I've never done this before."

Sophie gave her a quizzical look.

"What, exactly?"

"Slept with someone I've only just met."

"That's so sad. You must have missed out on so much."

"Are you teasing me?"

"No...."

The smile returned to Sophie's lips.

"....well, maybe, just a little."

Melissa sat up and lifted her half of the duvet away, dropping it onto Sophie, completely covering her before she flung the whole thing onto the floor beside the bed.

"Are you going?"

Melissa swung her legs out onto the carpet and made her way over to a small pile of clothes that lay on one of the chairs.

"I think I should, don't you?"

Sophie thought about this for moment.

"No. Not really. This isn't like some girls' dorm. No one here cares where anyone spends the night."

While Melissa considered a suitable response to that invaluable piece of information, she decided to sit back down on the bed.

"Ok" was what she eventually said.

"Good. Then we'll have some breakfast. Fruit juice, cereal, or something more substantial?"

"Fruit juice and cereal will be fine, thank you."

Melissa felt that, on balance, it might be a good idea to get dressed after all, even though Sophie was showing no inclination to do the same.

"Just going to have a shower…."

Sophie got up and put on her dressing gown that lay along the foot of the bed.

"….unless you'd like to…."

She nodded in the direction of the bathroom.

"No, that's fine. I'll shower when I get back to my room."

"Fair enough. Won't be long. I expect you can find the kitchen if you want to help yourself."

And without another word, Sophie disappeared into the bathroom leaving Melissa to go in search of breakfast. On one wall of the living area there were four Andy Warhol prints, the obligatory Marilyn Monroe and Soup Cans plus Debbie Harry and Elizabeth Taylor. On a shelf opposite the prints, there were various small items of pottery and an art deco figurine of a ballet dancer.

She walked through to the kitchen and was impressed by how tidy it was, recalling the one in her own town flat which was much more random in every way. She smiled as her thoughts returned to her modest little place that she had, over the years, made her own and wondered if she would ever see it again. But, before any sadness or longing could take hold, she began a hunt for the bowls and cereal and by the time Sophie appeared in the doorway, wearing a towelling robe and a small bright pink towel wrapped around her wet hair, Melissa had finished preparing the breakfast table.

"Can you be here every morning?"

Melissa gave the hint of a curtsy before they sat down to help themselves to the jug of orange juice, box of muesli and fresh fruit. Melissa wondered how she'd feel, this being the morning after the night before, whether she'd want to leave as soon as possible, or struggle to find any kind of conversation. But she didn't feel anything like that. Sophie had something about her, something far beyond the physical, that made Melissa not only attracted to her but comfortable with her.

"So do you often let strange girls pick you up in clubs?"

Melissa's expression as she asked the question showed that it wasn't meant to be taken too seriously.

"Mmm, well...."

Sophie finished her mouthful of cereal before answering.

"....I suppose it depends on the girl, and how strange she is. Actually, Danika is a pretty decent actor. She obviously had a good idea of 'my type' and played her perfectly. I didn't suspect for a moment."

Sophie picked up the jug and refilled Melissa's glass.

"She's certainly a force to be reckoned with, isn't she?"

"I think the word is 'driven'. I've seen her at her most violent, close-up, no prisoners taken. I might even go so far as to say that some of the violence is gratuitous. She would have killed the man in the alley if I hadn't begged her not to."

"You believe she *enjoys* it?"

Sophie slowly shook her head.

"No. Not enjoys, exactly. I think she needs it. She needs to take out her anger on them, but it's a controlled, focussed anger. Cold and clinical."

"I watched her in the arena. She had such a gentle way with the horse, she rides with real feeling and understanding."

"Yes. I've seen her too. Danika's quite the paradox, isn't she? But I don't think anyone knows the whole story, no one is allowed to get too close, with the possible exception of Verity."

Melissa took her last spoonful of muesli before selecting an apple from an overflowing fruit bowl. "Well, according to Verity, Danika and I might be going out for a ride together sometime soon."

Sophie looked suitably impressed. "And do you ride?"

Melissa had to think about that. "I have ridden, and I was ok, but it was a few years ago."

Sophie gave a dismissive wave of her hand. "Oh, you'll be fine then. Don't worry."

Melissa took a bite from her apple, thereby using the intervening silence to bring that particular subject to a close. Silence, of course, except for the sporadic crunch of the apple.

"Yesterday, you recall what you said about Layla...."

Having decided that she'd rather be talking about the young girl than her prospective equine adventure with Danika, Melissa took her chance to question Sophie further.

"Mmm mmm."

"....well, I get the confidentiality thing, absolutely, but I wondered if there was anything at all you could give me, if I were to have the opportunity...."

Sophie picked several grapes from a bunch in the fruit bowl, studying them thoughtfully as she considered how she could best reply.

"Harley Quinn."

"I'm sorry?"

"The DC Comics character. Batman? The Joker?"

Melissa wasn't quite sure whether she and Sophie were still on the same page.

"Ok. What about them?"

Sophie finished her last grape and considered taking a few more.

"Not 'them'. 'Her'. Harley Quinn. Layla loves anything and everything to do with her. She has books, Blu-rays, figurines, pictures, you name it...."

"And you think her interest...."

"Obsession," Sophie corrected.

"....her obsession might offer a way in, could possibly be used to get her to open up?"

"Oh, if only it were that simple…."

She gave in to her desire for more grapes.

"….or maybe for you, it might be."

"Meaning?"

Sophie shrugged.

"Meaning perhaps nothing. I was thinking out loud and I shouldn't have. Forgive me."

"Nothing to forgive. Go on. I won't repeat anything you say."

A short silence followed as Sophie decided whether she should 'go on'.

"I don't believe Layla will say what she so badly needs to say to either myself or Verity. In fact, I don't think there's anyone else here who has the kind of empathy she's crying out for. Verity represents the ultimate in authority, and I'm the professional who'll ask the clever questions designed to catch her out. However much kindness and understanding we try to show her, she's unable to see past those preconceptions. That's why the last thing I should do is offer you any advice, Melissa. Layla's very smart. She'd spot any input I might give you a mile off. In fact, even you knowing about the Harley Quinn thing might make her suspicious."

Melissa listened intently to Sophie, knowing now more than ever that she had to try to help the girl. But still she had no definitive answer as to why. Was it just a desire to do the right thing? Of course, she'd like to think that was the case. But, somehow, she knew it wasn't. There was another imperative pushing Melissa and, even though she was still unable to identify it, she was now absolutely certain of its existence.

"I'll try to be careful."

"Then…."

Sophie popped another grape into her mouth.

"….I wish you good luck. Now, lovely Melissa, it seems we've finished breakfast so you will doubtless use this as your cue to politely make your excuses and leave. Or maybe not?"

Sophie held her gaze, waiting for her to answer. She didn't have long to wait.

"Ok. Maybe not."

Chapter 21

Melissa closed the laptop and gave her eyes a quick rub before taking a sip from her mug of coffee. After some hours sat in front of the screen she knew she needed a break and some fresh air. She had returned to her apartment after leaving Sophie, having made a decision. Her time with Sophie had been an unexpected but extremely pleasant and enjoyable distraction, and it had also served to make her even more determined to try to help Layla. Sophie had given her permission to fail but, more importantly, permission to try.

The laptop had been provided by Verity just a few minutes after Melissa had phoned down her request, and she had set about interrogating the internet to find out as much as she was able about the DC Comics character, Harley Quinn. Formerly Doctor Harleen Quinzel, Harley made her debut in September 1992 in 'Batman: The Animated Series'.

Melissa had followed the history of the character up to, and including, the more recent films featuring Margot Robbie. She had no way of knowing the depth of Layla's Harley Quinn knowledge but knew, from her brief meeting with her, that the young girl was clearly intelligent enough to see through any poorly planned attempt to feign a mutual interest. Could Melissa retain enough information to be convincing? There was only one way she would find out.

After her break she would search out the Margot Robbie films and spend the afternoon taking what she could from those. Melissa settled on 'Birds of Prey (and the Fantabulous Emancipation of One Harley Quinn)', which seemed from the reviews like a good place to start. She slipped her shoes on deciding, as she tied the laces, that she wouldn't need her jacket, trusting that it was as warm outside as it looked from the window. But, before she reached the door, there was a light knock on it.

"Hello Danika."

"Oh, you're just leaving. I'll come back."

She was about to turn away.

"No, don't go. We can either stay here or take a walk."

For a moment, Danika seemed unsure whether or not to accept the invitation.

"Ok. We could go wherever you were going."

Actually, Melissa wasn't sure where she was going.

"Why don't you choose?"

"How about the stables? I could show you some of our horses."

The suggestion reminded Melissa of Verity's idea that they should take a ride out together, which she was still unsure about. But maybe Verity hadn't yet had the chance to speak to Danika about it.

"That would be lovely."

"Good. And Verity tells me you'd like to hack out with me sometime, so we can choose a horse for you."

Ok. So she had had the chance.

"How kind. Thank you."

Melissa wanted to be as non-committal as possible although, strangely, she realised the idea was actually beginning to grow on her. Maybe it was the thought of being with Danika again. Although so very different from Sophie in almost every way, Melissa found her even more captivating, and realised that the attraction had probably been there from the moment she first saw her at the funeral.

Little was said as they left the house and made their way around to the stables beside the arena. The moments of silence between them gave Melissa the chance to reflect on what Sophie had told her the previous evening and, more particularly, how 'Caz' had rescued her from The Custodians. Walking with Danika now, she found it difficult to imagine her being anything other than Danika. And it proved impossible for Melissa not to raise the subject.

"I was talking to Sophie last night."

"Ok."

"She was telling me about how you saved her or, more interestingly, *who* you were when you saved her. BAFTA winning performance, from what I've heard."

Would she be happy to talk about it?

"Well look at me. Not exactly 'nightclub' am I? I knew I had to go in there as someone else if I was going to hook up with her before she left the club, mainly because of the possibility she was being observed in there. Our meeting had to seem credible and it worked, more or less."

Danika gave a dismissive shrug, as if that was the beginning and end of the story. Melissa, although happy to leave it there for now, knew she wanted to know more. The self-deprecation was still present, from not being 'nightclub' to having no friends, but there was, in the background, something darker, hidden from view. How had Sophie described her? 'Driven'? Yes, Melissa wanted to know more.

After she'd opened the large double doors to the stables, Danika beckoned Melissa to follow her into the building. The smell of fresh hay and straw, as they began to walk along between the rows of stalls, took Melissa back to her early teenage years. She had been lucky enough to have riding lessons and, although she had become competent in all the basic skills, she had never had the confidence to continue. Hence her initial reluctance when the possibility of riding was first mentioned.

"Here's Firefly. You saw me riding him yesterday."

Melissa held out a hand for the young horse to nuzzle, feeling the soft, warm, velvety skin and the gentle breath.

"He's beautiful. Aren't you, boy?"

She lightly stroked his muzzle, continuing to talk quietly to him while Danika looked on and patiently waited until Melissa was able to tear herself away from an appreciative Firefly. They continued down the line of stalls, most of which were empty.

"The rest are out in the meadow."

Danika offered in answer to Melissa's unasked question.

"Can we go and see them?"

"Of course."

Danika led her out of the door at the further end of the indoor stables and into a small courtyard. They walked past a mounting block and a long hitching rail before leaving the yard through a high archway. Across from a gravel path, in a gap between a row of tall conifers, was a wide wooden gate. Danika lifted its drop-down latch and pushed it open. In the distance, Melissa could see the group of horses, all heads down and eating the lush grass.

One of them looked up lazily as they approached but, on seeing Danika, returned its attention to the grass.

"I sometimes like to come here and just be with them."

Danika walked over to the nearest horse, a magnificent grey, and gently rested a hand on his back. Melissa watched, fascinated by the clear bond between human and animal. And while she watched, she found herself struggling to reconcile the person she saw now with the one capable of extreme, and sometimes lethal, violence.

"This is Magick. Isn't he wonderful?"

Melissa nodded.

"He'll come to you, just ask him."

Danika stepped back from the grey as Melissa did as she suggested. It took only a moment for the horse to look to her and slowly make its way to her side. She put a hand on his back, just as Danika had done, and could immediately feel his quiet power.

"You have a connection. I think you should ride him."

Without hesitation, Melissa replied.

"Yes please. When?"

"There's a saying, isn't there? 'No time like the present'?"

All thoughts of returning to her apartment to watch the film were suddenly gone. She would watch it, and she would talk with Layla but, right now, this was where she wanted to be. With the horses, and with Danika.

"Wonderful!"

"Good. Then we'll return to the stables and tack up. I'll ride Firefly."

Danika turned to head back towards the gate, calling over her shoulder.

"Magick!"

Melissa had been about to ask if she had a lead rope but, as the grey began to follow, she quickly realised using one wouldn't be necessary. The horse remained a few steps behind them all the way back to his stall in the stable block. As soon as Danika had ensured he was safe and content, she left Melissa with him to go and fetch his tack. Once alone with Magick, Melissa moved closer to him, running a hand down his neck while looking into his eyes. And she felt as if she'd known him forever.

Danika carefully lowered the brown leather saddle onto Firefly's back and fastened the girth before turning her attention to fitting the bridle and stirrups. Melissa stood back while Danika checked her work, not wanting to interrupt but recalling all those instructive and happy times spent at a local stable after school.

"Would you like to get Magick ready? His tack's just over there."

Melissa didn't need asking twice and hurried over to the pegs marked 'Magick', removing the saddle, bridle and reins. She had expected Danika to watch over her as she prepared her horse for their hack but, showing a much appreciated trust, she left her to get on with the tacking up without the added pressure of a critical observer.

"You'll find everything you need through there. All sizes. I'm going to get into my riding things and I'll be back in a few minutes."

Before Melissa could reply Danika had gone, leaving her to find some suitable clothing of her own. She walked over to the door that Danika had indicated, expecting the room behind it to be like others she'd seen. A chaotic jumble that needed rummaging through to find the right size and fit. She should have known better. Hats, jodhpurs, boots, gloves and body protectors were all sorted into sizes, and neatly displayed.

Melissa could have easily taken much longer over her choices but knew that Danika would probably be waiting for her. So, suitably dressed for the occasion, Melissa returned to the horses. She had, she thought, wasted no time changing but was still beaten to it by Danika, who was standing beside Firefly making a few minor adjustments to his bridle.

"Ready?"

Melissa wondered if she was. It had been quite a while. Had she been overly optimistic about retaining her riding abilities? Well, she was about to find out.

"I'm ready."

She walked over to where Magick was patiently waiting and took hold of his bridle, following Danika and Firefly out into the courtyard. Melissa, after a moment's hesitation, placed her foot in the stirrup and swung into the saddle. As her free foot found the other stirrup, she silently congratulated herself on a faultless start, but then remembered that pride sometimes comes before a fall, maybe literally.

Danika looked over to check that Melissa was happy and received a thumbs up. With the lightest of touches to his flank, Danika moved Firefly forward and on through the archway, turning left down the single track lane that ran alongside the meadow. Melissa remained a safe distance behind her until the track widened out and she was able to move alongside. They were now approaching an apple orchard, with the fruit trees on one side and meadows on the other. The horses walked on, content in each other's company and their surroundings.

"They both know the way."

Melissa noticed that Danika was giving Firefly just the lightest of touches on the reins, and so loosened her own grip, allowing Magick his own little piece of freedom. Some horses, she recalled, would immediately take advantage of such freedom, but the grey continued on his way without slowing, wandering, or attempting to stop and eat.

"Don't think it's all like this…."

Danika turned to her.

"….there'll be plenty of chances for a canter."

Melissa appreciated her not mentioning the 'g' word. Gallop. However good she was feeling at that moment, the thought that they might be going to race at top speed through the countryside would have caused her rediscovered confidence to all but evaporate.

"Have I properly said thank you?"

Melissa enquired as they arrived at the far end of the orchard.

"For what?"

"For saving my life."

Danika looked a little uncomfortable.

"Yes, well, probably. Anyway, you don't need to."

They negotiated a narrow gap in the hedgerow, having to duck down to avoid a low tree branch. Beyond the hedge, and running parallel to it, was a road that, although well maintained, was only wide enough for one vehicle. As the horses stepped onto the smooth tarmac their metal shoes began to make a steady, metronomic clip-clop on the hard surface.

Melissa wanted to say how much she *did* need to thank her but, reading Danika's body language, guessed that she would rather not hear anything approaching praise or gratitude.

"We won't be on the road for long, we're turning off just up here."

The lack of follow-up and change of subject confirmed to Melissa that she was right in her assumption. No matter. Perhaps by merely being an agreeable companion for her ride, she could offer her some form of thanks, however inadequate.

"We're heading for that wooded area."

They continued on until they reached the trees that Danika had pointed out minutes before. With the gentlest of coaxing, she guided Firefly in between two large oaks, whose leaves and branches spread their shade across the single-lane road. Magick, without any prompting from Melissa, followed them into the woods. There was a bridle path, of sorts, that led them between trees and shrubs, the horses carefully picking their way around the odd stray branch or, at one point, over the trunk of a fallen beech. Melissa thought how pleasant it was in the dappled shade, with the occasional breeze ruffling the horses' manes.

"Ready for something that's a bit more fun?"

Melissa could see the field ahead of them, beyond the last line of trees. She had thought that, when the moment came, she would feel anxious, even to the point of being too scared to allow Magick 'off the leash'. But she didn't. She felt nothing but a tingle of anticipation and excitement. It might have been Danika, or the grey, or both but, whoever or whatever was responsible for her new found courage, she didn't care.

"Yes!"

Her answer brought an enthusiastic nod from Danika and, as they neared the field's edge, Melissa could see Firefly in front of her sensing what was coming, and felt Magick tense in preparation for the run. As she cleared the trees, Danika brought Firefly to a stop, waiting for Melissa to come alongside. As soon as she was level, Danika gave her a smile of reassurance.

"Don't worry, he'll look after you."

She didn't wait for Melissa to reply but gently touched Firefly's flanks with her boots. The young horse, clearly ready for the command, remembered his schooling and took off in a beautifully controlled canter. Melissa waited for Magick to join the chase but, although obviously more than eager, he remained where he was until she too gave the signal.

Both horses followed the track across the middle of the field, with Melissa and Magick keeping a safe distance behind Danika and Firefly, even though Magick would have been perfectly capable of catching and overtaking Firefly had he not been listening to his rider. And, during the time it took to reach the far side, Melissa became lost in the moment, forgetting, however briefly, what had led her to be on that horse, in that field, with Danika on that beautiful afternoon.

"That *was* fun!"

Melissa pulled up alongside Danika, a broad smile on her face.

"Told you Magick would look after you."

She urged Firefly forward, guiding him onto the wide area of grass that ran around the edge of the field before beckoning Melissa to walk along beside her.

"Do you do this often?"

"As often as I can, although I'm normally alone, apart from my horse, obviously."

Melissa sensed the possibility of a conversation, but didn't want to build her hopes up too much.

"Do you prefer to be alone?"

Might she let her in, just a fraction?

"I usually am."

"That's not quite what I asked."

Melissa wasn't sure, after she'd spoken, whether it had been a good idea to push it, but Danika's smile quickly told her that no harm had been done.

"I'm enjoying your company."

There was an honesty in those words which Melissa found quite touching. For all the superficial remoteness she sensed that, just below the surface, there was so much more.

"The feeling's mutual" was all that Melissa could think to say and probably all she needed to say. Several minutes passed in silence, with just the sound of birdsong and the breathing of the horses making up the soundtrack of their ride. Above them a red kite circled, scanning the grassland for its next meal, while a young fox scurried along the bottom of the hedgerow.

As they reached the five bar gate in the corner of the field, Danika leant forward over Firefly's neck and deftly released the catch that was holding it closed. She pushed it open and beckoned Melissa through before following her and then closing it behind them.

"Our little river's just down here. It's the one that flows into our lake. We can sit for a while, if you like, and the horses can have a drink and rest."

It seemed to Melissa that she was being taken to a favourite place, somewhere that Danika knew and loved, somewhere that might allow the barriers to, if not fall, then maybe lower just a fraction. Side by side they walked down a shallow slope, moving into the deep shadow cast by tall oak trees before emerging into the warm sunshine once more, the sound of the flowing river now clearly audible a short distance in front of them.

"We'll lead them from here."

As Danika spoke so, in one fluid movement, she dismounted, holding Firefly's bridle and walking beside him along the grassy path. Melissa slipped from her saddle, maybe not quite so elegantly, but nevertheless managed to achieve the same result. Together they led their horses down to the riverbank. Melissa watched as Danika secured Firefly's reins before releasing him to make his own way to the water, where he began to drink before abandoning the river in favour of the grass that grew in abundance along the bank. Melissa, rather reluctantly, did the same with Magick who, once free, joined Firefly.

"If you're worried they'll run off, I can promise you they won't."

Melissa wasn't totally convinced of that, but Danika's confidence was enough to quell her fears. She sat down next to her on the riverbank. Danika had already removed her riding hat and undone her body protector. Melissa took that as her cue to do likewise.

"Do you ever bring others here?"

Danika was now lying flat on the grass and had closed her eyes.

"No."

160

That simple answer begged another question, didn't it?

"Then....?"

"Why you?"

Melissa nodded as she lay beside her.

"Mmm, well, honestly? Honestly, I just wanted to."

"Then I feel suitably honoured."

"Oh, please don't. If anything it should be the other way around."

Melissa now definitely wished she had persisted with the 'why me' question because those particular waters had just become even murkier, and that thought had obviously transferred itself to her expression because Danika didn't wait for her to ask the question.

"Verity's told you about Brathy Beck, about those involved and what occurred there...."

"Yes."

"....and so, if you recall, there was a leader, a woman the others looked up to and took guidance from."

Could she remember her name? Her mind raced back to Verity's account of the incident.

"Helen."

It came to her almost instantly.

"Then you need to know, Melissa, that you are the only direct descendant of Helen, the leader of the Brathy Beck Coven."

Danika allowed her a few moments to take that in.

"Why didn't Verity say something?"

"Because I think she felt she'd told you enough for the time being. You've had quite a lot to deal with these past few days."

Melissa wondered if her connection to Helen might explain the feelings she had experienced, her longing for understanding and her desire to help. It seemed possible. However, at that moment, she just wanted to lose herself in her surroundings and Danika's company. And so, with a warm summer sun above them, the sound of the river washing over its pebble bed, and their horses resting in the shade of a large willow, Danika and Melissa lay back on the riverbank, just existing in each other's presence.

"Do you know the question I had when I found out about all of this?"

161

Danika asked as she turned to Melissa, who tried to imagine what was coming next.

"Go on."

"I wanted to know...."

Danika was quickly warming to her subject and had now propped herself up so that she could look directly at Melissa.

"....about descendants. Verity had told me of my connection to Brathy Beck, and so I asked her. Given that our Order is exclusively female and that our overriding preferences are, er...."

"For each other?"

Melissa kindly offered, and Danika nodded.

"So, I asked, well, how are there any descendants?"

Melissa had to admit that, of all the obvious questions, that one hadn't occurred to her.

"And what did she say?"

"It was quite simple really. They all had husbands."

Danika lay back down and closed her eyes once more, as if that was a definitive end to the subject, but Melissa had no intention of leaving it there.

"Did they know?"

"Did who know?"

Danika asked lazily, as if she'd just woken from a deep sleep.

"Did the husbands know that their wives were....were...?"

"Lesbian witches?"

Danika added, helpfully.

"Yes" Melissa replied, unable to come up with a description more suitable.

"Shouldn't think so. Possibly. Maybe. I don't know. Anyway, it doesn't matter, does it? The men that are chosen will only ever be a means to an end. A necessary evil. Nothing more. Sort of 'lie back and think of the coven'."

Danika gave her a brief sideways glance.

"And is that what we are? Technically?"

"What? Technically lesbian, or technically witches?"

Melissa rolled her eyes and tried not to smile.

"Witches. I asked Verity and she said something like it wasn't a given, but was likely."

"There you are then. I can't really add anymore to that. And, anyway, I think that, deep down, you know. Don't you, Melissa?"

She opened her eyes and looked at her. There was a glint of something in that look that challenged her to deny it.

"Verity also told me how she rescued you and brought you here."

If Danika recognised the change of subject for the diversion it was, she had the good grace to simply accept it.

"What exactly did she tell you?"

Melissa briefly recounted the rainy night, Danika's violent encounter with The Custodians, and Doctor Pamela Flynn. Danika listened intently without interrupting, as if reliving each moment as it was told. When Melissa stopped talking her voice was replaced by the sound of the river and the breeze in the trees.

"Except...."

Danika said, now speaking more softly.

"....that, of course, was just the end of the story."

"I'd like to hear the rest of it."

Melissa waited, wondering if Danika had intended her to ask.

"The rest of it? Mmm. The rest of it. Well, most of that can be summed up by telling you that my father was Polish, my mother English...."

Which explains her exceptional command of the English language, Melissa thought to herself.

"....I was born near Lublin, in a village called Osmolice, south of the city. My childhood was happy and carefree. I came to England when I was eighteen with a mind to find a career, something a little different. After I'd finished college, I trained hard, took professional courses in unarmed combat and close protection, then found myself work in the Personal Security sector."

"A bodyguard?"

"In a manner of speaking. Although at that time, of course, I had no idea that there was something coming for me, and for my future."

Her words hung in the air, filled with an emotion that she hadn't allowed to surface until that moment. It was there, and then it was gone.

163

In a spontaneous gesture, Melissa reached out and took her hand, giving it a reassuring squeeze. It seemed to her that it was the right thing to do, the kindest thing.

"I want to listen, if you want to tell me."

Danika turned her gaze to the horizon, her eyes focussed on the far hills that were bathed in the afternoon sun.

"Yes, I want to tell you" she said.

Chapter 22

~Danika~

On the table in front of her lay the padded envelope that had dropped onto her doormat a short time ago. With no indication of sender or courier, Danika had torn it open and found that it contained a small mobile phone and a single sheet of A4 paper. She sat down and picked up the piece of paper. There was no address on its header, and no surname for the sender. The signature at the foot of the page was written with a flourish, while the text was word processed.

Dear Miss Pacek

You don't know me but I feel I already know you. I shall not waste time with a pointless attempt to either introduce myself or, indeed, justify what I am about to tell you, except to implore you to trust me for the sake of your own safety and wellbeing.

I have used, in this first instance, what I believe to be the safest way of contacting you. In any future communication I must insist you only use the mobile I have enclosed. It's what is known as a burner phone and is untraceable and, eventually, disposable. Programmed into its memory is the number of my own burner. That is the only number you may call on that phone. Why? Because, Miss Pacek, your life depends upon it. It is as simple as that.

My aim is to meet you and immediately remove you to a place of safety. Please believe me when I say that I am your only hope.

We shall speak very soon.

Verity

Danika re-read the letter. A natural reaction might have been to put the letter, phone and envelope in the bin and dismiss it as the work of some kind of crank. There was no way she faced a threat as serious as the one described in the letter. She'd know about it, wouldn't she? And anyway, even if there was such a threat, she knew she was more than capable of looking after herself. Even if this Verity, whoever she was, had contacted her with the best of intentions, she was clearly deluded if she believed she could possibly help her. And yet Danika didn't put anything in the bin but, instead, placed the letter next to the mobile and sat back in her chair. Her head was telling her to throw them away and forget all about Verity, but her heart? Her heart was saying something else entirely. And that she couldn't explain.

Still staring at the phone she'd just been sent, Danika reached out to pick up her own mobile.

"Dani! Hi!"

The sound of her voice always made Danika smile.

"Elise. Great to hear you again. I've left it too long, haven't I?"

"No problem."

She laughed. And that was Elise. Nothing was ever any problem. She had always accepted Danika's absence without any complaint or hint of irritation and, in the times they were together, was the perfect confidant, friend, and lover. They had met soon after Danika left Poland and came to England. Elise had not long been in the country herself when their paths crossed. It had been in a café. Elise's shoulder bag had knocked over Danika's cup of coffee as she had been heading for the door. After profuse apologies and the purchase of a replacement coffee, they had spent a beautiful afternoon together. From that day on, their friendship had grown and evolved into something that suited both their desires and their desired lifestyle. Neither wanted to live in each other's pocket, each valuing their freedom to live their own life but taking comfort in the knowledge that one was always there for the other. It was an arrangement that worked well. And so, on receipt of the mysterious letter and phone, Danika knew there was only one person whose opinion on them she would trust. Her dearest friend, her only true friend. Elise.

"Can I come over?"

"Do you have to ask?"

166

No, of course she didn't. She knew that, but she also knew Elise. More likely than not she'd be on her desktop computer with its two monitors, working on some obscure programme to do with cyber security, or something like that. But, whatever it was, she'd never say she was being interrupted, or try to put off a visit.

"I'd value your opinion on something."

"Oh, and I thought you just wanted to spend some time in my scintillating company."

"That too, of course! Ok. See you soon."

"Dani?"

"Yes?"

"Love you."

Before Danika could respond, Elise ended the call, leaving her with those two words. If Elise hadn't closed the line might she have said the same to her? At that moment she liked to think so, and even felt regret that she hadn't. Picking up the letter and both phones, Danika collected her car's keypad and a jacket from the back of a chair before making her way down to her car. It was a short drive across the city to Elise's second floor flat. Luckily, the traffic was light, lighter than she would have expected, and she made the journey in a shade over twenty minutes.

Danika walked through the open main door, probably left unfastened by one of the other residents, and into the modest foyer, heading for the staircase. Without so much as a glance around her, she took the two flights up to the second floor. Elise's door was at the end of a short corridor and, as she approached it, Danika was surprised to see that it was half open. She knew that Elise took her safety and security very seriously and, even though she was expecting Danika, she wouldn't have opened the door until she knew that her friend had arrived. Danika reached out and pushed the door fully open.

"Elise?"

She walked into the small living room, a place that held many happy memories and had a cosy familiarity. Except that what she now saw was anything but familiar, or cosy. The room was a mess. Chairs had been upturned, the table was on its side, and several vases lay smashed on the floor.

"Elise!"

Danika called out again, this time much louder. She ran from one room to another, hoping to find her or, perhaps, hoping she wouldn't. She quickly established that Elise wasn't anywhere in the flat. There was no sign of a disturbance elsewhere so any struggle, and any violence, had been confined to the living room. She stood in the centre of the room, slowly turning a full circle as her mind raced to decide what she should do. She had just come from the street and there had been no sign of Elise. Danika walked back out into the corridor, looking up and down the stairwell, but there was no one to be seen and only silence but for the faint sound of traffic from the road outside.

Could there be something in the flat she hadn't noticed that might give a clue as to what had happened to Elise? Returning to the living room, Danika set about a careful search but found nothing that offered any answers. She removed her phone from her jacket and was about to call the police, but something stopped her, a thought, distant and fleeting. She replaced her own mobile and reached into another pocket for the burner phone that she had been sent just hours ago. She had intended discussing it, and the letter, with Elise, but it now seemed that was a conversation that wasn't going to happen.

Danika held the mobile in her hand, staring at it while she tried to make up her mind whether to do what she was thinking of doing. It was madness, wasn't it? Contacting this woman, this Verity? How could she possibly know anything about her, about any danger she might be facing? And yet Elise, who had been expecting her, had disappeared and there were signs of violence. Was that a coincidence? Danika selected the only number programmed into the phone's memory and pressed the green button. It connected.

"Hello Danika. I must admit I hadn't expected you to make the first call."

"Are you Verity?"

Danika made no attempt to conceal the mistrust in her voice.

"I am. Danika, has something already happened?"

She hesitated before answering, still unsure whether she should continue with the call or go with her first instinct and contact the police.

"Yes."

"Tell me...."

Another silence.

"....Danika? Tell me what's happened."

Verity listened as Danika quickly told her what she'd seen in the flat.

"....and I don't know what I should do about Elise. I couldn't see any sign of her outside. Look, I'm sure you want to help, but I really think I should call the police."

"No!"

Verity's emphatic response shocked Danika.

"I don't understand."

"You have to believe me when I tell you that you can't trust anyone, the police, the authorities, anyone."

"Except you, I suppose?"

"Except me, Danika."

No reaction to the edge of sarcasm in Danika's question. Just a statement of fact. And it prompted an immediate apology.

"I'm sorry, but I'm so worried about Elise."

The line went ominously quiet for a moment.

"Listen to me, Danika. It's you we have to worry about now."

"What are you saying?"

"I'm saying that there's nothing we can do for your friend right now. I'm sorry. We have to put all our efforts into getting you to safety. You have to get away from Elise's flat, and stay away from your own home. You can't return there."

Danika felt her world suddenly spiralling out of control, and it seemed she was powerless to stop it. But she had to fight a growing sense of dread that was threatening to overwhelm her. She needed to survive for Elise, to be there for her. She refused to believe that she would never see her again.

"Tell me what I should do."

There was no other option.

"Leave the building and go to a public place you know well. I'm about two hours away and it'll be dark before I arrive. Is there somewhere I can easily find you, somewhere out in the open?"

Danika thought for a moment before giving Verity directions to a courtyard near some offices, a place that should have a steady flow of people through it at that time of day. Having

169

closed the call, Danika quickly descended the stairs and made her way back out onto the street. She glanced around her, perhaps hoping that Elise would suddenly appear from a side street or doorway. She didn't.

Danika, in the time it took her to reach the pavement, had been trying to come up with a location where she could safely wait until it was time to go to the courtyard and meet Verity. She made the short walk to her car and, as she climbed behind the wheel, decided that she would head for the castle. It would certainly have people in and around it, being a well-known and popular tourist attraction.

As Danika started the engine she tried to overcome the thought that she was about to abandon Elise. Was this how she was going to treat her? To run away when she needed her most? There were tears in Danika's eyes, as she steered the car out into the traffic, as she realised that she hated herself for leaving without her.

As dusk began to creep in, the floodlights, which were located around the perimeter of the castle, switched on. Danika walked through the main gate, showing her pass to the uniformed attendant in the kiosk near the entrance. The castle and grounds would be open for another two and a half hours, just long enough to get her to her meeting time with Verity.

This was a place that Danika knew well. It was a destination she often sought out when she wanted somewhere to relax in quiet surroundings. But this time, in her present circumstances, relaxing was the last thing on her mind. She hurried up a short flight of wide stone steps, heading for her favourite part of the old building. The room housed a detailed model of the castle, each point of interest illuminated in turn, with corresponding information displayed on one of several small screens around the model. Danika looked at one of those screens, seeing the text appear in front of her but not reading a word of it. While appearing to be concentrating on improving her knowledge of the castle, her attention was actually being directed towards a man who had just entered the room. She had first noticed him the moment she had climbed from her car. He had been following her, discreetly and at a distance, almost professionally. Almost, but not quite.

Every aspect of Danika's training was now kicking in, her senses fully engaged, her body tensing as she tried to come up with a plan of action. She had to push all thoughts of Elise into the background and concentrate. She needed to be sure that her 'follower' wasn't simply an innocent visitor who happened to have the same interest in the castle's history. She tried to convince herself that might be the case but every instinct was telling her otherwise.

Danika spent another few minutes pretending to study the model, occasionally referring to the screen for further information, before she casually walked away and left the room. As soon as she had turned the corner into a narrow passageway, she ran along it to the second room, quickly darting through the open doorway before kneeling behind an exhibition cabinet containing various artefacts from archaeological digs around the castle.

She waited, trying to keep her breathing as shallow and as quiet as she could. She was certain she couldn't be seen from the door but had to take care that, in attempting to get some kind of view out into the passageway, she didn't make herself visible. It was at that moment she noticed the cabinet was on locked castors, which had the effect of raising it several inches off the floor. Danika realised that, by getting her head as near to the stone floor as she could, she had a very restricted, but adequate, sight of the doorway. If he came in to study the exhibits and turned out to be an innocent tourist, Danika was ready with her 'I lost my contact lens' line. But if his only interest was Danika and she could remain out of sight, then he would move on immediately, believing she had spotted him and decided to run.

She didn't have long to wait. From under the cabinet she saw his brown Oxford shoes, expensive, probably bespoke. She had made a mental note of them when she first noticed him. But they were visible only for a moment as he paused in the doorway before he was gone, hurrying away along the corridor. Danika could hear his quickly fading footsteps on the stone floor. She stood and walked slowly over to the door, carefully looking up and down the passageway. There was no one in either direction and she realised that, if she had expected to be surrounded by other visitors to the castle, then she hadn't reckoned on the time of day and time of year. It was late, almost dark, and she recalled feeling one or two raindrops on her face as she had walked from her car. It was hardly likely, if she had paused to think about it, that there would be more than a few determined tourists in the grounds.

Danika made her way cautiously along the passageway in the direction her follower had taken. She had no intention of continually having to look over her shoulder, regardless of what was going on. In fact, as thoughts of Elise surfaced once more, she was determined that the hunter was now going to become the hunted.

The passageway took a sharp, ninety degree turn in front of her and, as she approached the blind corner, Danika heard more footsteps, this time coming towards her. She stopped just yards from the turn, realising she was now too far down the passageway to be able to return to the first room and hide again. Her body tensed, ready to deal with whatever was coming her way.

Seconds later, the castle attendant turned the corner and walked briskly past her, giving her a courteous smile as he did so. Danika, who had been holding her breath, let out an audible sigh as the attendant disappeared from view.

She entered the main hall, a part of the castle now used for anything from modern art installations to science exhibitions. Currently, it was housing a touring display of theatrical and film costumes which would, in any other circumstances, have held Danika's interest. But not today. She walked past a particularly striking Tudor gown from a recent BBC production, all the time keeping her senses alert to any possible threat. There were two other people at the far end of the hall, a woman and a younger girl, probably her daughter. As Danika approached them, the woman turned and smiled before continuing to read the information board in front of a colourful roaring twenties dress.

Near the mother and daughter was the way out of the main hall, an open doorway that led into another, much shorter, passageway. Beyond it, a visitor could either continue into various other exhibition rooms, or follow the signs for the spiral stairway that led up to the castle wall and the central tower. It was somewhere that Danika knew quite well, having enjoyed views over the city from the circular walkway that ran around the upper part of the tower.

She hesitated at the signs as she made her decision as to which way she should go. What would *he* do? It was now dark and Danika could see the raindrops running steadily down one of the small windows that lined the passageway. She decided on the tower. It was the least likely place someone might go on a wet night and therefore, she was guessing, he'd think that she'd choose there, in the hope that he'd continue searching the maze of rooms in the body of the castle.

The temperature dropped as she came closer to the narrow, ancient stairwell. Danika gripped the rope that was fastened to the circular wall enclosing the time-worn, spiral steps. Slowly she began to climb, carefully making sure she put her boots onto the widest part of each step. Although there was lighting from the base to the top of the tower, it was far from bright and only seemed to add to the cold, forbidding atmosphere.

She was over halfway now and could just see above her the small door that led out onto the tower's external walkway. A thin shaft of light from an outside lamp shone across the topmost steps, indicating that the door was slightly ajar. If indeed he had gone up to the walkway to look for her, it would only take him moments to discover that she wasn't there, which meant that he'd be coming back down in a matter of seconds. Danika knew that if that happened she would be at a big disadvantage with him above her. He'd be able to send her back down the stone stairwell with one well-aimed kick.

She made the decision to take the narrow steps two at a time, needing to reach the small door before he appeared. Seconds later and Danika was standing on the top step, with the small door directly in front of her. She pushed it, causing it to swing slowly outwards. She felt the steady rain and the night breeze on her face as she made her way out onto the circular walkway. There was no one to be seen. Danika held onto the hand rail as she edged her way around the tower, while below her the city lights shone bright.

"Very predictable."

Danika spun round, momentarily releasing her grip on the safety rail. The man had appeared from behind her, his eyes fixed on her, his gaze unwavering.

"How so?"

She tried to sound confident and assured.

"It was obvious that you'd come after me. You wouldn't be content to merely hide, hoping to avoid being taken. You'd be angry. You'd want to take the initiative. Of course you would."

Danika had to make a conscious effort to stand her ground.

"Where's Elise? What have you done to her?"

He took a step towards her but she remained motionless.

"Right at this moment, Ms Pacek, if I were you I'd be more concerned about what we'll do to you."

He moved closer.

"Then why? Why me? Why Elise? Why are you doing this?"

He smiled.

"That's a lot of 'whys'."

Danika didn't feel like returning the smile.

"Then try answering just one of them. You owe me that."

"I don't owe you anything...."

Closer still.

"....but I'm generous. I'll give you something. You need to understand that you and your kind have a price to pay. A debt is owed."

"My kind?"

"Oh, really, feigning ignorance doesn't become you."

His voice was cold, void of any emotion and it chilled her to the core. There would be no point in attempting to reason with him, no point in hoping for any kind of mercy. She knew he would show none.

"Do you want me on my knees begging you for my life, for Elise's life? Is that what you want? Alright, then I'll beg you."

Danika had been watching him closely as she had been speaking. She judged that he was now within reach. She suddenly dropped to her knees and, in the same movement, brought her fist hard up into his groin. He stumbled forward, colliding with her and knocking her back against the wall of the tower. It took her only a moment to recover from the impact but, in that very short time, he had regained some of his composure

174

and was preparing to come for her, his eyes wide with anger. Danika pushed herself away from the wall, her hands wildly reaching out for the handrail. Her first attempt missed and she pitched forward, almost hitting her head on the topmost rail. In the same moment that he swung his fist towards her, Danika succeeded in getting hold of the handrail. She pulled herself around just in time to avoid the incoming blow, his fist glancing painfully against her shoulder. Having missed his target, the unchecked momentum of his failed attack had the effect of throwing him forward and over the top rail.

Despite Danika taking only a fraction of a second to react, her lightening response was almost too late. She just managed to grab his arm as he fell, but his weight pulled her violently into the safety rail. Somehow, with a superhuman effort, she just managed to hang on to him and stop herself from being pulled over the top rail and onto the concrete path far below. But she knew it was only a matter of seconds before she would lose her grip.

"Where's Elise? Tell me!"

She felt his arm begin to slip through her fingers.

"Tell me!"

Danika looked into his eyes, desperately wanting to see some spark of humanity, but instead she saw nothing but a deep, pure hatred. What had she done, what was she, to provoke such an extreme loathing?

"She's in Hell, just like you!"

Whether his arm slipped from her grasp, or whether she made a conscious decision to let go, Danika wasn't sure and didn't care. She watched him fall and moments later heard the sickening sound as he hit the concrete path. He hadn't cried out. He had plunged to his death in silence, and it was the silence that she would remember.

Danika made her way as quickly as she could back down the spiral stairs, almost slipping on the smooth stone in her haste to get away from the tower. She ran along to the far end of the passageway and into the women's restroom. There was no one else in there. She went to the furthest sink and turned on the cold tap, splashing her face until it felt numb from the icy water. After she had taken a paper towel and wiped her face dry, she found herself looking at her own reflection in the mirror above the sink.

Did she know the woman staring back at her? Because she saw in her eyes something that hadn't been there just a short time before.

She saw a simmering, intense anger directed at those who had forced her to become what she now knew she was. Someone who hated, someone who was emotionally untouched by the proximity of death, and who now had a desire to inflict pain and suffering on those who had taken Elise from her.

Danika looked down at her watch. There was still a while before she was due to meet Verity in the courtyard a short distance away. Should she stay in the castle and hope that the man's body wouldn't be discovered straightaway? He had fallen into a poorly lit, private area of the castle grounds, so there was a good chance that the alarm wouldn't be raised immediately. But the risks in staying were high. There might be others nearby, and clearly the castle was no longer the safe place she had initially hoped it would be. She decided that her chances would be improved, and her options increased, if she were out on the streets.

She turned away from the mirror and slowly opened the restroom door. She looked along the length of the passageway and then back towards the entrance. All was quiet. There was no sign of any alarm, no sound of approaching sirens. Nothing. Danika fastened her jacket and prepared to go back out into the rain. She knew it wouldn't be a good idea to make straight for the courtyard and wait for Verity to arrive. If there were others, then her presence would only serve to lead them directly to her.

Having left the castle, Danika walked towards the main gate. As she neared the kiosk she continued to look straight ahead, not wanting to catch the eye of the attendant she had seen earlier. At any moment she expected someone to shout 'stop!' and be physically prevented from leaving the grounds. But she walked on, unchallenged.

She could see her car in the distance but wasn't about to take the risk of returning to it. Instead, she walked briskly in the opposite direction, away from the castle and away from their meeting place. To take the route she was going to take, Danika knew she might make herself late for her rendezvous with Verity, and that scared her because she was now convinced that a woman she had never met, and didn't know, was her only hope.

Chapter 23

"And I think Verity's told you the rest, hasn't she?"

Danika lifted her head and looked over to where the horses were lazily eating the riverside grass.

"Yes. She told me how you eventually made it to the courtyard, quite badly injured apparently."

"I wouldn't say 'badly'."

Danika obviously wanted to play down that part, and Melissa was perfectly happy to let it go.

"She also mentioned you had a nightmare about Elise. Do you want to talk about her?"

Danika returned her gaze to the sky. A few small clouds had begun to appear, making their way slowly over the horizon and high above them, a passenger jet was painting a white vapour trail across the bright blue. She watched as the trail gradually thinned and finally disappeared. Something there and then gone.

"No. Not right now. Shall we ride again? I think Magick and Firefly need to be woken up!"

Both horses were looking very content and were showing no sign of wanting to move on. However, as soon as Danika stood up, they were suddenly alert and ready. Danika and Melissa swung themselves back into their saddles, guiding Magick and Firefly onto the oak-lined single-track road.

"What are you going to do when we get back?"

Danika asked, steering the conversation in another direction.

"I'm going to watch a film. Do you want to join me?"

"Depends what it is."

"It's Margot Robbie in…."

Melissa needed to start getting this right.

"….Birds of Prey (and the Fantabulous Emancipation of One Harley Quinn)."

Danika's raised eyebrows showed her surprise.

"Not an answer I expected."

"What did you expect, some weepy love story about a wronged heroine trying to make good against all odds....?"

Danika shook her head.

"No, I'd got you as more of a 'Texas Chain Saw Massacre' sort of girl."

Danika's expression remained impassive for some seconds before the grin that she had been holding back finally broke through.

"Admit it, for a moment you thought I was serious, didn't you?"

"Maybe."

Melissa gave her best 'I really don't care' look as Danika nudged Firefly off the road and onto a path that led through a single line of silver birch trees. They continued on into another meadow that was bisected by a bridle way.

"I might pass on the film, if you don't mind."

Danika looked over her shoulder, giving Melissa an apologetic smile. And, although it would have been very pleasant to have enjoyed Danika's company for a while longer, being alone would allow Melissa a better opportunity to concentrate on the finer points of Harley Quinn's Emancipation, Fantabulous or not.

"No problem. Got something more exciting planned?"

"Well...."

Danika urged Firefly forward along the bridle path, flicking another glance behind her to make sure Melissa was keeping up.

"....if you count working in the stables as 'more exciting' then, yes, I have something more exciting planned."

"You really love horses, don't you?"

"Yes. I find they give me a reason to wake up in the morning."

Was it really like that for her? Had her experiences and the loss of Elise taken its toll to that extent?

"But the good you've done, Danika, and the lives you've saved. You must find some comfort in that?"

She didn't answer until they reached the far side of the meadow, where she waited for Melissa to come alongside her.

"But it's never the ones you get right, is it? It's always those you fail that live with you, that are always there in the shadows, reminding you. And I miss her so much."

Perhaps in that moment, with those words, Danika had allowed her in, allowed her a glimpse of the pain she felt.

"If you want to talk about her…."

Melissa looked into Danika's eyes and saw not only the pain but, existing alongside it, the love.

"She was so alive. So beautiful. She….sparkled."

Melissa hesitated, wanting Danika to say more, but maybe that was all she needed to say.

"She sounds as if she was an exceptional young woman, and such a pretty name."

"Her grandmother was French and she was named after her. Elise Juliette."

Melissa realised that she could hear the river once more, its gentle rippling again providing its soft background to their afternoon. Moments later, the riverbank came into view, this time with a broad pathway running beside it. Wide enough, in fact, for them to ride next to each other with room to spare.

"And you loved her?"

Melissa now felt she was on safer ground mentioning love, and she wanted to give Danika every chance to say anything she wanted to about Elise.

"Yes. I did."

Danika had turned away from her, perhaps trying to hide the emotion she was in fear of showing. Melissa nudged Magick a little nearer so that she could reach out and gently rest a hand on her shoulder. It was the simplest of gestures but, in that moment, it was all that Danika needed to help her push back, just a little, against the sadness and anger that pursued her relentlessly and without mercy.

Chapter 24

As soon as Melissa returned to her apartment she began to immerse herself, once more, in the world of Harley Quinn. It had been with some reluctance that she had finally left Danika at the stables, realising just how much their time together had meant to her.

Melissa spent a short while on her laptop, recapping on some of the information she had read earlier before settling down in front of the large screen to watch 'Birds of Prey' and hopefully get to know Doctor Harleen Quinzel a whole lot better. As she watched so she jotted down the odd note or thought, bullet points that would provide a basic aide-memoire. But she knew that she mustn't, for a moment, lose sight of who this was really about. Layla. A young girl who found herself in a frightening situation following whatever terrors had brought her to the sanctuary. She was dealing with it alone, despite Verity's best efforts, in the only way she knew how, by shutting out as much as she could and withdrawing into a world of her own. But that, anyone could see, was neither desirable or sustainable. With both parents gone, Layla needed to face those terrors so that she might, eventually, find some kind of future. There were no guarantees, of course there weren't, but Melissa knew she had to try to somehow break through those defences that were being fuelled by unimaginable grief and loss.

Much to her surprise, Melissa really enjoyed the film. She had initially found some of the language and content not wholly appropriate for a girl of Layla's age, before having to remind herself she risked sounding like an out-of-touch, boring adult. Something she needed to avoid at all costs. In the film, Margot Robbie certainly made the role of Harley Quinn her own. She played the part with a joyous relish and it was impossible not to be drawn in by its story and characters. As the end credits began to roll though, Melissa felt less than confident that she could hold her own in the presence of a true fan.

There were also the 'Suicide Squad' films that featured Harley, and Melissa had to trust her initial instinct regarding which one might be Layla's favourite. But she also knew she had to be wary of over thinking the whole thing. To be convincing, she needed to know *something*, not *everything*.

Melissa switched the screen off, shut down her laptop and got up from her armchair. She picked up her notebook from the armrest and took it through to the kitchen, dropping it onto the table. After pouring herself a smoothie from the fridge, she sat down and began to read through what she'd written. As well as notes regarding the film, Melissa had also jotted down various snippets from trusted internet sources. By the time she'd finished her drink, she felt happy enough to close the notebook and drop it into a drawer, out of sight.

As she was about to leave her apartment, Melissa's thoughts returned to something Danika had mentioned earlier that afternoon. Could she really be the only direct descendant of Helen, the coven leader, and might that be the origin of her desire to help Layla? She'd like to think that she would have wanted to try anyway, out of common decency and a wish to do the right thing. But she couldn't deny that she felt there was something else, something that she wasn't yet fully understanding. And that 'something' had to be, in some way, connected to Helen and her duty, as she had seen it, to care for and protect those women who had looked to her for leadership all those centuries ago.

Melissa had decided to go to Verity's office, wanting that final nod of approval, confirmation that her idea of 'the right thing' still coincided with Verity's. Because, regardless of who her ancestor might be, it was still Verity who was in charge.

She knocked on the door.

"Come in."

As she entered she saw that the chair behind the desk was facing away from her. Slowly it swung round.

"Melissa. How lovely to see you again."

Harriet beamed at her as Melissa noticed her walking stick propped up against one end of the desk.

"Oh, Harriet. I hadn't expected….isn't Verity here?"

"I'm afraid not, my dear. I'm minding the shop in her absence, as it were. Can I be of any assistance?"

Could she? Of course she could. She was as qualified as anyone, including Verity and Sophie, to offer a valid opinion. And so, as concisely as she could, Melissa explained her thoughts regarding Layla, and how she wanted to try to help her. Harriet listened intently, occasionally nodding, and always engaged with what Melissa was saying. When, after a few minutes, she finished speaking, Harriet sat back in her chair but remained silent as she gave careful consideration to her reply.

"It's clear to me that you have Helen's blood running through your veins. And I see from your expression you understand what I mean by that."

Melissa acknowledged the compliment.

"I may, of course, fail completely. I've talked to Layla. She's an intelligent girl."

"But you will have tried, Melissa. That's all any of us can do, isn't it?"

She smiled her thanks and turned to leave the office.

"Oh, Melissa?"

Melissa returned to the desk and waited as Harriet opened one of the drawers. After taking a moment to check she had hold of the correct item, she then handed over a brown envelope.

"It's something Verity obtained for Layla. I believe it was her intention for her to have it sooner rather than later, and I can't think of anyone more qualified to deliver it."

Melissa took the large envelope from Harriet.

"May I know what's in it?"

Harriet smiled.

"I'm given to understand it's a particularly rare edition of a comic which features our friend, Harley Quinn."

Melissa regarded her with more than a degree of suspicion.

"Did Verity ask you to give it to me specifically, Harriet?"

Melissa had no intention of leaving without an answer.

"I think you know that you have Verity's full backing, regardless of outcome, and she felt you might require an 'in'. I believe that's the word she used."

Melissa took a moment to think about that.

"You knew, you all knew, I was going to do this, didn't you?"

"Let's just say we've encouraged you to make a decision that you were going to make anyway."

Harriet's gaze held hers, waiting for the comeback. Would she be angry at such passive manipulation? Perhaps she had a right to be.

"Ok...."

Once again, Melissa turned and headed for the door.

"....then wish me luck."

She didn't wait for Harriet's reply, but left clutching the envelope. After she had gone, Harriet whispered 'good luck' before closing the desk drawer.

Chapter 25

The more Melissa thought about it, the more she realised that it shouldn't have come as any surprise to her. She had suspected that Verity's concern for Layla went far deeper than she would ever admit but, perhaps, to talk about that concern beyond a mere acknowledgement of its existence, would only serve to bring memories of her own childhood far too close for comfort.

Melissa stood outside Layla's apartment door. She recalled the day of her own arrival, when Danika had brought her along this corridor for the first time, and she caught a glimpse of Layla, who had been eager to avoid her then, and not overly enamoured to be in her company since. Would now be a good time? Would there ever be a good time? Melissa took a deep breath before giving two quick knocks on the door. She waited. After what seemed an age but was probably no more than a few seconds, the door was opened just far enough for Layla to see out.

"Oh. Melissa. What do you want?"

The question hadn't been asked with any degree of annoyance, but merely as a polite enquiry. So far so good.

"Layla. Lovely to see you again. I have something for you from Verity."

The door opened a little wider.

"What is it?"

The question was loaded with suspicion, and Melissa was about to tell her but just managed to stop herself in time. Why would she have been told what was in the envelope? She wouldn't have any reason to know, would she?

"No idea. I'm just the messenger."

Layla took the envelope from her.

"Thank you for bringing it."

She stepped back and was about to close the door. As Layla moved aside, so Melissa saw the figurine standing on a shelf behind her and, in that moment, made her decision to commit, and test the saying 'there's no time like the present'.

"Harley Quinn!"

Layla turned to see where she was looking before nodding her head, the suspicion still there.

"That's right."

She said, waiting for a follow-up comment before offering anything more by way of conversation.

"Are you a Harley Quinn fan?"

Melissa immediately regretted using the word 'fan'. It was possible that Layla may not like to be described as such. Not everyone did.

"I think she's cool."

"Me too."

Layla looked as if she wasn't sure she believed that.

"Really?"

Melissa nodded enthusiastically although, she hoped, not too enthusiastically.

"Yes. Really. Although I like the films more than the cartoons or comics. Margot Robbie's just so good. I love her in 'Birds of Prey'."

Layla pulled her door open a little wider, regarding her now with a mixture of begrudging respect and more than a hint of mistrust as Melissa wondered if she'd mentioned the film a little too soon.

"My model's from that."

"I thought I recognised the gold outfit and the mallet."

"Do you want to have a better look?"

"May I?"

Could this be going any better? But Melissa knew she had to rein in the optimism. She was still walking on eggshells.

"Yeah. Come in."

Layla turned back into the hallway, beckoning Melissa to follow. As she entered, the first thing she noticed was how neat and tidy everything was. She glanced through to the living area and saw that there wasn't a cushion, chair, or ornament out of place. The tidiness seemed to Melissa to be almost obsessive. She stopped in front of the figurine.

"It's beautiful. So detailed."

It was indeed a superb likeness of Margot Robbie's Harley. As Melissa was studying it, Layla opened the envelope she had just been given and removed the comic.

"Oh wow! This is super rare. Wonder how Verity got it?"

She looked to Melissa, who gave a shrug. All she could truthfully offer was

"She's a very resourceful lady."

Layla placed it with great reverence onto a nearby table before returning her attention to Melissa and the figurine.

"I love that film too. I think it's the best. What's your favourite bit?"

The question was probably asked in all innocence but, nevertheless, it put Melissa on her guard. Was it a test, just to see whether she had actually seen 'Birds of Prey'? Possibly, or she could just be seeing monsters where there were none.

"Near the start, in the nightclub, when Harley throws up in that woman's handbag!"

That seemed, judging by Layla's reaction, to have been an unexpected answer, and she actually smiled.

"Mine's when she drives that truck into the chemical works, after the Joker's dumped her, and at the end when Cassandra finally goes to the toilet! That's so funny!"

Melissa quickly began to build on what Layla was saying, adding her own comments and opinions, making it a discussion of a mutually loved subject enjoyed with good knowledge and humour. Melissa tried to tell herself that it was too soon to assume the beginnings of a friendship, but it was difficult to play down the progress she felt she'd made with Layla in such a short time. So was now the time to walk away?

"Lovely to talk, Layla...."

Melissa said when there was eventually a pause in the conversation.

"....but I think I should leave you in peace to spend some time with Verity's gift."

"Leave me in peace?"

Layla looked at her with a puzzled expression.

"It's a saying. I just meant, I'll leave you alone now. That's all."

A cloud seemed to pass over her, and she looked away for a moment. It appeared to Melissa that there was a battle going on inside her between what she was used to saying, and what she really wanted to say. Melissa waited to see which would gain the upper hand.

"Do you have to go? I mean, if you do, that's fine. I won't mind. Really."

The subtext of those few words was clear to Melissa, and surprising. Behind the 'go or stay. I don't care one way or the other' there was a barely disguised anxiety, a keenly felt hope that she wouldn't go, at least not yet. But Melissa wasn't going to make her say as much. The conflict inside her didn't need its flames fanning, it needed them slowly and gently extinguishing.

"Actually, I was hoping we could talk some more, but I didn't want to outstay my welcome."

Layla shrugged, still wanting to put on an outward show of indifference.

"Ok."

Melissa smiled, quietly impressed at how well Layla, for someone so young, played the role she had chosen for herself.

"Do you want to stay here, or shall we take a walk?"

"Have you seen the butterfly room?"

"I was there with Justine and Sophie a little while ago, but I'd love to go back."

As they walked together along the corridor and on to the butterfly room, Layla remained silent. Melissa thought about trying to push the conversation on, but didn't want to risk everything she'd gained by going for too much too soon, and it wasn't until they were sitting together, surrounded by the flowers, plants and butterflies, that Layla spoke again.

"Aren't they beautiful?...."

She looked around the room, her eyes wide with wonder, like a child half her age. She held out a hand and it took only moments for a butterfly to settle on it.

"....I think I like it here almost as much as being with the Brathy Beck stone."

Melissa thought about mentioning her mother, recalling their previous brief conversation there, but decided the last thing she wanted now was to make some clumsy, ill-considered comment and lose any hard won trust.

"Do you usually come here on your own?"

Layla's gaze never left the butterfly as she replied.

"I could never be alone here, when I'm surrounded by these wonderful little things, could I?"

But there was something underlying those words, in the way they were said, in the presence of the word 'here' and its implication. Melissa found that incredibly moving. A thirteen-year-old girl shouldn't have experienced something that had caused such a depth of sorrow and hurt. Melissa felt tears welling in her eyes, and had to fight hard to keep them at bay as another butterfly landed on Layla's shoulder.

"Is that how you feel everywhere else, Layla? Lonely?"

Had Melissa read too much into her words? She had made an assumption and could only wait to see how Layla would brush aside the unwanted question. Would it be a direct denial, or something more nuanced?

"Apart from at the stone, yes. It is."

She spoke those words quietly, as if she had finally accepted that there was no point in running anymore. No point in fighting something she could never defeat. Melissa was reminded of Danika. Danika and Layla. Two broken souls. She took her hand and held it. A simple gesture that said 'I'm with you now, and whenever you want me to be'.

As if reading the moment perfectly, the two butterflies flew away from Layla, finding a new resting place on one of the plants. Layla turned to Melissa. The look in her eyes was enough to prompt Melissa to put her arms around her and hold her, saying nothing and saying everything. It might have been minutes before she gently released her embrace. As she held her at arms' length, Melissa saw that there were tears on Layla's cheeks. She carefully wiped them away.

"I think your Mum was very lucky to have a daughter like you."

Melissa gave her a warm smile, hoping she'd said the right thing.

"I miss her."

Of course she did, and it must hurt like hell. But was she ready to take the next step? That had to be up to her.

"Would you like to tell me about her? About what happened?"

Layla looked over to where the two butterflies had settled, her eyes staying on them as she began to speak.

Chapter 26

~Layla~

She watched as the waves rolled in, broke, and finally died away into shallow ripples on the shore. Behind her, some way from the water, lay a man and a woman. Both were on their backs, their eyes closed against the fierce sunlight.

Layla had never really understood why adults would lay for hours, just for their skin to get a little darker and even, possibly, burnt. Apparently, a 'beautiful tan' was the thing to have. It made a person more attractive. It made others envious. But no. She still didn't get it. Lying still and doing nothing wasn't an activity that, Layla had decided, was ever going to appeal to her. The beach wasn't her favourite place but she was with her parents, and that made it all ok.

She wandered a little way into the water. It was warm and inviting. Over to her right, a green, tree-covered headland reached out into the calm sea. Layla could just make out some people standing on the furthest point. They were facing towards the coastline beyond, which was hidden from her view by the headland. To her left, the beach stretched away into the distance, its white sand dotted along its length with tufts of marram grass that were gently swaying in the light summer breeze.

The surrounding peace and beauty wasn't lost on Layla. Without doubt, she appreciated such moments and never ever took them for granted. And, as she stood in the water, the waves softly lapping at her legs, her thoughts turned, as they usually did at such times, to her parents.

In truth, Layla's world revolved around her mother. That's not to say she didn't love her father. Of course she did. But there wasn't the connection, the empathy, the 'something', that she had with her Mum. There was something different and very special about their relationship. She hadn't realised at the time that this wasn't the case with every mother and daughter. Perhaps one day her mother would have told her. Maybe she would have sat down with her, as she had done on many other occasions, and gently explained, as best she could, who she was and what she was. But, tragically, they never had that moment.

A cruise ship appeared on the horizon, making its way to its next destination. Layla watched it for a short while before deciding to return to her parents and, hopefully, an ice cream or something equally scrummy. She waded back through the shallows until she felt the dry, warm sand beneath her feet. She ran up the beach and, as she reached her parents, she dropped to her knees beside her mother.

"Can I have an ice cream now?"

Whenever she wanted anything Layla would always try her mother first, putting on her best 'butter-wouldn't-melt' act. Even though her mother always saw right through it, it usually worked and so, without opening her eyes, she pointed at the ice box before letting her arm fall back to her side.

"Take whichever one you fancy, darling. But only one!" she added with a smile.

"Thanks Mum."

Layla set about searching the box, quickly finding a rather delicious looking strawberry and cream flavoured lolly. After carefully fastening the lid, she sat back and set about enjoying her treat. She looked back to the ship, wondering about all the people who might be on it, and allowing her mind to populate it with her own cast of characters. Her mother actively encouraged such flights of fancy, often telling her that her dreams should only be limited by her imagination. She was, and always would be, a free spirit, she told her. That is what her ancestors would want for her, she said. Layla had never understood the bit about her ancestors but had usually nodded, with a serious expression, as if she did.

She finished the lolly and would have loved another, but her mother had said only one. Now if she had been told by her father, that might have been different. Put simply, she had never felt anything for him. Love, respect, a desire to please. None of it. And yet, he had done nothing to deserve such an absence of feeling. He had been kind, attentive, supportive. How could she not love him? Outwardly, Layla said all the right things, did all the right things, and any casual observer would have no idea of the emotional vacuum in her heart. Did her mother know? Layla suspected she did, but she had never said anything to her, and she often wondered why. Might it be that she already knew why her only daughter felt nothing for her loving, caring father?

The ship had now sailed out of sight. Layla got up and, not wanting to disturb her parents further, quietly placed the lolly wrapper into the litter bag before making her way back towards the sea. Maybe, she thought, she might go and look for a rock pool. She had spent hours in the past studying the tiny creatures that lived in and around those little aquatic worlds. And, as Layla made her way to a group of boulders near the shoreline, she could have had no idea just how she would recall this day, and those like it, with such joy, and such infinitely deep sadness.

As the nights grew longer and the days colder, so Layla sensed the approaching shadows. However, what form those shadows were taking, and what threat they held, she didn't know. Several times she had thought about talking to her mother, but she couldn't describe what was troubling her, she couldn't give it a name, or even why it scared her so much. So what could she tell her? And what could her mother do to help even if she could find a way?

Layla stared up at her bedroom ceiling. She lay on her bed, a book by her side. She had come up to her room with every intention of reading but, once alone, she found she was no longer in the mood. She closed her eyes, maybe hoping that sleep would take her away from the anxieties that were following her like ghosts, ever present, floating in and out of her thoughts and not allowing her to find peace, even in the quietest moments.

It was two days ago that her father had received the phone call. She had heard her mother questioning him about it, and about the sudden need for him to go away. It wasn't unheard of. He had spent time away before. But this seemed different because *he* was different. After the call everything seemed to change. The way he spoke to her appeared colder, as if any love that he had for her had suddenly faded away.

Layla had wondered if she was imagining this 'cooling' or, at least, the extent of it. Perhaps she was being over sensitive and too ready to allow her ghosts to twist her perspective on other things. Yes, of course, she should have taken all of this to her mother and shared her fears straightaway. She should have given her the chance to help. The fact that she didn't was a regret that haunted Layla, together with all of the other 'what ifs'. Had she had that conversation then might it all have turned out so differently?

Layla, on an impulse, suddenly jumped up from her bed and made her way back downstairs. She looked through the open door to the study and saw her mother sitting behind her desk, her attention fixed upon the screen of her laptop.

"Mum. I'm going to the wood. I won't be long."

In reply, her mother held up a hand to show that she'd heard her. Layla grabbed her jacket from the hall coat rack as she pushed open the front door. Outside, it was a cold, bright afternoon, the sun low in the sky. The wood that she had referred to was no more than a five-minute walk from the house, and could be seen from Layla's bedroom window.

It was a place that she would often go whenever she wanted to clear her head of whatever was troubling her. It might have seemed strange to anyone who couldn't understand, but Layla felt an affinity with the wood and everything within it. It had spoken to her from an early age, called her into its heart, and given her comfort and peace when she could find solace nowhere else. She was sure that her mother knew about the wood and what it meant to her, although she had never said as much. Could that be added to the list of things her mother seemed to know without being told?

Layla kicked at the drifts of fallen leaves as she walked along the path that led past the first line of trees. Once through the trees, she left the path and made her way in amongst the undergrowth, taking a route known only to her, deep into the wood and completely hidden from view. After another few minutes of steady progress, Layla was nearing her destination. Just beyond a rather forbidding gorse bush, which she negotiated with the minimum of fuss, was her objective. An ancient, imposing yew tree.

She approached it with reverence. If the wood was her world of comfort, then the yew was its beating heart. Layla recalled the first time she felt its power, and how it had frightened her. But, as time passed, an uneasy acceptance had slowly replaced the fear until, without Layla noticing, any lingering anxieties had completely disappeared.

She knelt, feeling the soft ground give slightly under her. A breeze had picked up since she had entered the wood and was pushing and pulling at the branches above, making the yew seem alive, as if it was reacting to her presence. Maybe, in her young imagination, that's exactly what she believed. And, although she would never tell her, Layla sensed her mother's presence whenever she was there, with her yew. It wasn't the same when they were at the house together because, there, she always felt the shadow of her father. A shadow that seemed to bring with it a sense of foreboding.

But was that fair? He had always provided for her, and said he loved her. And Layla was sure he believed what he said. But she had always sensed that there was something else there, or something not there. She didn't know which.

All was now quiet, the breeze disappearing as quickly as it had come. Layla closed her eyes. It helped to heighten her other senses, bringing her into even closer communion with whatever it was that existed within the wood. As she allowed herself to fall under its spell, she recalled the first time her mother had shown her the yew. She had led her by the hand until they had stood together in front of it, but she had said nothing by way of an explanation as to why she had brought her there. It was as if she knew her daughter belonged, and that belonging was enough. No words were needed.

It took only moments for the familiar sense of tranquillity and wellbeing to wash over her. She allowed herself to become one with her surroundings, and to accept the comfort and feeling of safety that the yew gave her.

But, in one moment, all that was good, all that had been protecting her, was gone, shattered into a million pieces and thrown into the fast approaching darkness. Layla jumped to her feet, not knowing at first what she should do. She looked around her, but everything was as it had been. So where was the danger?

And then it came to her. The house! She had to get back to the house!

Layla ran, as fast as she could, almost falling at one point when her foot caught a tree root. As she reached the path that would take her back home, a low branch flicked across her face causing a scratch on her cheek and, by the time she reached the driveway, flecks of blood had begun to appear from the wound. Still running, she burst through the front door and into the hallway.

"Mum!"

She called out as she ran towards the study. The laptop was still open and running but there was no sign of her mother, however the chair she had been sitting on was now lying on its side behind the desk. Layla stared at it, her young mind no longer able to keep the darkness at bay. Eventually she turned away. Running out of the study, she hurried into the kitchen and then the living room.

"Mum!"

Still no answer. She tried to fight the panic, but it was a battle that was lost before it had begun. Frantically, Layla ran up the stairs. Her mother might be in the bedroom. Maybe she'd fallen and had to go and lie down. But just as Layla reached the landing she was grabbed by an arm and dragged into her parents' bedroom. Layla screamed out, using a word that a young girl shouldn't even know. And then she looked over to the bed. Lying on it was her mother. She might have been sleeping, except that her eyes were open and she wasn't blinking. Her body was still. Lifeless.

"Mum?"

Layla whispered as she slowly walked over to her. She reached out and touched her hand.

"Mum!"

This time she shouted, using both hands to shake her mother's body. But she knew. Despite all her efforts, she knew. Layla, the tears now streaming down her face, turned to face her attacker.

"Dad?"

Her voice faltered in disbelief.

"Did you kill Mum?"

She asked the question, not wanting to hear the answer.

"It had to end like this. There was no choice."

His voice was quiet, with an air of weary resignation. Layla took a few paces towards him, not stopping to consider whether she should try to run from the room.

"What do you mean?"

Make him say it. Make him own his crime.

"I'm sorry, Layla."

She slowly shook her head.

"I don't think you are. I think you hate us both. You've always hated us. Haven't you? Haven't you?!"

She screamed out the last two words, her voice full of anguish and fury. The sudden change in her took him by surprise and, instinctively, he took a step back before regaining his composure.

"Do you know what your mother was? Do you know what you are, Layla?"

The question seemed to momentarily calm her. She stared directly into his eyes, remaining silent for some seconds, until finally she said

"I'm your daughter."

Layla spoke quietly, without any trace of emotion. He had been about to respond. He tried to respond. But, for some reason he was suddenly struggling to speak as her eyes held him.

"You....you and....your mother....you....are...."

"What am I, Daddy? Tell me."

But she knew he couldn't. Her eyes followed him as he dropped to his knees, and the anger and hatred rose, unchecked, inside her. She watched as the blood began to flow, from his nose, his mouth, his eyes, and ears. She watched as he fell forward, his head hitting the floor just inches from her feet. And the sight of his blood made her smile, a cruel, cold smile.

They lay on the bed together, mother and daughter. Layla held her mother's hand as her tears flowed. How could everything have been so perfect just a short time ago? Except, of course, it wasn't. It never had been, had it? The clock had been ticking from the day that her father had planned his first meeting with her mother. Because that's how it must have been. The witchhunter marries the witch knowing that, one day, he must

196

kill her. And his daughter. A family destroyed. For a moment, Layla caught herself believing that his love for her might have stopped him. But, in truth, she knew there was no love. There never had been. Layla turned her head to look at his body. There was no pity in her eyes, and no regret for what she'd done.

She had no idea how long she remained next to her mother's body, with her thoughts going to ever darker places. And hidden by the grief, and the pain of loss, was a void that now existed in her soul. What was going to happen to her? She didn't care, because nothing mattered anymore. She would just stay where she was and die next to her mother. That's all she wanted. She closed her eyes.

"Layla?"

The voice, although soft and measured, startled her. She sat up and looked over to the door.

"Who are you?"

The woman walked into the room, glancing down at the man's body and taking care not to step in the blood that had pooled around his head.

"My name's Danika. I'm so sorry that I couldn't save your mother. We only learnt about your father when he met up with a contact today. Again, I'm sorry. But you need to come with me now, Layla."

She sat down on the bed beside her.

"I want to stay here, with Mum."

Danika reached out and gently broke Layla's hold on her mother's hand.

"I know you do, my love. But what do you think your mother would want for you now? She'd want you to be safe, wouldn't she? I can take you somewhere safe."

Layla turned to face her. Danika had never seen such desolation in one so young.

"Will I be in trouble?"

"For that?"

Danika nodded in the direction of the man's body.

"Yes."

She sounded genuinely scared.

"No. I won't tell if you don't. But you know, very few of us can do what you did, Layla. That makes you very special."

Danika gave her a sad, sympathetic smile before she tried again.

"So will you come with me?"

Layla looked around her, to the bodies of her mother and father, and back to Danika. Reluctantly, she got up from the bed and walked over to the door.

"What'll happen to my Mum?"

Danika joined her in the doorway, taking her hand as she did so.

"I'll make sure she's looked after. I promise."

Together they made their way down the stairs and out onto the driveway. As Danika led her towards her car, Layla took one last look at the house. Her eyes fixed on the first floor bedroom window for some seconds before she got into the passenger seat. Danika closed the car door, walked around the front of the blue Jaguar and climbed behind the wheel. Without a glance back, she steered the car out of the driveway and onto the narrow country lane.

"Did you mean what you said, about me being special?"

Danika nodded.

"Of course. You get that kind of power from your Mum."

Danika's immediate regret at having mentioned her mother must have shown in her expression.

"It's ok. Really. It's ok."

But it wasn't. It could never be ok, could it? However, as the journey went on, so Danika found that Layla's conversation became less and less. It was as if she were gradually closing down any thoughts of what had just happened, putting them in a locked room and throwing away the key and, when they eventually arrived at the sanctuary, Danika's suspicions were confirmed.

"Danika? Please promise me something."

"What is it?"

Layla's eyes fixed and held hers.

"Promise me you won't tell anyone about what I did at the house. Not anyone."

"You'll be asked about it, by people who'll be trying to help you."

"Promise me. Please?"

Could she do that? Would it be right to do that? Danika hesitated before answering, knowing that, once said, it couldn't be unsaid.

"I promise, Layla, I promise."

As she spoke, Danika led the young girl towards the sanctuary's front door.

Chapter 27

"So your father was a Custodian?"

Melissa lifted a hand so that another butterfly, that was flying around them, could settle onto it.

"Danika's found stuff out. She tells me about the stuff she finds. But, whatever, she always goes along with what I want and she doesn't stop anyone from believing what they want to believe about me."

So it seemed Danika had stood by Layla, and her wishes, from the beginning.

"And, yes, he was what you said, but I don't want to say it. The only reason for him being with Mum was so they could have someone close to one of us, and I'm the result of that. Then he got the call to end it. So he did. And I ended him."

She said it with a barely disguised revulsion, and Melissa understood. The 'overwhelming shyness' and 'barely controlled anger' that had been attributed to her was an obvious reaction to everything she'd suffered.

"Could we go out to the Brathy stone together tomorrow?"

"Why not? If you're happy for me to come with you?"

Layla nodded.

"I want you to be with me, because I want to tell you something there, something I haven't told you. I want to tell you the most important thing of all."

The next morning, they made their way to the place where the Brathy stone rested, and together they stood near the wild flowers that grew in a beautiful randomness beside it. Layla turned to Melissa and smiled.

"When I first told you that I didn't have any favourite places, when we were here, I lied. This is my favourite place."

"I can see why. This really is somewhere special. I can sense it."

"But do you know why it's special to me?"

Layla looked at her, waiting for an answer.

"I'm afraid I don't."

Melissa had no intention of guessing.

"It's special because my Mum's here."

"I remember you told me you come here to talk to her."

"Because she's here."

Layla repeated, trying hard not to let the impatience she so obviously felt show through. But it was the moment when she pointed down at the wild flowers that Melissa suddenly understood.

"She's *buried* here?"

Layla nodded.

"The flowers grow for her. Danika brought her here and helped me plant the flowers."

Melissa, at that moment, didn't know what to say. And so she decided to do what she always did in such moments. She said nothing, instead she took Layla's hand and gave it a gentle squeeze. Maybe nothing more needed to be said right then. Maybe all that was needed was their presence in that place, and Layla's love for her mother.

After agreeing that they would watch 'Birds of Prey' together soon, Melissa left Layla at the stone and returned to her apartment. She hoped that now it might be possible for Layla to begin her own process of accepting and healing. Certainly, the shadows that had been haunting her seemed to have retreated, but Melissa knew that she needed to stay close and vigilant. Layla's full recovery wouldn't happen overnight, and there would be times when her ghosts would try to return. Anyone so young, who had faced such trauma, would inevitably experience setbacks. All Melissa could do was to try her best to mitigate the severity of those setbacks.

She found herself a small tub of ice cream in the freezer and sat down at the kitchen table. As she worked her way down the tub, Melissa reflected on the previous day and how personally satisfying it had turned out to be. She felt much closer to both Danika and Layla, now with a much greater understanding of their own personal worlds, and what made those worlds such dark, hostile places.

And then, of course, there had been Sophie. She had been so concerned about Danika and Layla that Melissa had completely forgotten that she'd woken up in her bed the previous morning. The memories of that, and the night before, brought a smile to her lips. And what might Sophie be doing tonight, Melissa wondered? She quickly decided to stop wondering and go and find out.

Maybe Sophie might fancy a meal in the dining room, or possibly something somewhere more intimate. No, that was assuming too much. She was allowing her desire for her own gratification to lead her into making assumptions about someone she had, more or less, only just met. Melissa revised her expectations downwards, thereby hoping to avoid any disappointment in the form of a polite refusal from Sophie.

Having given herself one last check in the hallway mirror, Melissa reached out to pull the door open at exactly the same moment that her apartment phone began to ring. She considered ignoring it, after all, it couldn't be anything important, could it? However, despite her temporary frustration at the unwanted interruption, she had never been able to leave a ringing phone. With a sigh, Melissa walked over to the handset and lifted it from its cradle.

"Melissa."

"Hello Melissa. It's Verity. Melissa, could you do me a favour?"

"Of course."

"Could you find Danika and bring her to my office, please? I suggest you try the stables."

"Ok. Shall I just let her know you want to see her?"

Melissa knew that wasn't exactly what Verity had asked her to do, but she thought it might be worth checking.

"I'd like you to accompany her, if that's ok? And I'd be grateful if you could be as quick as you can."

"Ok. I'll go now."

"Thank you."

The line went dead thereby preventing any further questions such as, why didn't Verity just call the stables and tell Danika she wanted to see her? Melissa replaced the handset, somewhat disappointed that her Sophie search would, it seemed, have to be put on hold.

Melissa made her way to the stalls, where some of the horses were waiting to be taken to the meadow. Looking up and down the row, she hoped to see Danika. She said her name softly, not wanting to startle either her or the horses.

"Over here!"

The voice came from one of the furthest stalls. Melissa arrived to see Danika busy making up a straw bed, forking the huge drifts of straw into a thick, even carpet that covered every inch of the stable floor as well as a foot or so up each wall.

"That looks comfy. I wouldn't mind sleeping in here!"

"Hello. What's brought you over here?"

Danika kept working as she glanced over in Melissa's direction.

"Your presence is required in Verity's office."

"Now?"

Melissa nodded.

"Afraid so."

Danika made no attempt to hide her irritation.

"Tell her I'll be there as soon as I've finished this."

"I've been asked to accompany you. Right now."

Her annoyance became even more obvious as she flung a last forkful of straw across the stall before returning the pitchfork to the storage cupboard.

"Ok. Let's go."

Melissa followed Danika out of the door, feeling like a teacher escorting a naughty schoolgirl to the headmistress. As if using some kind of twisted telepathy, Danika turned to her.

"Do you think I'm going to get the cane?"

"I don't think that happens anymore."

"Oh. What a shame. I thought I might have something to look forward to."

Danika replied with a fleeting twinkle in her eyes.

They walked on, Melissa now unable to deny that her feelings for Danika were growing with every second she spent in her company. Should she mention Layla? She decided against it, not wanting to cross the fine line of trust that Layla now had in both of them. If Layla wanted to tell Danika at a later date, then that was up to her.

"Do you know what Verity wants?"

Melissa shrugged.

"Not a clue."

They made their way through the reception area and down the corridor that led to Verity's office. Danika knocked on the door, just as she had done on the day she had brought Melissa to meet Verity for the first time.

"Enter."

Danika walked in, closely followed by Melissa. Surprisingly, Verity wasn't sitting at her desk but waiting for them just the other side of the door.

"Melissa, thank you for delivering Danika in such a timely fashion."

Melissa nodded and turned to leave.

"Could you remain here, just for a short while?"

She nodded again, doing her best to hide her desire to be on her way.

"Verity?"

Danika's expression showed that she had picked up on the tone in Verity's voice. There was a serious edge to it. An edge she had seldom heard.

"There's someone here who'd like to say hello."

Verity stepped aside, allowing them to see that there was indeed another person in the office, sitting in the chair in front of the desk. She stood and walked over to them.

"Hello Dani."

Melissa heard Danika's sharp intake of breath and saw her hand fly up to cover her mouth. When she answered it was in no more than a whisper.

"Elise?"

Elise opened her arms. As they embraced, holding each other as tightly as they could, Melissa could see that both women had tears streaming down their faces. Verity beckoned Melissa to follow her out into the corridor.

"I wanted you to be here because I knew what a shock it would be for Danika. I didn't know how she'd react."

"I'm not sure I understand. Danika thought Elise was dead or, at least, that's how she spoke about her."

Verity glanced back into her office and smiled.

"Well, I think she knows differently now."

"So what happened? I mean, how isn't she dead, and how did you get her back?"

"Wait here a moment."

Verity returned to her office.

"Danika, can you look after Elise if I have a short walk with Melissa?"

She re-joined Melissa in the corridor.

"They have a lot to discuss, so shall we take that walk? I think Elise needs a little time to explain one or two things to Danika."

Verity led her back out into the morning sun as, somewhere in the nearby woods, a red kite flew up into the clear blue sky.

Chapter 28

~Elise~

"I'd value your opinion on something."

"Oh, and I thought you just wanted to spend some time in my scintillating company."

"That too, of course. Ok. See you soon."

"Dani?"

"Yes?"

"Love you."

Elise closed the call before Danika could reply, wanting to avoid the awkwardness that she knew she'd feel, having heard those words. It was one of the things that she adored about her, that underlying shyness that was made even more endearing because of Danika's outward confidence. And what might she want her opinion about? Elise had a good idea, but couldn't let on to her friend and risk everything unravelling. She guessed Verity had contacted Danika with the intent of getting her to safety before she was caught up in the fallout from their plan.

Elise recalled the day they had first met. How, as she had been leaving the café, her shoulder bag had knocked over Danika's cup of coffee, and how Danika still believed it was an accident when, in fact, it had been quite deliberate. Elise had thought about telling her many times, and had nearly done so on several occasions. But, somehow, she had never been able to. And now, as time had passed, she had convinced herself that there was no point in saying anything. What did it matter how they had met? Fate often needed a little helping hand.

What had it been about Danika that had made Elise do what she did? There was the obvious, of course. A physical attraction that Elise quickly discovered, much to her relief, was mutual. And that, at least initially, might have been enough for both of them. Except that, for Elise, her overriding motivation for finding Danika was something far more powerful than lust, or love. It was the certain knowledge that they were both descended from the Brathy Beck Coven, although Danika knew nothing of the bond that connected them.

Elise had been twelve years old when her mother had told her. She had explained the legacy, and what it could mean for her, the good....and the bad, and she had instilled in her daughter a desire to seek out others with that legacy. So, years later, when Elise had become what is known as a 'white hat hacker', that is, someone who uses their computer skills for good, rather than for criminal purposes, she used her technical abilities to make deep searches in her quest to find those 'others'. She followed many dead ends and experienced countless setbacks, some thanks to her own mistakes in not spotting well-constructed barriers or deliberate smokescreens. But, finally, she managed to achieve some modest success.

That success had taken the form of two names, one being Danika Pacek, and the other being Verity Trask. And so, as her personal relationship with Danika had grown and flourished, unknown to Danika, another kind of relationship had been built with Verity. Up-to-date knowledge and understanding of The Custodians and their aims had been shared between them and together, over time, Elise and Verity had formed the plan that was now about to be played out.

Elise had set about using her computer skills to create an online profile for herself that she hoped would prove to be irresistible to The Custodians. If they found the profile, which she made sure they would by laying a carefully fabricated trail, they'd see that Elise was a prize worth having. They'd believe that she had detailed knowledge that would prove invaluable to them and, so her thinking went, would make her too valuable to simply dispose of. It was a chance to get closer to The Custodians than any of her kind had ever done before. A chance to discover information that might be used to oppose and disrupt. That was the theory. Verity had taken some convincing and Elise had been forced to admit that, in practice, it had the potential to go dangerously wrong.

There was, though, something that concerned Elise far more. When the time came, and it surely would, how might Danika react to her deception? She had been so worried that, as they grew emotionally closer, she had even considered abandoning the plan.

There was a knock on the door. Elise knew it was too early to be Danika. She walked slowly towards it, taking a deep breath as she did so. All the indications were that The Custodians were about to make their move, and although Danika's imminent arrival was undesirable, Elise knew that, had she tried to put her off, she would only have succeeded in arousing her suspicion. She just had to hope that Verity would be able to meet her at some point soon and get her away to safety. Elise, although concerned for Danika's wellbeing, knew her well enough to be certain that she was quite capable of looking after herself, if necessary. But was she capable enough? It was too late now to do anything about that.

Elise hesitated before releasing the catch on the door, knowing that she was probably about to let in the devil. Even though she was expecting the onslaught, the force with which the door was kicked open took her by surprise. She was knocked back against a table and chair, the impact causing some small vases to fall and smash on the floor.

She lay still, waiting for the assault to continue. And, at that moment, her plan to make herself appear too valuable to kill, didn't seem to be quite as clever as it once had. Elise lifted her head in an attempt to see her attackers but, before she could get a good look, she felt the needle slip into her arm and, just moments later, her vision closed down to black.

Was it the bed that was gently moving? She slowly opened her eyes. No. It was the whole room. Elise sat up and looked around her. The room was small, its walls and ceiling were made of highly varnished wooden slats and it was lit by a bedside lamp. The bed itself was set against one wall while above it there was a window. Elise stared at it for a moment, knowing that 'window' wasn't the right word for what she saw. What was it? Her head still ached as she struggled to think.

Porthole! That was the word. The small, round window was called a porthole, and she was on a boat! Elise swung her legs over the side of the bed and made her unsteady way to the door.

She turned the handle but it didn't open. She was about to call out but stopped herself. Best not to attract any attention until she felt more able to deal with whoever might come through that door.

As she returned to the bed, almost collapsing onto it, she couldn't help thinking how much she'd like Danika at her side right now. Except, of course, she wouldn't. She wanted her as far away from these people as possible. She just had to hope that, by doing what she was doing, she might make things safer for all of her kind. Was that the height of naivety? Suddenly, it seemed as if it was.

Elise became aware of the pain on the side of her head where she had fallen against the table in her apartment. She lay back down, trying to bring some order to her thoughts, to be ready when they came for her. She had discussed with Verity what she could give them, what would make them think they were getting something while being given next to nothing. Clearly they had believed the fake profile she had put out there, otherwise she'd be dead. That was a fact worth holding on to, she told herself.

She fell once more into a light sleep. Minutes, maybe hours, passed before the click of the door lock pulled her back into consciousness. She opened her eyes and forced herself back to her feet, feeling some relief that her headache had now receded to a more bearable level. Elise waited for the door handle to turn and for someone to step into her cabin. Why were they coming? To see if she was awake so that they might begin some kind of interrogation? She was about to find out.

But nobody came through the now unlocked door. It remained closed and there were no further sounds from the other side. Elise, very cautiously, made her way over to it, expecting at any moment to be confronted by whoever had done the unlocking. She pressed an ear against the polished wood, listening for the slightest sound behind it, but she heard nothing except the low hum of the boat's engine.

Elise tried the handle again, and this time she felt the door move slightly. She pulled it towards her until it was half open. She stepped out into the narrow passageway, looking to the left and right. No guards. No welcome committee. No one. She decided to go right, for no particular reason. It was a fifty-fifty choice and she had no way of knowing who, or what, lay in either direction.

The passageway was lit along its length by ornate wall lamps. Elise recognised the style as Art Deco. As she reached the far end, she saw the steps that led up to another door. She took a glance behind her before gripping the handrail and climbing them but, before she could make it to the top step, the door opened.

"Miss Elise Calvert, I presume. Welcome aboard. Captain James Turner at your service. I'll be your captain for the duration of the journey. Anything you require, anything at all, please don't hesitate to speak to one of my crew."

Elise took another mouthful of her light breakfast. Although she didn't feel particularly hungry, she thought it might be a good idea to eat something from an impressively extensive menu. In fact, the hospitality on board had been exemplary. She was being treated like an honoured guest, the only guest, and it had been made clear that nowhere was off limits. Of course, she could hardly escape, not without drowning, and so this was the perfect way to take her to wherever their destination might be, and that piece of information, it had been made clear to her, was not going to be revealed however many times she asked.

After her meal, Elise decided to go up on deck, wondering if she might be able to learn something of their route from any visible landmarks. It was a bright, benign morning, and the sea was calm. Elise could just make out land on the horizon, but it was impossible to see anything that might be recognisable, and she had no idea how long they had been on their voyage.

With the outward view not yielding any clues as to her whereabouts, Elise turned her attention to the boat. And it took only moments for her to realise that calling it a boat was to do it a great injustice. A medium sized luxury yacht would be much more accurate. The overwhelming impression was one of gleaming white and chrome. Elise had seen such vessels in films and documentaries about the wealthy but had never imagined she would ever be a guest on one. Except, of course, she wasn't quite a 'guest', was she? Elise had to remind herself not to be seduced by the luxurious surroundings and artificial bonhomie. She knew she was in a perilous situation.

As she walked along the deck she noticed the name of the yacht written on the side of its lifeboat. *The Witcher.* It brought a wry smile to her lips as she climbed one of the external stairways onto the upper deck. Since there seemed little else to do but sit back and enjoy the ride, Elise decided to find an easy chair on the sun deck to do just that and, still experiencing the aftereffects of whatever drug they had used on her, soon fell asleep once more.

When she awoke, the sun was higher and the land was closer. Close enough for Elise to now see that what they were approaching was an island. She could just make out a jetty reaching into the sea from a small bay and, as she continued to watch, it became clear that was exactly where they were heading. And, as the jetty got nearer, so Elise saw that there was a single figure standing about halfway along its length, watching as the yacht began manoeuvring into position for mooring.

Elise made her way back down to the main deck, to where one of the crew was standing by with a mooring rope. She gripped the handrail, her eyes now fixed upon the person standing on the jetty. The woman, wearing a mid-length dress that seemed to shimmer in the sun, removed her sunglasses as the yacht was secured and the gangway lowered and fixed into position. She walked forward and stood near the end of the gangway, while the yacht's captain, who had appeared by Elise's side, gestured that she should be the first to disembark.

She hesitated before making her way down the narrow walkway, using the side ropes to steady herself. As she drew closer to the woman she could see that she was smiling warmly, which had the effect of putting Elise very much on her guard.

"Elise Calvert? How lovely to meet you. My name is Liv Rann, and I am the leader of The Custodians."

Chapter 29

~*Elise and Liv*~

Elise tried hard to hide the shock that she felt at hearing that introduction, but couldn't stop herself from saying

"You're a woman."

"Apparently so. Well, at least I can be sure that your recent experiences haven't affected your powers of observation."

She gently rested a hand on Elise's back, guiding her along the jetty and on towards a Jeep that was parked near the end of the walkway. In seconds they were hurtling along a dirt track, a cloud of dust billowing into the air behind them.

Every so often Liv glanced at Elise and smiled, maybe wanting to be sure that she was managing to hang on through some of the sharp bends and inclines. But Elise's thoughts were elsewhere. The journey, Liv, and the complete absence of any hostility or suspicion in her treatment and welcome, had only served to add to her feelings of confusion and concern.

After several minutes of Liv's expert driving, they pulled up outside a luxurious single story building that was almost completely hidden by lush green vegetation. Conversation had been limited on their short journey, mainly because of the noise from the Jeep's engine as it powered them along the track.

"Follow me."

Liv jumped from the vehicle and waited for Elise to join her. They entered a large, open plan living area that was a continuation of the exterior, with plants and shrubbery in every direction amongst the minimalist furniture and décor. In one corner there was an ornamental waterfall dropping onto several different pebble-covered levels.

"I take it, from the look on your face, that things are not quite as you expected."

Liv led her on, through what appeared to be a dining room, and out onto a veranda at the rear of the building. It overlooked a wild garden filled with flowering plants and vegetation, hardly any of which Elise recognised. Suddenly, seemingly from thin air, a man appeared carrying a silver tray. He was dressed smartly, in a well-cut suit and perfectly matched tie. He stood still, his gaze fixed upon Liv, awaiting instructions from his mistress. She has a butler? Really? Although Elise said nothing, her thoughts must have been plainly written on her expression.

"This is Holcroft."

He gave a curt nod in Elise's direction.

"Could we have something cool and refreshing to drink please, and also some of those exquisite canapés? Thank you."

He turned away and they were alone once more.

"Let's both sit here, shall we?"

Liv made her way over to a wide swing seat that was suspended from the roof of the veranda. Elise hesitated, perhaps because of her proximity to Liv should she accept her offer.

"Don't want to get too close to the enemy, mmm?"

She smiled, making no attempt to hide her amusement at Elise's discomfort, instead patting the empty space next to her.

"Not at all."

Elise sat down as confidently as she was able.

"Good. That's nice. Now we can have a lovely chat. We'll soon have something to eat and drink, so what could be more pleasant?"

In any other circumstances, Elise would have readily agreed with her. But was all of this, the whole 'warm welcome for an old friend' act, meant to be part of the disorientation process?

"I must admit...."

Elise was now close enough to smell the scent Liv was wearing. It was subtle, and suited her. *Krigler* maybe? Elise wasn't absolutely sure.

"....I was, I am, shocked. How could you be the head of such a violent, evil cult?"

"Well, of course, *I* might be violent and evil, mightn't I? Then I'd be perfectly suited to the position. As to the practicality of becoming The Custodians' head, I inherited the title from my father. He had no other children so, when he died...."

"But you didn't have to take it!"

Liv shrugged.

213

"No, I didn't *have* to, but I wanted to. That's why I killed him."

"Excuse me?"

Elise wasn't sure she'd heard that correctly, but before she could ask her to repeat it, Liv continued

"And I believe you'd agree with me that this whole thing needs to be stopped. I've just begun that process."

Before Elise could respond, they were interrupted by the arrival of their food and drink. Holcroft deftly placed a small table in front of them before wheeling in a trolley filled with a selection of light bites. On its lower shelf were several bottles and an array of fine crystal glasses. He was about to start serving the food when Liv held up a hand.

"It's ok, thank you Holcroft. We can take it from here."

He nodded and left them alone on the veranda. Elise was now impatient to hear Liv elaborate on what she'd just said but, for the moment, she seemed far more interested in the contents of the trolley. She passed a plate and a glass to Elise.

"Plenty of choice. Help yourself."

As Liv proceeded to follow her own instructions, Elise realised that there would be little point in trying to move the conversation on until she had sampled the hospitality. She took two of the smoked salmon canapés and, avoiding anything alcoholic, poured herself a chilled pineapple juice.

"How didn't we know about you?"

Elise asked after she'd eaten the two canapés and reached out for a third, realising that she was, regardless of what lay ahead, quite hungry. It hadn't been the question she had intended to ask, recalling what Liv said just before Holcroft had returned.

"You didn't know about me because I didn't *want* you to know about me, at least not until I was ready. Unlike you, dear Elise. You definitely wanted to be found, didn't you?"

"Was it that obvious?"

Liv took a sip of her champagne cocktail and put her glass down before replying.

"Oh, don't feel bad, it was very well done. But there was 'find me' writ large right through your profile. The pudding was, shall we say, a little over-egged. However, anyone without my exceptional IT abilities wouldn't have spotted it."

214

Liv said it without any hint of vanity or arrogance.

"I'll try harder next time."

"Hopefully there won't be the need for a next time because, as I believe I mentioned, I've put myself in a position to stop this destructive, wasteful, misguided enterprise."

There it was again. Elise hadn't imagined it.

"I really don't understand."

Liv held up a hand as she ate her canapé, indicating that she was going to answer, but not until she'd finished her food. Finally, she gave a last swallow and then took another drink from her glass.

"Sorry about that. My father always told me never to speak with my mouth full, before I killed him, obviously, although not directly before. I'm not that tetchy."

A joke about killing her father? Elise was now even more unsure about this woman.

"Your plate's empty. Keep going, Holcroft won't want to take anything back to the kitchen. Now, where was I?"

"Stopping the killing?" Elise prompted.

"Oh yes. I've wanted to for years but have never been in a position to act, until recently."

"But the killings are still going on, aren't they? My kind are still being threatened and dying at the hands of The Custodians."

Liv hesitated as she searched for the right metaphor.

"Do you know how long it takes to bring a super tanker to a stop from normal speed? No? About twenty minutes. Well, I'm at the bridge of this super tanker and I'm doing all I can to stop it, but it's not going to happen with a click of my fingers. However, Elise, it can happen more quickly if you agree to help me."

"I have nothing but your word for all of this. How do I know I can trust anything you say? And why would you want to stop it anyway? Why would you want to destroy something that your father so clearly believed in?"

Liv emptied her glass and looked as if she was considering refilling it. Instead, she pushed herself up from the swing seat.

"Come with me."

Without waiting, she made her way back into the house and headed purposefully towards a door in the far corner of the living

215

area. Elise, several paces behind, followed her into what had to be the library. Like the other rooms, it was very modern. Unlike the other rooms, two walls had floor to ceiling shelves filled with books. Elise walked over to one of the book-laden walls and began to glance through the titles.

"Are you surprised?"

"At what?"

Liv stood by her side.

"That, in this cyber world, I should still value such a thing as a book?"

Elise shook her head.

"No. Not at all. Books are wonderful. Absolutely."

"Except I've only read a handful of them. They make a good background for a Zoom call though. Gives the illusion of intellect. You must have seen people do it on the news and in documentaries."

While Liv had been speaking, she'd been running a hand along one of the lower shelves until, about a third of the way down, she stopped. Reaching between two large volumes, she pushed at a well-hidden spot on the wall and stood back. Moments later a whole section of shelving slid back revealing a passageway behind it. Liv beckoned Elise through but this time, instead of going on ahead, she waited so that they could walk together along the corridor.

"I feel I should apologise for the experience overload, however, time is pressing."

In front of them there was another room, only this one didn't have any windows and was lit by subtle up-lighting, with two lamps positioned on each wall. It was sparsely furnished, thereby maintaining the minimalist motif from elsewhere in the building. There was a large desk in the centre on which stood three desktop computers, each with its own keyboard and monitor.

"This is where we're going to create chaos and end this vendetta once and for all. If you agree to assist me."

Liv quickly added the last sentence, not wanting to appear to take Elise's cooperation for granted. Elise, however, seemed more interested in the computers, sitting down in front of one of them and studying the icons on the front screen.

"I believe you're quite the talent where these things are concerned, if what I've read about you is correct?"

Liv sat down next to her, watching her closely.

"I know enough. Probably not as much as you."

Elise remembered to add. She wanted to remain non-committal, although she would readily admit to being extremely intrigued.

"Oh come on. Don't undersell yourself, especially not to me, Elise Calvert, white hat hacker."

After some seconds, Elise pushed her chair away from the desk and swung around ninety degrees to face Liv.

"If what you say is true, then of course I'll work with you. I'll do anything to stop this evil persecution. But I think the operative word there is 'if'. I'm ready to listen, but you need to tell me more. A lot more."

Chapter 30

~Liv~

She watched the Land Rover drive off and knew it had to be now
or never. Her father was so rarely away for long that it was
unlikely she'd have another chance like this. What she was about
to do would either confirm her worst suspicions or tell her not to
be so ready to jump to conclusions in the future. She desperately
hoped it was the latter.

Liv had decided to wait for at least an hour after her father's
departure, just in case there was a problem with the yacht, or
anything else for that matter, that might bring him back to the
house prematurely. She feared being discovered, but she had to
know, once and for all.

It hadn't been one single incident that had brought her to this
day. It had been snippets of overheard conversations, visitors
coming and going without introduction, the obsession with
secrecy and the sidestepping of questions when asked. But,
above all, it had been an overwhelming feeling, an intuition, that
had finally made up her mind. She had no choice. She had to act.

More than an hour passed. Liv took one last look out onto the
driveway. No sign of the Land Rover. She took a deep breath
before removing her phone from her pocket. Over the past few
weeks she had taken to 'accidentally' leaving it in the library,
partially hidden by some pot plants, with its camera trained on
the opposite bookcase.

Liv had noticed how her father had often locked the door
when he had gone in there and, when questioned, had quoted the
rather vague excuse of business confidentiality. Maybe that was
true, Liv had thought, but couple the door-locking with all the
other little anomalies....

She entered the library before finding the video her phone had recorded. She had already watched it more times than she could remember, but she had to be sure. The last thing she wanted was to make a mistake that might trigger some kind of remote alarm.

Liv located the two books and carefully reached between them. This was the bit that the video didn't reveal. What was behind the books that she needed to find? After a few seconds her fingers brushed over what felt like a light switch. She closed her eyes as she pressed it. If she had overlooked something, then she was about to find out.

The whole bookcase began to slide sideways, just as it did in the video. Liv paused as she saw the short corridor with the room at the end of it. Even at that moment, she had to take a deep breath and force herself forward, feeling that her courage was about to fail her. She hurried on to the room knowing that, as the bookcase slid back into its normal position, she was now committed, regardless of the outcome.

The first thing she saw was the desk and computer. She sat down in the chair and booted it up. Within seconds it was asking for a password. So far so predictable. Liv took out the memory stick from her pocket and plugged it into one of the desktop's USB sockets. She then sat back and waited. It took just under a minute before the computer displayed its front screen, all of its security temporarily bypassed. Liv removed the memory stick and put it back in her pocket, its job done.

She studied the rows of icons. It soon became apparent to Liv that the majority of them were folders containing administrative and financial records, everyday housekeeping. But there were a few that looked a little more interesting. The first that she decided to open had the label 'BB'. The document within had the full title as its header. Brathy Beck.

She began to read, intrigued by what seemed to be an account, real or fictitious, of an incident that occurred centuries ago. What could that possibly have to do with her father? By the time she had finished reading it, Liv had to admit that she was really none the wiser. She enjoyed supernatural horror stories and this one had held her attention as well as any she'd read. But the story, as far as she could tell, didn't offer her any answers, and she failed to see any relevance to her father or to anything that might interest her.

Liv closed the 'BB' folder and opened the one next to it which had the equally enigmatic title 'CNS'. Inside that folder were various documents, each one seeming to relate to a subject named 'The Custodians'. Liv clicked in and out of a few, noting titles such as 'Aims', 'History' and 'Targets – Acquired and Potential'. Well, there was no point in trying to guess, was there? She had come this far and so Liv set about reading each document in turn, missing out nothing and taking in everything.

It had been like a descent into Hell. By the time Liv had finished the last document there were tears rolling down her cheeks. But something far more destructive than sorrow had been building inside her. There was now an anger that had been growing as she had read of the persecution, of the significance of Brathy Beck, and of the plans still being made. Finally, Liv closed the last 'Custodians' document and returned to the front screen. She scanned the rows of icons one last time and had been about to shut the computer down when she saw an icon set apart from the others. It was annotated 'L'. Just 'L'. She opened it. The document it contained was a report. It didn't have a title, and consisted of just a few short paragraphs. She read it.

It took one sentence for her to realise that the 'L' stood for 'Liv'. Her father had commissioned a report on her! But the shock of that was completely overshadowed by the contents of the third paragraph. 'It is therefore confirmed that your daughter is a direct descendant from one of the members of the Coven of Brathy Beck. There is no possibility of error.'

Liv remained staring at the screen for some minutes, trying to take in everything she'd just seen. Reading between the lines, she had sensed her father's shame. He felt ashamed of her, and of her mother, his wife. It must have been the harshest of blows to discover that, within his own family, there were those of the kind he spent every day hunting down. A cruel coincidence. But, the more Liv thought about it, the more she considered that it might not be such an accident that blood relatives found themselves on opposite sides of the divide between hunter and hunted. The fate of the witchfinders and their quarry had been intertwined for centuries. It would have been no different for the women of Brathy Beck and their pursuers. Liv, with her new found allegiance and understanding, could now imagine how the lines of separation might, over the years, have become blurred and, perhaps, that blurring had only served to increase her father's desire to intensify The Custodians' persecution of their kind. Of *her* kind.

As she turned the computer off and ensured everything was left as she had found it, a plan had already begun to form in her mind. Her father's shame and his desire to keep his dirty little secret to himself would lay the foundations for his, and The Custodians', termination. She would bring the whole edifice down, stone by stone if she had to. She would do it for herself, for her mother, and for all those who had been, and would be, persecuted. It would undoubtedly be a long game but, maybe, there was a way to make it shorter.

She made her way to her room and, as she booted up her own laptop, she couldn't think of anyone but her mother and began to question the circumstances of her death. The death certificate had said heart failure, together with other associated medical complications. At the time, in the midst of her grief, Liv had accepted that. Why wouldn't she? But now she was wondering, and her imagination no longer had any borders.

Knowing what she *wanted* to do, however, was one thing. Actually making it happen was another, and she would have to accept that, while her strategy played out, the killings would continue. But Liv understood enough now to realise that, once she was the head of The Custodians, having another of her kind by her side might help lessen the time it would take to bring all of it to an end.

It was then, as Liv started her search for that potential accomplice, that the words 'once she was head of The Custodians' repeated themselves over and over. Did she really believe that was even a possibility? And yet, everything she had planned rested upon that possibility becoming a reality. It had to happen and, for it to happen, her father had to die, because Liv believed she now knew enough about this organisation to use its own credo against it. The Custodians were built upon a bedrock of tradition, and tradition said that the role of leader was an inherited one, maintaining a continuity that went back to the times of the witchfinders.

The fact that her father clearly hadn't spoken to anyone about her gave her an advantage, a clean slate. She could become whoever she needed to be, whoever they wanted her to be. The witch could become the witchfinder. Or appear to. It was the least she could do for the father that she now hated so much.

As Liv entered her laptop password she was reminded of the memory stick she'd used on her father's computer. She removed it from her pocket and returned it to its hiding place, wedging it firmly at the back of a drawer. Having recently obtained it, illegally and at some cost, Liv wasn't about to let it fall into anyone else's possession. But it had done its job for now. It had unlocked the darkness and allowed her to look into the abyss.

Three weeks after her father died, Liv located the one she'd been hoping to find. Her name was Elise Calvert. She also had an incontrovertible blood link to the Coven. However, it seemed to Liv that finding her was a little too easy and that she wanted to be found. No matter. That might be made to work in her favour. She would arrange a pick-up and hope that the goods weren't damaged in transit.

Liv didn't underestimate the size of the task ahead. Innocent women would still come under threat, and some would die. It hurt to accept such a thing, but Liv was also realistic enough to understand the inevitability of her situation. The long game would be played out, the super tanker would eventually be stopped, and those who still wished to hold on to the doctrine would be destroyed. She made that promise to her beautiful mother, and to all those who had suffered, and who would suffer, before this was over.

The first step was taken on a bright, warm morning along the coast road some five miles from the house. An eyewitness (that was unfortunate) said they thought the Land Rover exploded *before* it crashed. However, later investigations concluded that the explosion most likely occurred upon impact with a crash barrier, after the driver lost control of the vehicle. Any further enquiries were deemed unnecessary by the authorities after private discussions with the deceased's daughter. Liv considered that the saying 'It's not *what* you know, it's *who* you know' was never more appropriate.

In the following weeks and months there had been some within The Custodians who had voiced misgivings, and others who made no attempt to hide their naked hostility towards her but, as Liv hoped it would, tradition finally won the day and five months after her father's death, she became The Custodians' leader.

Liv knew she had been taking a calculated risk, and that the price of miscalculation might be as high as her own life. But dissent against her succession had been, not extinguished, but quelled by those who argued that the bloodline *had* to prevail in the matter of leadership.

It was then that the hard work began. The work of surrounding herself with a hard core of those she could trust, those who would obey her regardless, and stand by her in the face of any opposition. Achieving that proved relatively easy compared to beginning the gradual undermining of the command structure and instigating a quiet disruption by sowing the seeds of suspicion and doubt where they would do most harm.

It was a period of time that tested Liv's authority to the limit, and she knew she had to find an ally from within the Coven descendants. Find her or fail. On the darker days, those days when she would receive reports of the death of another innocent, she felt her resolve weakening as she questioned her ability to achieve her goal. Maybe she would fail, maybe it had been the height of conceit and madness to believe that she could succeed. And yet, she *had* to succeed. Any other outcome was unthinkable.

"Her name's Elise Calvert, and I want her brought here alive. Yes. Here. Do you understand? That is non-negotiable. You can deal with any other complications as you see fit. But Elise must come to me unharmed."

Liv closed the call, knowing that her orders would be questioned at lower levels. Questioned, but not challenged. Of course, she had no way of knowing if she had read the situation correctly. If, as she presumed and hoped, Elise wanted to be taken, then she would put up a minimum of resistance. But, if Liv had got that wrong, then she might have just signed the young woman's death warrant.

Her investigations had also indicated that Elise had a close friend, possibly lover. Danika Pacek. She was the potential complication that Liv had referred to in her phone call. Danika was an unknown quantity. Although Liv had basic information regarding her background, she had no way of predicting her actions, and her ability to stop Elise's abduction being carried out cleanly. It was just one more way that her plan could fail. However, if Liv had also given orders that Danika should not be harmed, then alarm bells would definitely have rung in places where she couldn't afford them to ring. Had she just thrown Danika to the wolves? She didn't want to think about it.

And so, it had come down to this. Liv stood on the jetty and looked out to sea. She could just make out the yacht on the horizon, bringing Elise ever closer. Did her approach represent justification and salvation, or misjudgement and, ultimately, disaster? Could she convince Elise to believe her and be her ally? Liv would soon have the answers.

She watched as *The Witcher* drew nearer, the sunlight reflected from the glistening white of her hull. Liv could now make out a woman standing on the upper deck. She was looking in her direction and probably already making up her mind about her. Liv had to remind herself not to allow her growing anxiety to show through, at least not as a first impression. She had to radiate confidence, to appear every inch the leader.

As the yacht came alongside the jetty, the woman descended to the main deck and made her way to where the gangway was slowly being lowered. Liv took a deep breath. She had played this moment over and over again in her mind but, now it was here, now *she* was here, suddenly nothing seemed as certain as it once had. The woman walked down the gangway. Liv smiled as she approached.

"Elise Calvert? How lovely to meet you. My name is Liv Rann, and I am the head of The Custodians."

Chapter 31

The grounds of the sanctuary were silent, except for the sound of water gently lapping the shores of the lake and birdsong drifting in on the breeze. Layla had asked Harriet if she would paint a canvas of the wildflower clearing near her mother's grave. There had been no sorrow in her request, none of the darkness that had overshadowed her every visit to that place. She knew that such a painting, hanging on the wall in her apartment, would now bring her nothing but comfort. Of course, the pain of her mother's loss would never leave her, but she was now able to live alongside that pain. It was no longer an all pervading shadow that blocked out all light, and all hope.

So, as the sunlight crept its way into the clearing, Layla began to set up Harriet's easel and canvas, positioning it so that she had the best view of the wildflowers with the Brathy stone in the background. Finally, happy with her efforts, Layla turned her attention to preparing the brushes and paints. She was so engrossed in her task that she didn't immediately notice Melissa, who had appeared on the pathway that emerged from the woods.

"Good morning! I see Harriet's found herself a very able assistant. Or are you setting everything up for yourself?"

Layla explained about the painting as she continued to busy herself. Melissa had never seen her so animated and engaged.

"Melissa?"

"Yes?"

Layla stopped what she was doing and walked over to where she stood.

"I don't believe I've thanked you. Mum always told me to say thank you."

"What for?"

Layla smiled.

"For going to all that trouble just for me. All the time you must have spent learning about Harley Quinn, reading stuff, watching stuff."

Melissa sighed.

"How soon did you guess?"

"Fairly soon. I mean, almost straightaway really."

"But you still went along with it?"

Layla thought about that for a moment.

"My Mum also told me to be polite, and I haven't really done that since I've been here. I thought you'd be a good place to start."

Melissa put her arms around her and hugged her. It seemed the most natural response to the way she felt. She half-expected Layla to 'politely' push her away but, instead, felt the young girl pull her even closer. All emotional barriers had now disappeared and she had given herself permission to move on.

Leaving her to await Harriet's arrival, Melissa continued with her walk that took her on past the tennis courts. Rumour had it that there was to be a rematch between Justine and Sophie that afternoon. As Melissa made a mental note not to miss the game, so her thoughts turned back to Sophie. The hoped-for assignation had never happened. By the time she had left Verity, Melissa had no longer been in the mood to go searching for her. Well, maybe another time, because Melissa's immediate concern was for Danika. She couldn't imagine the shock it must have been, to be suddenly faced with someone so dear to her, someone she believed she'd lost forever. She hadn't been able to sleep for worrying about her, and how she might have reacted to Elise's story. Would she see her as some kind of hero, or would she see the situation as nothing more or less than a personal betrayal by the woman she had loved? And it wasn't only Elise was it? Could any kind of trust now exist between Danika and Verity?

Melissa fully understood why Verity and Elise had done what they had. To achieve their goal, it made absolute sense. They would both have seen it as a price worth paying. But how would Danika see it? It would be a tragedy if that price turned out to be the loss of a friendship and the consequences of that loss. It was clear how much Danika meant to Verity, they had something close to a mother and daughter bond. Melissa had already made up her mind that her morning walk would take her to the stables, where she would doubtless find Danika. But she wasn't looking

226

forward to whatever conversation might follow. Could she talk her round? She wasn't confident, but she had to try.

And yet, if it was over between Danika and Elise, what then? Melissa's thoughts began to run in directions she wouldn't confess to another soul. Did she really have those kind of feelings for Danika? No. Absolutely not. She would deny it to herself, and to others. She was going to see her for purely altruistic reasons, there was no hidden agenda. There just wasn't.

As Melissa neared the stable block she thought she could hear voices. She walked on in silence towards the tack room, the voices now louder and more distinct. In fact, the sound she could now hear was that of gentle, affectionate laughter.

The door to the tack room was slightly ajar. She carefully pushed it a little so that it opened just a fraction more. From where she stood, Melissa could see Danika and Elise. They were embracing each other, and both looked very happy.

Melissa quickly turned away and hurried from the stables, not stopping until she was once more on the path that led back to the house and to her apartment, which was where she wanted to be right at that moment. She jogged back through the main doors and headed for the stairs, not wanting to start crying until she was safely shut away from the rest of the world.

"Melissa?"

She spun round to see Verity entering the reception area. 'Please, not right now' was what Melissa thought but, with a forced smile, what she actually said was

"Hi Verity. Can I help you?"

"I just wondered if you were going to the tennis this afternoon? They've both been practicing I hear."

"Oh, yes. Sure. I'll be there."

"Are you ok?"

She managed another smile as she nodded, maybe a little too vigorously. She turned and took the stairs two at a time, not wanting to enter into any kind of prolonged conversation. As she leant against her door to push it closed, so the tears began. Her feelings for Danika had taken her by surprise. Perhaps it was that she owed Danika her life. That might explain it. Or maybe it was the times they had spent together, just the two of them. Had Melissa picked up on something that was never there? Anyway, it was all irrelevant now. She knew she should feel happy for them. Danika and Elise. But the guilt started to flood in on her. Guilt that she didn't feel happy. Guilt that she'd slept with Sophie and never given Danika a thought. That now somehow felt like a betrayal, except that there was nothing to betray. Melissa lay down on her bed and closed her eyes hoping that, in the quiet and solitude, she might be able to bring her thoughts and emotions under control. After some minutes, she fell into a fitful, light sleep.

There was a knock on the door. She considered ignoring it, pretending to be out, anything to avoid talking to another person. There was another knock. Slowly, reluctantly, Melissa rose from the bed and walked over to the door.

"Yes?"

"It's Danika. May I come in?"

What was she going to say? No? Although she did momentarily consider it, Melissa pulled the door open and beckoned her in. "Sit anywhere. Would you like a drink?"

Danika chose one of the armchairs and dropped into it.

"No thanks. Verity suggested it might be a good idea if someone dropped in to check that you're ok."

She should have known that Verity would have seen right through any attempt to hide her feelings.

"I, er...."

She really wasn't feeling ready for this, for being told first-hand about her and Elise, and losing something she never knew she wanted so badly.

"I expect you're up to speed on everything that's happened recently...."

It was a statement rather than a question.

"....but Verity wants it emphasised that it isn't over. The official line is that although Liv and Elise have been largely successful over the past months, a residual threat remains and so it's requested that we all stay at the sanctuary until such time as it's deemed safe enough for us to leave. Of course, anyone that wishes to stay on permanently regardless of the level of threat will be more than welcome...."

Danika took a breath.

"....I think I've remembered that correctly."

"Well done." Maybe in a previous meeting, Melissa might have made some attempt at humour but, right at that moment, she really didn't feel like it.

"So are you ok?"

"I'm sorry?"

"Verity wanted to know if you're ok and, come to that, so do I."

She could lie, of course she could. But what would that achieve? Danika would know, and she would feel no better for having done so.

"I'm going to miss you." Melissa said the words quickly, before she had the chance to change her mind.

"Miss me? I don't understand."

'Oh Danika, please don't make me say it' Melissa thought and nearly said out loud.

"You'll be leaving with Elise soon, won't you?"

She couldn't disguise the sadness in her voice, nor did she want to, but her words brought an even more puzzled expression to Danika's face and she shook her head.

"Elise has already gone. She's on her way back to Liv."

It was Melissa's turn to say, "I don't understand."

In response, Danika beckoned her to come and sit with her.

"We're no longer together. Elise has told me that she's in a relationship with Liv now. It was inevitable, I suppose, working with someone so closely for so long."

This had the effect of turning Melissa's thoughts into a maelstrom of confusion.

"But I saw you both this morning...."

Melissa hadn't intended to mention her presence at the stables but now it didn't seem to matter. Danika leant forward and took Melissa's hands in her own.

"By 'this morning' I expect you mean at the stables?"

Melissa nodded.

"We were saying goodbye, and we were wishing each other well. That was it."

"But I can't believe that in the space of just one night you accepted all of that so easily. The woman you loved, who meant so much to you, tells you it's all over and you say 'oh, that's fine'? You do nothing to try to convince her to stay with you?"

She felt Danika squeeze her hands tighter as she replied. "At first I wanted to. I wanted to remind her of what we had and what we could have. But, as we talked I began to realise something. While she was telling me about Liv, I realised that I had a Liv, someone I knew I needed to be with more than anyone else, even Elise. I think I always knew it but couldn't, or wouldn't, listen to my true feelings. That's always been one of my many failings."

Where was this going? Melissa now felt more confused than ever. "I'm not sure I…."

"The times I've spent with you have been some of the happiest of my life. I've only just been able to admit that to myself. Of course, I have no idea if that feeling's mutual."

A few seconds passed before Melissa took Danika in her arms and held her, a moment that had seemed an eternity away just a short time ago. But Melissa knew that there was something she had to say, for her own peace of mind. If it meant losing what she now had then so be it. Better to lose it all now than later, when the pain would be so much harder to bear. And there was no point in trying to sugar the pill.

"I slept with Sophie."

Danika released her embrace, held her at arms' length, and the silence that followed was like slow torture for Melissa. Eventually Danika spoke.

"That's ok. So have I. She's quite fun, isn't she?"

Melissa's inward sigh of relief was transferred to her expression in the form of a smile that grew broader as it mirrored Danika's.

"Verity's asked if I'm going to the tennis match this afternoon. Will you come with me?"

Danika nodded. "Of course. But there's at least a couple of hours before then. The horses are all fed, watered, and turned out. Your diary's probably empty. So…."

Melissa didn't need any further prompting. She took Danika's hand and led her through to the bedroom, softly closing the door behind them.

Chapter 32

Verity rose from her chair and walked over to the window that looked out across the grounds of the sanctuary. Could this really be the beginning of the end? She didn't dare hope, but it seemed that the risk she and Elise had taken might just have paid off.

However, there was something that could leave their success tainted. She needed to find Danika, to explain and to apologise. Verity had asked herself many times how she would feel in Danika's place, and the answer was never a happy one. Now was the time to face up to the cost of her deception. She found Danika on her way to the stables and they walked together to the meadows where some of the horses had spent the night. Verity had rehearsed her apology and her plea for forgiveness, and she would just have to hope that Danika might be able to see the bigger picture and understand the reasoning behind it all.

"….and so I wouldn't blame you if you were angry with me. I deserve it for letting you mourn Elise when I knew the truth. But I couldn't tell you because if you had been captured they might have made you talk, and that would have signed, not only Elise's death warrant, but probably Liv's too, and have lost us our only chance to end this. There was just too much at stake…."

Verity waited for Danika's response, preparing herself for the oncoming storm. Danika, who had been stroking Magick's neck and mane while she listened to Verity, finally turned to face her.

"I've always looked up to you, Verity. I've carried out your wishes and orders without question, and never regretted that for a moment. I've always believed in you. From the moment I found you in that rainy courtyard, my life has been blessed by knowing you. Seeing Elise last night in your office was a big shock to me. Of course it was. And believe me, since that moment my emotions have been to Hell and back…."

Verity looked away, not wanting Danika to see the tears that were threatening to come.

"....but my emotions set against what might have been lost? You had no choice Verity. In your position I would have made exactly the same decisions. I have no anger for you, or Elise. You did the right thing, as you always do. I respect you, admire you, and love you just as much today as I did yesterday. That's why I hope *you* won't be angry."

Verity looked confused.

"Why would *I* be angry?" she asked with some trepidation.

Danika avoided eye contact as she replied.

"Well, you see, we've arranged....that is, Melissa and I, we've arranged something. I was sure about it at the time, but...."

"But now you're not?" Verity asked, helpfully, but before Danika could respond a voice called out from the gate behind them.

"Verity!"

She turned, standing motionless and silent for some seconds. "Pamela?"

Leaning on the gate, Doctor Pamela Flynn waved as Verity said her name, while her young daughter stood beside her, transfixed by the sight of the horses.

"Go and say hello, then."

Danika put a hand on Verity's back and gently encouraged her forward, relieved to see her growing smile as she ran over to where Pamela was waiting. While, unseen, a butterfly settled on a nearby buddleia, its satin wings shimmering in the morning sun.

The End

232

Milton Keynes UK
Ingram Content Group UK Ltd.
UKHW010712050224
437294UK00018B/700